TEMPORARY TALES

OF MAGIC AND HOPE

N.V. HASKELL

CONTENTS

FORWARD

First and foremost, thank you dear readers, friends, and family for your support over the last few years.

When I returned to writing in 2019 I wasn't thinking about plot, theme, or pacing. Neither did I consider if those stories would ever be read by anyone who wasn't related to me. Having my work published seemed implausible and I certainly never expected to win an award (The Mystical Farrago/Writers of the Future, Volume 38) or to have a story on the Nebula recommended reading list (A Murmuring Darkness/September 2023/Strange Horizons). No, I wrote for the sheer enjoyment of creating other worlds and characters that were both foreign and familiar.

Along the way, I met some amazing people and can honestly say that my writing might not have come along so quickly if it weren't for the influence of the late, great David Farland, whose kindness as a mentor is something to aspire to. There were other well-established writers who influenced me including Kevin J. Anderson, Rebecca Moesta, Todd McCaffrey, Wesley Dean Smith, Martin Shoemaker, Tim Powers, and Jody Lynn Nye, amongst others. If it weren't for my fellow writers, critique partners, and beta readers I don't know where I would be. I have so much gratitude for my Writers of the Future and Superstars Writing Seminar cohorts and friends turned loyal readers that there are far too many people to name without fearing I'd accidentally leave someone out, but I hope they know who they are.

My biggest supporter is my husband who is the quiet force of a steady sea that keeps me upright during those sinking moments of self doubt.

In this collection are new and previously published stories, including the first story I sold that, reportedly, made people cry. 'The War Within' was inspired by a couple I knew who were dealing with dementia and remains one of my favorites. There are stories about step-parents with unyielding love and siblings trying to understand and forgive each other. Tales about choosing another life when the one you've been living no longer fits. Stories of strength and self-discovery, sitting with grief until you can breathe again, finding grace in self-acceptance, and love that isn't necessarily romantic, glamorous, or celebrated.

My favorite themes have always revolved around resilience, persistence, forgiveness, and healing. Here are stories rich with strife, misunderstanding, and the deep, often unspoken bonds of generational trauma. There are tales of lost love, love lost, love persevering, strength, revenge, letting go, and a bit of humor. But always, always there is hope. And in that hope, there is *magic*.

I hope you find something magical in these Temporary Tales.

~N.

CHAPTER ONE

THE WAR WITHIN

Originally published in the final issue of Deep Magic ezine, Summer 2021. Edited by Jeff Wheeler.

Arene kicked up dusty clouds with each step, her gaze trained on the grey sky. Sol, walking several feet behind, noticed the silt sticking to his robes and suspected she did it on purpose, a remnant of her teasing nature. There was a lightness to her steps, as if she didn't remember they'd been walking for a week. Sol felt the weight of each day growing heavier. Unlike his wife, he remembered all that she forgot. The monastery was his last hope of saving what was left of her fractured mind.

The scarf covering her head slipped to her shoulders. Unruly salt and pepper hair escaped, blowing softly in the breeze. She made no attempt to adjust it. The fabric was so thin it offered no protection from starling, but she wore it out of habit. It was something to cling to with each episode of confusion, which came several times a day now.

Sol's staff kicked up dirt as well, but there was no one behind them for miles. As his knees and back protested loudly, he required the staff to take more of his weight. He paused to catch his breath, admiring Arene's familiar movements.

Her head jerked one way, then the other, tension tightened her shoulders. Sol froze, powerless to stop the change occurring. His temples throbbed as she turned towards him, eyes frantic. She looked as if she might dart away, but she never did. Arene always chose fight over flight. It was her nature.

"Arene?" He opened his palms upward in deference.

"Who are you?" She asked, suspicion crept into her face. Her hands balled into fists.

"Sol." Calming his voice, he lay one hand over his heart.

"Do you know me?" Her eyes darkened, a storm in a blue sea.

The breeze gusted, flinging dust into Sol's face, though he made no move to stop it. "My love, if I were blind, I would know you. You are my home." He said, but her expression didn't change. She had lost him again.

Sol swallowed. "You found an old dog once, injured and bleeding. Do you remember?"

She stared, not responding. He continued. "You named him Jun. He was brown with white paws and a white…"

"Tail." She whispered, the storm in her eyes settling. "I brought him with me when I…where did I go?"

He offered his hand to her as he stepped forward, smiling. "Across the mountains. We have a farm there."

Familiar blue eyes met his. She took his hand as they continued walking. "I can't remember what happened to him."

He kissed her knuckles, the wind settling. "He lived a long life and loved you above all others. It was a long time ago."

He held her hand as long as she would allow, knowing the moment would pass soon enough, and he would be forgotten again. Each time it happened his chest grew heavier, tighter. Drawing her back had become increasingly difficult as the disease progressed. She had forgotten their home and their children. Could not comprehend that there were grandchildren. And even though she didn't always remember him, or the thirty years they shared, she remembered the dog they'd saved when they were on the run. She was a saver, she saved that dog and the man who followed her repeatedly over the years. Sol wondered if the memory of pets lingered in a different part of the brain and if, perhaps, they had their own type of magic.

Near midday they rested under a lonely tree, the first descent shade they'd been granted all day. The clouds burned away by unforgiving starling shine left them parched, their skin tender pink.

Sol's food was dust in his mouth as he closely monitored each bite she took, gently encouraging her to take another. She drank, but not enough, and ate even less. The curve of her collar bones jutted from the shoulders of her shirt, her sternum visible as sharp lines below her neck. Her clothing draped upon her frame, so loose he couldn't sew them in further.

Tucking a lock of her hair behind her ear, he adjusted the scarf around her face to protect her thinning skin. Sol had routed them onto less travelled roads two days prior and they had been fortunate to not encounter others. It was only another day or two more to the monastery.

He kissed her forehead. "I love you, Arene."

She smiled, the same sly smile he remembered. Her fingers interlaced with his. "I love you, too." She looked at the clear sky and frowned, sniffing the air. "Rain coming soon."

He nodded. "I feel it too. A needed reprieve."

"No, it's not." She scowled. "They are trying to stop us."

He quieted, swallowed instead of speaking and studied his worn boots.

"The ones who did this to me." She said, answering a question not asked.

Lacking the energy to argue, he stifled a sigh. He measured his words as he stood. "I am sure, when the time comes, you will be able to stop it."

She glared at him. "I don't think I know how anymore."

He tugged her gently to her feet, gently patting her shoulder. "Let's move on."

The day continued in a pattern of walk, rest, and eat. She forgot him once more and had to be led back to Jun's memory. Sol had tried memories of other pets they shared over the years, but Jun worked the best.

As dark clouds slid across the sky, Arene cursed and spat, the wind weaving around them. Cold rain stung their burned skin as Sol wrapped his arm around her and pressed on. She struggled, continuing to curse the storm. They took shelter in a grove of trees as lightning crashed.

Pulling the scarf away, she stared upwards, a determined look on her face. "I can stop this." She said, her hands clenched and began to glow.

His vision blurred as he shook his head, gently covering her hands with his. "Please, Reny, please don't." He begged. Her fierce nature was a reminder of who she had been and aided in softening his tone with her.

The sadness on his face stilled her.

"Every time you use it, it makes you worse." He whispered.

"What do you mean 'it makes me worse'?" She spat, the pitch of her voice asking to fight again.

Sol's calm was unyielding. "You lose a little more of yourself each time you use your power." His voice trembled. "You've lost the children and our home. You keep losing me." He said. "I'm afraid I won't be able to bring you back next time."

Arene stared at him, her eyes tracing the deep grooves around his eyes, lingering on his graying beard and thinning hair. Sol wondered when he had grown so old that she struggled to recognize him, but he hoped his words could still reach her. The glow from her fists faded and she leaned against him.

"We wait it out." He said, she nodded quietly. He held her until they drifted to sleep.

Sol woke alone in the quiet night. The empty place next to him was still warm from her. It was his first deep rest in many days, and he cursed himself for it. Gathering their belongings, he stumbled after her, arthritic knees and back arguing at his haste. Following muddy footprints, he called her name, but she did not answer. Her steps turned in a circle, lost, confused, then headed in another direction. Something not human screamed in the night. He ran, panic moving him forward.

Arene stood with her back to him, a long smear of dark liquid circled the ground around her feet. Sol inched forward, peering around her to the small deer that lay dead before her. It's soft eyes empty of life. She wrapped her arms tight around herself, shoulders shaking. Her fingernails dug into the backs of her arms.

"Arene?" He said cautiously.

She turned, eyes wide and wet. "She startled me." She gasped. "I didn't mean to, Sol. I swear I didn't mean to. It happened so fast."

He nodded and pulled her away from the sad scene. "It's okay," he said. "It's not who you are."

She cried until she forgot what she had done, and he did not remind her. He watched her sleep, calm and peaceful, while he chided himself for sleeping too hard.

What if it had been a group of travelers? Or a child that had wandered away from an encampment? If it were him lying dead on the ground, would she know enough to miss him? He rubbed calloused hands together, pushing the thoughts down.

They were almost to the village and then a short trek up the mountainside to the monastery. The Seers would help her, they had to, there were no other options.

It seemed a lifetime ago when she appeared on the battlements, drifting in on a hailstorm directed at their enemies. Her power was terrifying, and he loved her instantly. Having expected a thousand soldiers, not a young wind weaver, he should have been angered at the king. But instead found himself grateful. Of course, he heard rumors of a powerful woman able to block out the sky if she wanted. None of the rumors spoke of her truthfully, but none of them were wrong either. She was capable of easy horror, sweeping opposing forces away with gusts of sharp wind that painted the ground shades of red and brown. With a few sweeps of her hand she cleared the enemy like brushing crumbs from a table. Her black hair floated around her and, although she walked upon the ground, it was the wind that carried her.

Theirs was a professional relationship at first. She was not free to love or live, her life implicitly wrapped with the king's demands. But each battle drew them together and he saw she brought light to his darkness. Where he had spent years sowing seeds of bitterness, she ushered whispers of hope.

Sol had been in service to the king for a long while and knew enough of the political sphere to understand the impossibility of a relationship between them. He was several years her senior, a thought that made him more uncomfortable than not. What could he offer her that she could not receive from a more youthful and less bitter man?

She had a lively demeanor, despite the work they did, and he often found himself laughing in her company. Soon he noticed how often she looked at him. Some of the soldiers pointed out that he smiled more.

It was near the end of the war, victory only days away, when she entered his tent. He had resisted her, but she had persisted, and he found himself unable to say no to her, a pattern that lasted still.

She spoke bravely about her feelings. While he had cautiously held his tongue, like a coward. She laid a hand upon his chest and told him what she wanted. At first, he was reticent, but her conviction swayed him. They run and possibly die together if caught, or their deaths could anguish slowly over years, ever alone in the king's service.

The night the war was won, they fled before they could be labeled a threat to the king's power. They stole away to a neighboring land, finding a dog along the way.

Her eyelids fluttered in her sleep, Sol keeping guard beside her.

Arene was everything to him. Thanks to her, theirs was a quiet life with a farm that flourished. They had three children, healthy and brave, like their mother. And been blessed with four grandchildren. Their home was filled with love and laughter. There was no talk of war or what had come before and none of the king's assassins ever found them, so well had she hidden them.

Her first episode was quick and frightening and passed soon. But a month later there was another one, and then another, with larger lapses of memory between. Memory that did not come back.

Sol asked the children to hold the land and moved the two of them further into the forest after a disturbing incident with their son and grand-child. He hoped it would pass. She forgot to eat or drink, and he would wake in the middle of the night only to find her wandering far from home, lost and scared.

As her memory disintegrated, her paranoia increased. She believed the king had people everywhere, casting spells and stealing her thoughts. She could not see that it was her own magic that was doing the damage. With each spell there were repercussions, yet he could not convince her and arguing with her only increased her agitation. Mostly, he was silent or agreed with her to keep her calm. He was patient, focusing on his love for her when his frustrations threatened to break him. No matter what came, he would be with her until his end.

When starling rose, he woke her, managed to get her to eat a few bites before they continued their journey together.

"Where are we going?" She asked. "I know I should know, but I can't remember."

"It's all right." He said gently, pointing towards a looming point on the horizon. "Up there is the Zakon monastery. The Seers there will help us."

"Sol, what's wrong with me?" Fear edged into her voice.

He shook his head, pausing for a long moment before saying, "Your magic is taking its toll on your memory."

"Do you think they will help us?"

"They must," he replied, "or we will make them."

She walked beside him, eyes clearer than they had been in a long time. "If they can't fix me, what will happen?"

He didn't reply, his eyes fixed on the road. The weight in his chest kept him silent as emotions trapped his voice.

"I know what I am capable of." She slipped her fingers into his, "And so do you. If they cannot cure me, then I must be put down."

"No." He shook his head, pulled his hand away. "I won't do it and I won't allow it. Don't speak of this."

She pulled him back with a strength that belied her thin frame. "If left unchecked, I could kill thousands. I could kill all those we love and everything we have worked for. I could not live with that."

He shook his head again, dust in his eyes causing them to water. "I can't." He whispered.

She placed a hand on his chest. "You can. And you might have to. You might be the only one who could."

He refused to answer but gripped her hand as they walked. By the time they reached the village she had stayed with him nearly all day.

They rented a room at a tired inn that, Sol suspected, was not prone to crowding. They were dining on warm, hearty food when a young bard began to sing. He had prefaced it by saying it was an old song written before he was born, about a couple gone to legend. The general and the sorceress, whose courage and forbidden love won the great war and how she had spirited them away to a dark realm to live out their days in peace. It was done well, although the details were wrong, and perhaps a bit more romantically imbued than the reality had been. But the singer had a gifted voice. Arene clapped along, no recognition of the tale in her eyes. Sol watched her. No matter what the song said, this was the greatest war they would ever fight, this war within her.

Arene slept fitfully in the small bed, tossing, and crying out. She'd thrown open the window at one point, but Sol had been there to close it. He rested in a chair propped against the door, alerted by every sound she made.

When morning came, they gathered their bags and started up the steep road that led to the monastery. Sol paused repeatedly, catching his breath as the air thinned and the temperature dropped. Every day of his sixty-two years, and every sleepless night he'd endured to bring them this far catching up to him. Arene raced ahead, unconcerned by the altitude and easily outpacing him. She did not hear him call her name.

The grade of the road increased, forcing him to lean heavily on his staff with each step. Starling was nearing midday, the light ushered through in wispy breaths between the clouds that surrounded the peak.

Lightheaded, he struggled for breath, as he continued to place one foot in front of the other. His teeth chattered in the dampness. Rounding a small turn, he met Arene's eyes, sharp and darkened with distrust.

"You've come to spy on me." She hissed, fists glowing softly in threat.

Sol raised a clumsy hand but was met with gusts of wind and snow. Clutching his staff, he planted himself against the onslaught and spoke of the dog again. He yelled over the howls of wind, feet slipping. He cast a wary eye over the edge where they stood, the gusts pressing him towards it. It took a long time for Jun's name to register, almost too long, before her assault slowed.

The wind died, she was herself again. Arene looked from him to the edge, then down at the fading glow of her hands. She sobbed into his chest when he wrapped familiar arms around her.

"It's okay. Nothing happened." He said. The dark corner of the monastery roof stood a quarter mile ahead, barely visible in the clouds and snow. Maintaining an arm around her, they continued up the road. By the time they reached the entrance, she had stopped crying.

After several forceful knocks, a stubble headed man wrapped in a dull green robe escorted them into the small compound. He led them to a meager apartment and asked them to wait. The space was warmed by a fire in the stone hearth. Sol hung their wet cloaks on hooks near the fire and wrapped her in soft blankets that were laid out upon the couch.

The monk returned, settling a tray of hot tea and biscuits on a small table. He poured the tea and handed them their cups while he spoke. His name was Len, he informed them that the Seers had been expecting their arrival for some time but were currently in prayer. He encouraged them to rest and, offering a polite bow, left them alone. Sol heard the soft click of the lock in the door, but it did not concern him.

Sol sipped from the mug, grateful for the heat in his belly. His joints eased their complaints before the warmth of the fire, despite the damp clothing he wore. He caught his head nodding and shook himself. Arene smiled at him.

"What?" He asked.

"You are the most handsome man I've ever known." She said, raising the cup to her lips.

"Ah, my love, I fear you've lost your vision, too." He smirked.

"I see everything." She scooted next to him. "I knew when I met you long ago, covered in blood and scars, clinging to life but not embracing it." She patted his hand. "I knew that we would end up here someday. I could see our lives laid out before us."

He smiled, raising his eyebrows. "You knew we would end up in a monastery when we grew old? You truly are gifted, I never counted myself a religious man."

"Don't be ridiculous." She swatted him. "I knew you would be with me at the end. I knew we would take care of each other no matter what happened." She sipped her tea again. "And I was right."

He raised his cup in a mock toast. "I would have died without you a hundred times, having never known how to live, if we hadn't met. I ought to send the king my thanks, if I wasn't so sure he still wants us dead." His smile faded, his tone turned soft and serious. "You are the best of me, my dear."

She shook her head. "You are wrong, again. How could I marry a man who is wrong so often?" She winked. "I would have been the one to fall long ago if it weren't for you."

He frowned. She took his hand, tracing the lines on his knuckles with the cool tips of her fingers.

"How long do you suppose wind weavers live?" She asked.

"I don't know. Same as everyone else, I guess." He shrugged, shifting in his seat.

"No. I have outlived the oldest one I ever heard of by fifteen years. I never wanted to make my burden your own, but I suppose there was no way of avoiding it. My plan was to slip away in the middle of the night when I first noticed the decline- but it came so suddenly that I forgot to leave." She scowled as she continued to study his hand. "You were right, you know? About the magic stealing my mind." She cleared her throat. "It's the price extracted for such a gift. The more you use, the faster your mind erodes. If I maintained my employment with the king and continued to meet his demands, I might have lasted another ten years." Her gaze drifted towards the fire as she continued. "Ten years of service and he would have put me down like a rabid dog, probably before I lost myself. It's the way it has always been for those like me."

He studied the delicate line of her jaw, the black and gray curls that framed her face and, although her skin was spotted by years in the starling and her cheeks grown hollow, he could only see the beauty that was her, looking back at him. He opened his mouth to speak, but she stopped him.

"I need to get this out while I am still here, before I am gone again." She gripped his hand, eyes bearing into his own. "If it weren't for you, I would have had no life at all." She continued. "I would not have known motherhood, or a simple life. I would have been used up for the services I could provide. But you have such goodness and so much love. You say that I am the best of you but, truly, it has always been the other way 'round." The blue of her eyes was changing again, her clarity fading. "I only have one more request for you."

He stared at her. "I already told you no."

"It might not be a choice, dear. My rage grows stronger every time I have an episode." Her voice trembled. "The confusion, the anger, this power, these do not lend to good endings." She squeezed his hand again. "You might have to."

Sol leaned forward, resting his elbows on his knees, and shaking his head. The wood popped in the fireplace. Arene dropped his hand and stood, glancing nervously around the room.

"Where are we?" She asked.

He sighed and did not reply. He rubbed his forehead with knotty hands and squeezed his eyes shut, attempting to alleviate the steady ache behind them. Leaning back, he watched her pace around the room, pulling out books and running her fingers along each surface. She seemed unaware of his presence.

There was a small tap on the door. The soft release of the lock sounded, and Len ushered an older woman inside. Her robes were bright green, matching a scarf piled high on her head. She smiled warmly, although the smile did not reach her eyes.

Sol stood as Arene turned towards them, scowling. The woman swept past Sol and embraced Arene with open arms. Arene froze, caught off guard, her expression softened.

"It's good to see you, my dear," the woman said. "I expected you sooner, though." She took hold of Arene's hands and pulled her gently to the seat. She handed her the tea she had abandoned. The woman motioned for Sol to join them as the younger monk stepped outside.

"Do I know you?" Arene asked, an awkward smile crossed her lips.

"You should drink, dear." The woman's smile was steady. "You must be worn from your journey. We have plenty of time to talk."

Arene took a large drink, closing her eyes as she tipped the mug back. The woman gently took the mug from her hands and placed it on the table. Arene's eyes grew heavy as she reclined in the chair. She frowned slightly, tilting her head.

"It's all right," the woman said. "You can rest if you want. All will be well when you wake." The woman draped a soft blanket around Arene, who drifted to sleep. The woman turned to Sol, all warmth replaced by a serious demeanor.

"We have some time before the tea wears off." She said and extended her hand to him. "I am Kyra, the Abbess here."

There was strength in her grip. "Sol. This is Arene. The tea?" He asked, studying his mug.

"Len mixed it in her cup, per my orders. I thought it wise to temper any unpredictable elements." She smiled, continuing, "I know who you are, and who you were. Honestly, I always wondered if she would find her way here." Dark eyes swept over him, giving a quick assessment. "I believe I know why you are here, but you must ask for help before I can extend it."

He cleared his throat, glancing to Arene, noting the steady rise of her chest. "Can I ask anything?"

She nodded. "You may ask whatever your heart desires, but I give no guarantees that we will provide it."

"She's ill." Sol said, the words heavy on his tongue. The Abbess waited patiently, "She's lost large pieces of her memory over the last few months and is dangerous to herself, and others." He rubbed his hands together.

"She's gifted, you know. I had to isolate us after she didn't know our children. I was worried that she might…" he let the words fall and coughed again as his voice broke. "She's powerful, but it's getting harder to bring her back. She's asked me to end her, which I will not do. We thought, I thought, you might be able to…"

A lump rose in his throat. "Can you help her?"

Kyra's sharp eyes assessed him. "I understand how much she means to you, General. Arene is one of the most powerful weavers of recent history, and the fact that she has lasted this long is a true testament to her strength. Most weavers have gone mad by the time they are thirty."

He gave a knowing grin. "She's past that by more than a bit, but there's still a lot of life in her yet."

The Abbess studied Arene as she slept. "She asked you to put her down, and you refused?"

He nodded.

"Do you know the price for coming here?" She asked. He shook his head. "It's possible we could restore her mind," Kyra said, "but it won't be easy, and I make no promises." She looked at Sol. "It would be the end of her weaving. Do you know how she would feel about that?"

He swallowed hard, he didn't know nor did he care. He wanted her back; the weaving never made her more than who she already was.

"Do whatever it takes."

"Be careful what you say." She cautioned. "The cost may be greater than you can imagine. Are you willing to make a personal sacrifice to restore her mind?"

His arthritic fingers clasped together, trembling. "I am."

Her sad eyes studied him. She stood, "I will need to discuss this situation with my brothers and sisters. You may find me at starling rise in the main house. We can determine the option that best suits you both, and the means of payment."

"What if she has another episode tonight?" He asked.

She shook her head. "She is powerless within these walls. But if you would like to get some sleep, which you appear to need, she should sleep until mid-morn tomorrow. If she should wake, there is always one of us available and we would happily provide you with more tea."

Kyra locked the door behind her. Arene stirred as cool air kissed her cheek when the door closed. Sol wrapped the blanket around her and carried her to the bed in the corner. He kissed her forehead, then lay down beside her, draping an arm around her. The sound of her breath, the scent of her, the beat of her heart starling him to sleep.

He startled awake before starling rise, instinctively sitting up and searching for her. Arene slept peacefully beside him, her face serene.

A basin of clean water and fresh clothing waited for him near the fire. He bathed and dressed keeping a watchful eye on Arene as she slept. He chewed his lip, unable to recall the last time he had left her. As if on cue there was a tap at the door.

"I will watch over her while you are with our Abbess." Len said.

Sol looked back to the bed, hesitant. Taking a deep breath, he invited him in and set off towards the main house.

Starling crested in the eastern sky, painting it orange and pink. The mountain air was crisp and bitter cold. He watched the star rise and shivered, telling himself it was the cold and nothing more. He never recalled trembling in battle before, but now he found himself anxious regularly.

Sol opened an ornate door to the high peaked building, allowing a blast of frigid air in with him and snuffing out several candles that burned around the room. Kyra sat on the floor, legs neatly folded underneath her. Her eyes closed, hands folded in her lap, she wore the same green robes and scarf. He stood along the back of the room, unsure of what to do.

She let out a long exhale, opening her eyes. "Come and sit, please." She motioned toward a cushion in front of her.

He lowered himself to the ground, stiff knees and hips uncooperative. He needed to shift every few minutes or a different part of his body would ache or threaten numbness. The cold made it worse.

She waited patiently for him to settle. "How is she?"

"Still sleeping."

"Good. Hopefully, we can decide our course of action before she wakes."

He crossed his arms. "What can be done for her?"

"There are a few options for you to consider. Once we have decided on what will happen, we can discuss what payment is to be rendered."

He nodded, resisting the urge to rub his eyes.

"Option one is to leave Arene in our care. She can live out the rest of her days while being kept safe and unable to harm others."

"Could I stay with her?" He asked.

She shook her head. "No. Your presence would only confuse her as her cognition continues to decline, and it would torture you to witness it."

Sol was quiet, leaving her would feel like betrayal. "What else?"

"Option two would be that we strip the rest of her powers and let you return home with her. Her memory would not deteriorate further, however, neither would it be restored. The weaving would not steal anymore of her. This is the I option would recommend."

He sighed, wondering if he could continue to care for her like this for the remainder of his days? He was ten years her senior, what was the likelihood that he would outlast her? What would happen to her if he went first?

He slumped, his hands stilled their worrying. "Is there anything else?"

She pursed her lips. "There is another option, but I warn you, I do not think it is what she would want."

"Tell me."

"To restore her memory, we would need to remove yours. All thirty years of your experiences together, to be specific. Right now, her mind is like a field ravaged by fire, burned and charred. We need to plant seeds, memories, but to regrow them they must be authentic to her. We would remove her powers, so that the new memories would not deteriorate." She stared at him calmly as she spoke, awaiting his reaction.

"What would happen to me?" Sol asked.

"You would remember very little of the last thirty years."

"I would not know her? Or my children?" He rubbed his forehead, squeezing his eyes shut.

"No."

He was silent for a long time, the candles casting moving shadows around them.

"What is the price for this?" He asked.

"The extraction and keeping of her powers is enough. We can use the weaving to protect our compound." She said, "But it is a large sum for her to pay. And losing your own memories seems adequate payment for you."

He shifted uncomfortably. "Would I be permitted to stay here?" He asked. "I don't want to burden her."

"That could be an option." She replied. "But after the transfer it would be Arene's decision."

"There is no way to hide me from her? You could tell her I had gone, and she could return home without me."

"I would never allow that." Kyra's voice rose a fraction. "You forget your value to her."

He stared at the floor between them, working his hands together as she watched him weigh his options.

His eyes glistened in the candlelight. "I'll do anything to make her well again. It doesn't matter that I won't remember."

She sighed and gave a small nod. "I thought you might say that."

"How do we begin?" He asked, he shifted again.

She stood and held out her hand to him, the older woman helping him rise to his feet. "We start by having a cup of tea."

"Arene?"

"Will sleep through the entire process." She patted his arm. "It will be painless for both of you, don't worry."

"How long will it take?"

"It will take some time to siphon her powers, and a little longer to withdraw your memories. But it will take no time at all to give them to her."

Taking his arm, they stepped out into the cold morning. The sky was brighter shades of blues with hints of orange still lingering on the edges. Starling shone bright, illuminating the world around them, the birds sang sweetly.

"What will I remember?" He asked, staring into the sky and shivering.

"It's difficult to say exactly," she said. "Most likely, you will remember who you were before you met Arene. Your childhood memories and your time in the war, perhaps. You might remember the skills you had before you met her, but not much of what you learned since. I cannot say what else, it's different for everyone."

"Will I be able to make new memories?" He asked.

"It's possible, but there are no guarantees."

Sol's shoulders rounded as he gripped the railing and looked down into the precipice below. The wind swept away tears that escaped his eyes. His voice was soft. "I won't remember her at all."

Kyra placed a heavy hand on his shoulder. "You know, memory is a funny thing. I've found it is tied so closely to emotion that it can be unpredictable. For instance, although your exact memories will shift, the emotion tied to those memories remains. You may have a pleasant attachment to something without understanding why."

He did not reply, his thoughts his own.

She led him back to the apartment where Len greeted him, along with ten new faces, each with shorn heads and green robes. They served him tea and biscuits, speaking kind words of reassurance. When he felt the sedative take effect, he lay down on the bed beside his love, who still slept peacefully.

He held her hand, a small wetness rolling down his cheek. He did not brush it away.

A drum beat in his ears as he looked to Kyra and nodded. Closing his eyes, he drifted away, the thrum of chanting the last thing he heard.

Sol opened his eyes to dim light, though he could not recall where he was nor why his body ached so much. He groaned, looking around.

A woman sat on the edge of the bed, holding his hand. Her eyes were sharp, ice blue, and gentle. Her face wore a history of beauty, with salt and pepper curls falling past her shoulders. She felt familiar and, though he could not place her, he liked her immediately. Her smile was comforting as she brushed cool fingers over his brow. He found himself smiling back.

"Do I know you?" He asked, his voice hoarse.

"I am Arene." Her eyes shone. "And I am here to take you home."

CHAPTER TWO

AN UNTETHERED LIFE

Grandfather Hovan died peacefully in his sleep in his eighty-second year. As the patriarch of a family of necromancers, it was foolish to expect him to stay dead.

Lani's mother, Helene, found him in the morning when he didn't come to breakfast at the family table. There were tears, but the serene smile on his face lessened the pain of loss for everyone except Lani. With his passing came the realization that her life would drastically change, and she was powerless to stop it.

As news of the elderly necromancer's death reached nearby villages, those who owed him debts worried he would come to collect while they slept. An edge of trepidation rippled through portions of the superstitious populace, and the Hovan family hired guards to protect the funeral home and his body. The dead always struck fear in the hearts of the living - unless it was one of their own.

People didn't understand how necromancy worked and Lani's family had spent generations ensuring those secrets were well kept. Raising and controlling the dead took only a bit of magic. The real trick was putting them back to rest again. Grandfather said that was where unskilled necromancers struggled. He'd laid a long, worried look on Lani as he'd spoken those words.

For the past ten years, Helene had managed the family's necromancy and funerary business, and it was assumed that Bran, Lani's brother, would follow in her footsteps. He had a natural talent for necromancy and a suitable temperament for the job - much more so than his talentless younger sister. Lani had not reanimated the dead since she was young and, after that traumatic experience, she had no interest in it. Her mother believed that Lani simply didn't apply herself, but there was a deeper reason that Lani couldn't voice out loud - she felt uncomfortable profiting off of others' grief. And after what happened to her father, Grandfather supported her decision.

Lani knew that Grandfather had mixed feelings about his own demise. He'd lived too near death to fear it the way others did, but he'd worried about leaving her. As his body deteriorated over the past year, he relied heavily on the herbal painkiller devil's claw for relief. Each morning, Lani would prepare a batch of the pungent herb and mix it into his tea. Despite reconnecting with old friends through letters and putting on a brave face, his eyes betrayed the agony he felt. For Lani's sake, he endured the pain of life until his final breath, leaving her with a heavy weight of guilt.

With her role as caregiver gone, a new burden loomed ahead - an arranged marriage to whoever brought the best connections to her family. With their status and power within the tribe, there would be no shortage of suitors, although her mother would likely dismiss most of them for not being suitable for their family's image. Lani's own desires held little weight in this decision; it was all about what was best for the family, or more accurately, her mother's ambitions for tribal leadership.

Lani had wanted her family to wake Grandfather and speak to him one last time, but Helene had balked. Bran and his wife, Fala, had agreed. The old man was at peace and there was nothing more that needed to be said. Plus, they knew he wouldn't really hear them, anyway. In this matter, like so many others, Lani's voice didn't matter.

People died with things unsaid and undone every day but, according to the Hovan family's knowledge of necromancy, souls didn't worry about those issues. It was the people left behind that often struggled with closure. Sometimes with guilt, like when Siran's sister died while saving her from drowning. Or with anger, in the cases of adult children with abusive or absent parents. But most frequently, people feared that their loved one passed without knowing something. Why they'd done or said a particular thing in the past. Sometimes they worried the dead hadn't known how much they were loved. People worried the deceased had never forgiven or understood them.

Necromancy offered a chance to heal these wounds for a hefty fee. The Hovan family would reanimate the corpse and have it listen and comfort the living until their tears ran out. The deceased would rub a consoling hand along a back, pat a shoulder or, even, provide a hug. Then the body would be returned to its coffin and they would cast the inanimation spell. A funerary burn ensured it wouldn't rise again.

Providing closure was a highly profitable business. And though cus-tomers believed they were talking to their loved ones, the necromancers suspected that, in actuality, the corpses were nothing more than soulless meat and bones. Helene insisted that once the soul departed, there was no way to bring it back. But when Grandfather and Lani had been alone once, he'd admitted to having doubts. He theorized in a hopeful voice that perhaps some memories or emotional attachment lingered. Maybe the soul didn't completely depart, not if they had regrets. Then he'd shrugged nonchalantly, as if he'd said too much, and emphasized that no one really knew anything about life after death. Not even the necromancers, no matter what anyone said.

The morning of the funeral was stifling, made worse by the crowd that gathered to pay their respects. Neighboring provinces had sent representatives and gifts to honor him. The funerary ship was already stocked with flowers and waited in the river for the procession and lighting ceremony.

Lani stood in her best white funerary robe, the one that she and Grandfather had spent hours mending the seams on only a week prior. Bran stood tall and somber beside her with Fala and her swelling belly on his other side. Helene was at the rear of the receiving line, greeting everyone with a tightly controlled countenance that hid any signs of grief. Families with single men of marriageable age gripped Helene's hand and subtly glanced at Lani, laying the foundation for negotiations to come.

Lani squirmed. Helene would be in a hurry to get rid of her, especially since most of her peers had been married for years. The exception was Siran, Lani's closest friend. As the ninth of twelve children, Siran had forged her own path under the radar of her tired parents. She was fiercely independent and would probably shed blood before anyone forced her into marriage. Lani couldn't help but envy her for that strength. In another world or time, she would have been content staying by Siran's side forever, but she was bound by family and societal expectations.

Siran arrived at the wake shortly after the family did, dressed in her finest linen and had even smoothed down her usually unruly curls with oil. She politely made her way through the line despite receiving disapproving looks from Lani's mother. Bran cleared his throat when Lani held Siran's hand for too long. He said nothing directly, but he'd known where Lani's heart lay for a long time. Much like Grandfather had.

When the funerary hut was full of bodies ripe with perspiration, the family made their way forward for a last goodbye. Helene went first, squeezing her father's hand and brushing her stained red lips on his stiffened cheek. Bran was next. He placed a hand on Fala's belly and whispered last sentiments before wiping his eyes and moving away.

Grandfather's oaky complexion had turned ashy in death. His hand was stiff and unyielding in Lani's. The lump in her throat blocked her words. Sandalwood incense and a hint of devil's claw wafted toward her on a sultry breeze. Her vision blurred.

"Lani." Her mother's voice was sharp but hushed, meant to hurry her along.

With a swallow, Lani leaned over him. Her chest constricted. An electric pulse skittered across her skin as she kissed his cold forehead and whispered a final prayer. The sudden reflexive crush of her grandfather's grip made her gasp. She tried to pull away, but he held her. His eyes slowly opened. Grandfather stared at her vacantly with the milky coated eyes of the reanimated.

Helene hissed under her breath and stepped closer, blocking the view of the others in the room. Her face twisted into an expression of disgust, and tears welled up in her eyes for the first time since his death. Her voice shook with something uncharacteristically small and wounded. "What have you done?"

"N... nothing. I didn't do anything. I've never..." Lani's voice trailed off. There had been one other incident before, but she couldn't remember it. It had happened at her father's funeral when she was just three years old. Helene and Grandfather had taken care of the gruesome aftermath. It was something often referenced whenever Lani resisted her mother's demands. She couldn't blame Helene's resentment, not really. Lani had been grateful that she'd never shown aptitude for necromancy since then. At least not until now.

It was a little-known fact that only the person who awakened the dead could put them back to rest. If they could not do so, then more drastic measures had to be taken. A sick feeling churned in Lani's stomach as she silently begged her grandfather to return to his slumber, but he only squeezed her hand tighter. She winced in pain.

Bran appeared at Lani's side, struggling to undo Grandfather's grasp before it broke her fingers. "I didn't hear your spell," Bran said.

"I didn't say one. You know I can't do this. This can't be me."

"Well, it wasn't me or mother. And certainly, wasn't Fala," he said. He whispered his usual spell to make the dead slumber but, in response, Grandfather blinked once slowly, released Lani's hand and gripped the coffin's sides. The wood crunched beneath his fingers. The siblings exchanged horrified glances and took a few steps back.

Helene leaned in closer, ignoring the growing commotion from the concerned crowd, and cast her inanimation spell. She pressed a hand flat across his chest and made to keep him down, frantically repeating the mantra. But the corpse of Elder Hovan paid his daughter no mind. He sat up and, with a slight push, sent her hurtling to the floor.

Gasps and screams careened through the air as the dead necromancer sat upright. A crush of bodies shoved violently through the doors to the street, leaving only an elderly couple and Siran behind, each of whom looked more curious than afraid.

Grandfather threw a spindly leg over the edge of the coffin. Bran and Fala backed further away. Helene still lay on the floor, staring at the corpse as it came to stand on sturdy legs. His eyes were trained solely on Lani. She froze as grandfather walked toward her, but she had no fear. The man who'd raised and supported her more than Helene ever had stood before her and waited.

"Bran? What should I do?" she whispered.

"Put him back to sleep," he replied. He said the spell that he normally used slowly and Lani repeated it, but to no avail. Grandfather didn't move.

Helene rose to her feet. Her voice quivered as she spoke. "Fix this, Lani. Put him back to rest." Lani turned to her, catching the pained expression in her mother's eyes as she slowly shook her head. "I can't manage it again. It's brutal and messy and..." A small gasp escaped her lips. "Please, not to my own father."

"I don't know how. I...I'm sorry," Lani said. Grandfather stepped a little closer at the sound of her voice, as if her pain had beckoned him.

The Hovan family looked awkwardly at each other before a hoarse voice interrupted.

"There are other ways for him to rest." The elder woman who still sat on a bench said. Her companion, a man of a similar age, helped her stand. Sarin was gone.

Helene's eyes narrowed. "What do you mean? Who are you?"

The old woman shuffled forward, leaning on her partner's arm. "I'm Maris. Peri, my brother—maybe you've heard of him? — was a necromancer too. He and Elder Hovan studied together when they were young, before family obligations pulled them apart. He died last week. We came to deliver the news to Elder Hovan, but we were too late." She nodded at Grandfather. "Peri, rest his soul, sometimes struggled with the last step of necromancy. When he'd reanimated a child and couldn't make her sleep again..." She sighed and shook her head. "Well, I'm sure you can imagine the moral tortures that ensued. There's a village across the northern border known as the Deadlands. That's where he took her, and others."

"A village?" Lani's voice was thin. Grandfather mentioned Peri's name with curious frequency over the years, always with a hint of nostalgia.

"There's a route you can take that bypasses any villages and can help to avoid the less understanding," the old man spoke this time. "I can draw you a map."

Lani's stomach clenched. "Me?"

Helene moved closer to Lani and placed a trembling hand on her daughter's shoulder. "He'll only follow the one that woke him. You know that."

Lani hadn't been out of their province in twenty years. The thought of leaving the security she'd always known sparked something deep within her. "What will happen when we get there? Will someone tend to him?"

Maris sighed and replied reluctantly, "They will tend to him as he decays."

Grotesque images flooded Lani's mind and made her shudder. She turned back to face her grandfather's milky eyes, hoping to find some hint of warmth or recognition, but they were empty.

Helene grasped her hand. "You must do this. For the sake of our family."

Lani walked carefully down the overgrown path as thunder rolled through the dark clouds overhead. Cold rain stung her cheeks, but the old man didn't notice such discomfort. Devoid of soul or memories, Grandfather seemed like nothing more than an empty vessel that was drawn like a moth to Lani's light. He followed her because he had no thoughts of doing otherwise. After all, unintentionally or not, she'd been the one to wake him and should have been the one to make him sleep again. But every attempt had failed. Years of Helene's nagging echoed through her thoughts. She should have practiced.

Every so often, she'd take his hand, noting that the callouses born of seventy laborious years seemed smoother on his sallow skin. Only another twenty miles until they reached the border. Helene had wanted to send an escort for safety, but Bran had resisted. It was unlike her brother, who was usually so protective. But he'd hugged her fiercely before she left and told her he loved her.

If all went well, they'd reach the Deadlands by tomorrow's sunset. Grandfather would be safe, even if his body continued to fester.

Grandfather's steps were uneven. The left foot dragged irrhythmically and had already caused a fall. He'd landed hard on his hip but had carried on. If he broke a bone, she wasn't sure what she would do. He'd grown so frail over the last few years that she'd assumed he'd be as light as a child. Now, she worried the weight of rot would be too much to bear and, though his belly hadn't distended yet, Lani doubted she'd be able to carry him. She wrinkled her nose at the faint herbal scent that still clung to him.

Before Lani left, her mother promised that there would be changes upon her return. Helene's voice was filled with barely contained emotion, and Lani knew her future would be mapped out for her. She would be forced into a quick marriage with someone of high status and no great integrity. Helene might make her study necromancy again to ensure that mishaps like this wouldn't happen in the future.

These prospects made Lani consider staying as a caretaker in the Deadlands. It would be peaceful there, and she didn't mind taking care of her grandfather. It would certainly differ from the life she had to return to. Death may be messy, but the suffocation of familial expectations felt like no life at all. However, leaving Sarin behind was something she couldn't consider.

Sarin had vanished before the old couple started speaking, but Lani tried to ignore the sting of that absence. It had been a family matter, after all, and Sarin knew enough of her mother to respect that. There'd been no time to seek Sarin out and, after changing clothes and putting together a knap sack of essential items, Lani and grandfather had left after sunset. With decay setting in, they couldn't delay.

After three days of steady walking, a soreness had settled in her legs and back that intensified with each movement, only slightly lessened by the sharper sting of blistered feet. She'd slept a handful of hours but was too worried about grandfather wandering to allow much more than that, even though he was always in the same place when she woke. The lack of sleep made her careless in ways that had set them back almost a full day.

She'd misread the map and taken a wrong turn at a fork in the path. That error led them off route and they'd practically stumbled into a small village. Though she had seen no one, it didn't stop her from looking anxiously behind them every so often. Any fool with half sense would see what grandfather was immediately. There were stubborn superstitions about the dead and if they were caught this far from their province, they'd both be set on fire. Grandfather to make sure that he didn't rise again, and Lani for good measure.

So far, they'd been lucky. Other than the occasional call of vultures above, they'd been alone.

The soft rain morphed into stinging drops that forced them to shelter beneath a tree. She coaxed him to sit beside her and pulled a hood over his head before securing her own. It was better to wait than risk slipping in the mud. He stared at her in that unnerving way, as if waiting for her to speak. She stifled a sad sigh, knowing that the creature before her wasn't really her grandfather. It didn't have a soul. But doubt pecked at her and she kept thinking of those words she'd wanted to say at the funeral. Questions she hadn't been brave enough to ask before now.

Grandfather had mentioned Peri frequently over the years, usually combined with some story that brought a wistful smile to his face. Though they'd never visited each other in all of Lani's life, the men had exchanged letters regularly. Yet he'd rarely spoke of his wife who'd died during Helene's birth.

Lani wondered if Grandfather had always known about Sarin. He'd certainly never discouraged the affection. In fact, he'd invited Sarin to noonday meals when Helene was absent. He'd been fond of their friendship. Almost envious.

"Did you want the life you lived?" she whispered finally, her voice competing with the heavy drumming of rain against the leaves. Even knowing an answer wouldn't come, she feared it. What if he'd been strapped to an unwanted life because his parents dictated it and had tried to spare his granddaughter the same fate?

He maintained the same glazed expression he'd worn since he was animated. He couldn't answer. His vocal chords had probably rotted by now, anyway. But she needed to ask. She'd always suspected that the reason he'd loved her so much was because he'd seen himself in her. Lani bit her lip and looked upwards. The leaves danced in the rain. It would be dark soon.

"Did you love him?" A raindrop landed on her forehead. Lani couldn't look at him. If she did, she might remember that the thing she spoke to wasn't really alive. She might as well have been talking to the wind. "I always thought you and I had more in common than the others. A connection. The way you kept mother from marrying me off when I was eighteen, and discouraged her control without revealing what you must have known about me. About Sarin." She let the rain drip down her face onto her closed eyelids. "I just wanted to say—"

"Lani?" A familiar voice cut through the rustling leaves. Sarin stumbled into view. Her wide face, flushed with relief and exertion, was framed by matted ebony curls. Mud caked her boots up to her calves. Sodden dark robes clung to her tall frame. Sarin dashed forward with a cry and Lani stood to meet her. They embraced, and Lani shuddered, suppressing the unexpected tears that stung her eyes.

"What are you doing here?" Lani asked against Sarin's neck.

"I've been trying to catch up with you for two days," Sarin said. She pulled back, cupping Lani's cheeks with her cool hands. "I can't believe they let you do this alone. If your mother hadn't been so against me, I'd have caught you the day you left." Her gaze flicked to the old man, who watched the interaction impassively. She tilted her head and gave a wicked smile. "Helene's going to be mighty angry when she finds out that Bran told me where you went."

Lani pulled back but held Sarin's hands. "Bran told you?"

She nodded. "He was worried. So was I. You've never been this far from home."

Lani hugged her again, letting out a long exhalation. "Thank you."

They settled beneath the tree while the downpour turned to a drizzle. Sarin leaned against her and pulled out a small wooden box from her bag. She pulled out two buns, a small block of cheese, and a pair of red apples, splitting the portions with Lani before leaning back with a sigh.

"I lost you when you took that wrong turn, took me a while to realize those were your footsteps heading back." She nodded at the old man. "His legs getting worse, isn't it?"

Lani nodded. "He's fallen once. I've slowed our pace to accommodate." She bit into the apple, savoring its sweetness before she spoke again. "Did you see anyone?"

Sarin shrugged. "Not exactly." Lani gave her a questioning look. "I didn't see anyone, but there were other footprints. Too big to be yours, too even to be grandfather's."

A shiver worked its way down Lani's spine. "Where?"

"On the other path. They disappeared northwest into the woods before the split."

If they'd been seen, Lani would have expected an attack by now. That the tracks veered in the same general direction they were heading made her nervous.

"You look tired," Sarin said with a concerned voice. "You should get some rest."

She shook her head. "Grandfather—"

"I'll watch him. You're not alone in this anymore."

Lani bit her lip to keep it from trembling and squeezed Sarin's hand. "Thank you."

"Bran sent a letter too, but you can read it when you wake up." Sarin gave a compassionate smile. "Go to sleep."

———— ✦ ————

For the last five years, Lani had been conditioned to wake at any sound that might suggest her grandfather needed help. So, when she opened her eyes to the misty pre-dawn light, she was not prepared for what she saw.

Sarin leaned against the trunk beside her, eyes closed, breathing deep and calm. Grandfather sat facing away from them, his spindly legs crossed, staring into the brush with a rigid back. His posture should have alerted her that something was amiss.

She pushed away from the tree and gasped. A machete lay on the ground at her feet. Its blade coated in blood. A severed hand still gripped the handle. Lani screamed and kicked it reflexively away.

Sarin immediately sprang to her feet, panic filling her wide eyes as she scanned their surroundings. A dagger shook in her grasp as she scanned the clearing. The sudden movement sent nesting birds surging into the sky.

"What happened?" Sarin asked, spinning cautiously around until her eyes landed on the machete. "Who...?" Her voice trailed away.

Grandfather still sat, unmoving. A spatter of crimson that hadn't been there the night before dotted his robes. Lani knelt beside him, noting the shades of red and brown beneath his nails. She hesitated before gently turning his hands over to reveal sticky blood smears.

"Grandfather?" Lani asked softly. He shouldn't have been able to do anything without her orders, and she only knew how to make him sit, stand, or follow. According to long held necromancy teachings, the dead were incapable of acting on their own. But the gore on his hands said otherwise. Maybe she'd made him act while she dreamed, but that made little sense. She would have remembered something, and she definitely should have woken up when he'd stirred.

Sarin pried the fingers from the machete's handle with a morbid curiosity. Lani's thoughts flicked to the village she'd almost stumbled into. Just because they had seen no one didn't mean that no one had seen them.

"Where's the rest of him?" Sarin asked, nudging grandfather with her knee. Although his head turned slightly toward her, his eyes stayed focused on the woods. Dropping the severed hand to the ground, she followed his gaze. Gripping the machete in one hand and the dagger in the other, Sarin stepped toward the brush.

"What are you doing? You're no fighter," Lani said.

Sarin glanced back at her. "I'm better equipped for this than you are."

While Lani had spent most of her time doing domestic tasks and simple chores, Sarin had made a living doing labor-intensive jobs like chopping wood, digging trenches, and repairing roofs. She was stubbornly determined and hated being told what she couldn't do - qualities that Lani admired about her.

Sarin darted into the bushes. After making a quick assessment of their immediate perimeter, she found nothing and returned.

Lani helped Grandfather to his feet. "We should go. Maybe we can make it there by nightfall."

They moved steadily down the road. Sarin walked at the rear of the group behind grandfather. The machete hung from her belt, one of her hands rested upon the hilt of her dagger.

The sun burned through the clouds by midday. Suffocating humidity clung to them like a shroud. They made it eight miles before resting. The concerns of threats around them had displaced Lani's physical discomfort.

The worry that her grandfather might have murdered someone at her behest, she kept to herself.

Sarin tipped a gourd back, taking a long gulp of water as they rested beneath a patch of thick shade. Lani wiped the sweat from the back of her neck with her sleeve while watching the old man.

Grandfather had been acting strange since that morning. It wasn't anything specific that she could point out, but his eyes seemed slightly clearer. His movements were more focused and, again, she got the feeling that he was on alert.

"Should reach the border by —" Sarin's words ended with a startle. Grandfather had spun to face her, much too quickly for either a man of eighty-two years, or a necromanced body. He gripped her arm to keep her from falling backward, then yanked the machete from her belt.

Before Lani could reach for him, he raced away. Sarin stumbled. The gourd dropped to the ground as grandfather disappeared into the surrounding foliage. He barely disturbed the greenery. Lani cried after him and started to follow, but Sarin held her back.

Sarin shook her head and brought a finger to her lips, motioning Lani to stay behind her. The women crept through the brush, following the old man's offset footsteps. Ahead, there was a muffled cry and a man's yell.

"Got him!"

They crashed through a row of bushes and into a small clearing. Grandfather was on his knees, flanked by two brawny men. They wrapped a rope around his neck and tied his arms behind him. A third man lay on the ground gripping his side where blood seeped between his fingers. The machete lay beside him, the blade newly slick and coated red.

"Let him go!" Lani said. Sarin stretched an arm out to keep her from rushing forward. The largest of the men held an axe, the other a long sword. There was kindling piled high around the base of a tree, and another loop of rope already around it. They'd come prepared.

The larger man spat on the ground upon seeing the women. "Looks like we don't have to go hunting for them after all."

The other man finished tying grandfather's wrists and then turned towards them, sword at the ready. Sarin shielded Lani behind her and raised her hands cautiously. "Please, there's no need for violence. Just let him go and we'll leave peacefully."

"No need for violence?" scoffed the man with the axe. "He's already killed one of our own."

Lani shook her head in disbelief. "That's impossible."

"Protecting you, I assume," he sneered. "Thought you could pass through our territory with that abomination?"

"He's not an abomination," Lani said as she tried to push past Sarin, who gripped her arm.

The axe-wielding man shook his head in disapproval. "Nothing good comes from bringing back the dead."

Lani softened her voice, trying to calm the escalating tension. "That's why we're taking him to the border."

The other man pointed his sword at them. "What do you think, Javi?"

Javi shrugged. "This is as far as they go."

"But—" Lani started.

"Anyone who travels with the dead is tainted with darkness. Bad luck follows. We can't let you leave," Javi said.

Sarin lunged sideways, beneath the man's blade. Her shoulder collided with his gut. He sprawled on the ground, sword landing several feet away.

"Run, Lani!"

Lani's feet refused to move. She screamed Sarin's name. Grandfather turned slightly, eyes momentarily focusing on the grappling bodies.

Sarin sent two swift punches to the man's face. His eyes dazed before instinct took over. He flipped Sarin onto her back, pinning her. His fist crunched into her nose.

"Sarin!" An electric surge rippled across Lani's skin. She raised her bag above her head and charged forward.

A second punch met Sarin's eye. She choked and squirmed, trying to block the next blow.

The injured man on the ground grabbed Lani's leg as she passed. She tripped, the bag flew from her arms as she landed face down. Energy pulsed through her, reaching down into the ground as she screamed for help. Lani tried to rise, but Javi stomped on her back and held her down. Another blow knocked Sarin's head to the side.

Sarin didn't move. Her breath gurgled through a bloody mouth. The man panted over her. He looked back at the others with a twisted smirk.

Lani continued to yell desperately while clawing the ground to reach Sarin. Javi stomped again. Pain shot through her ribs. The pulsing in her ears quickened and grew louder as another sound reached her—skittering claws and shifting dirt.

With his arms still bound behind him, Grandfather stood. The rope strung around his neck like a noose. He turned and stopped, waiting. The men shifted, confused, as the noise escalated.

"Javi?" the man atop Sarin said. He tried to rise from his knees and gasped. A small set of sharp, dirty teeth jutted from the ground and pierced his hand. His eyes widened. He shook his hand until the skeletal head of a rodent dislodged and flew a few feet away. The rest of the body climbed from the dirt. Another set of sharp nails clawed the man's legs. He yelped and rose to his feet as more figures broke through the surrounding ground. They climbed up his legs as he danced frantically.

The man who'd tripped Lani screamed. In an instant, small bones of rodents and birds covered his writhing body, tearing off bits of flesh and pecking at his eyes.

Javi stepped away from Lani and gripped his axe, a perplexed expression on his face. He then turned to stare at the old man.

"You!" Javi charged towards the man with his axe held high, but stumbled when a loud crash shook the ground. Sinewy rotting muscle and patches of dark matted fur clung to the enormous bear that entered the clearing. Filtered sunlight caught the squirming maggots that feasted on its flesh. Its jaws opened wide, baring sharp teeth and a black, gooey maw. Javi stumbled backward. The bear launched forward and knocked the dancing man to the ground. Skeletal rodents scurried over him, biting and clawing as his wails increased.

Javi's axe met the bear's skull, knocking some of the fur away. But the blade made no difference. Its jaws clamped down on Javi's arm as he screamed. Blood oozed down his arm through the bear's jaw to the ground below. A loud snap echoed through the air as Javi's scream escalated. Then the reanimated bear dragged the man into the woods.

The dead creatures created a perimeter around Lani as she crawled toward Sarin and rolled her onto one side and cleared the blood from her mouth. Sarin took a deep breath. Lani cradled her head in her lap before looking around her.

Grandfather watched them from where he stood. His shoulder would dislocate from the tension of the bonds. As her gaze fell on the rope around his neck, the skittering claws and snapping jaws escalated their assault on the remaining men whose voices slowly died.

Lani gently lay Sarin down before lifting the rope from grandfather's neck. She was untying his arms when a sudden crash came from behind. She turned. Javi lunged forward, his face caked in blood. Expression frenzied and wild. He raised his axe with one arm. She covered her head and screamed.

But the blow never came. Instead, a wet gasp greeted her ears. The sword that had been lost earlier jutted through Javi's chest. His life dripped from the point.

Javi fell to the ground as the blade withdrew. A gaunt, sallow-skinned man stood behind, holding the sword. He wore the flat, empty expression of the dead. A soft sound passed through grandfather's lips, akin to an exhalation or a sigh.

Lani untied Grandfather and turned back to Sarin. The noise of claws and teeth had died with the men. Most of the bones crawled slowly back into the ground, a few lay broken and still. Sarin moaned, blinking one eye open. The other bloomed purple and swollen.

Lani kissed her forehead. "I told you, you're not a fighter. Fool. What were you thinking?"

Sarin's attempt at a smile resulted in a wince. "Someday I'll listen." With Lani's help, she sat up, taking in the mangled bodies and upturned dirt. "Did Grandfather do that?" Then her eyes cleared enough to see the two men. They huddled together. "Where'd he come from?"

Lani shrugged. "Don't know. He saved my life."

"What should we do with him?" Sarin said.

Grandfather's fingers intertwined with the other man's. The two figures leaned toward each other, the same way Sarin did in Lani's arms.

"We take him with us."

They reached the village of the dead the next morning, having to allow for extra time and rest. An old woman dressed in frayed light blue robes parted the gates for them when they neared. A look of relief swept across her face.

"There you are, ya' rascal!" She said, then nodded to the women. "He escaped yesterday morning. They can move quick when they want. Searched for him well into the evening. Thanks for bringing him back."

Lani paused. "I thought they could only move when they were commanded."

The old woman smiled. "That's true for some, but others, the smart ones, come prepared."

Sarin and Lani exchanged a confused look. "What do you mean?" Lani asked.

The old woman took one of grandfather's hand. She sniffed the air around his neck and nodded. "He'd been taking devil's claw before he died?"

"Added it to his daily tea for months to help with pain."

The old woman smiled slyly. "Pain, huh?" She shook her head. "Also works as a sort of preservative. From what we've seen with this one," she motioned to the other man. "Helps keep some of their faculties and memories, too."

"And if they had magic before?" Lani asked. She'd been hoping that it was grandfather's bit of necromancy that had animated the bones in the clearing.

The old woman shook her head. "Nah. Magic dies when they do, love."

"Even if it's necromancy?"

She cackled. "Necromancy? Is that what he was? Then he knew exactly what he was doing, didn't he?" She glanced between the men. "Funny thing, though. This one was in the business as well." She nodded to the other man whose hand had returned to Grandfather's.

A curious dread settled in Lani's chest. Something she'd suspected finally finding words. "I brought him back without meaning to."

The woman sighed sympathetically. "Happens more than you'd think. Grief, fear, anger, love. All the potent emotions can make it happen with the untrained." She gestured behind her. "That's how many of these people wound up here. It's hard to let go of those we love."

"Who brought him back?" Sarin asked, gesturing to Grandfather's companion.

"Sister. He'd discouraged her from learning the craft. I think he was relying on her emotions to do the trick."

Lani paled. Grandfather had protected her, supported her decision to not learn necromancy, knowing that she'd be unable to end the spell if it happened again. It had forced her to leave the village and bring him here. But that wouldn't have been possible if Maris hadn't come to the funeral home, and she wouldn't have come if Peri hadn't died when he did. The way the men's fingers intertwined made Lani consider the full scope of the situation with fresh understanding.

"Do you have anything else you'd like to say to him?" The caretaker asked.

She swallowed, that familiar lump in her throat stifling her voice. Lani wrapped her arms around her grandfather's bony frame and whispered, "Thank you for loving me."

His hand patted her back once before he eased away. With hands still clasped, the caretaker ushered the men through the gates. "Come on, Peri. Let's get you cleaned up. And whose blood is that? What have you been doing?"

Lani stared through the slats of the gate and watched them shuffle away. She wiped tears from her eyes. The comforting weight of Sarin's arm slung around her shoulders.

"Oh, I almost forgot." Sarin pulled out a wadded piece of parchment from her pocket. "From Bran."

Lani,

Father once said that life was too short to be tethered to the weight of other's expectations. And Grandfather had his own regrets, that you may have guessed by now. He drank too much wine one night when you were still small and talked a lot about the things he missed.

I want you to know that the family will be fine. Fala, the baby, and I will be fine. Helene will survive. This is an opportunity for you to go and live the life you want.

I love you.

Bran

Lani slumped into Sarin's arm, sobbing with relief and sorrow. It was a long time before Sarin spoke.

"What do we do now?"

Lani sniffed and smiled. "It doesn't matter. As long as it's together."

CHAPTER THREE

THE DYING BOOK

Originally published in the Misfits of Magic Anthology with Three Ravens Publishing, August 2022. Edited by William Joseph Roberts.

The babe's high-pitched screams ensured that no one slept, and I had given up any hope that the wagon's rocking would soothe her. After three solid hours of wailing discontentedness, it was clear that she would not be settled. Not by me at least. I was becoming convinced that she hated me, and her hate would be justified.

I took her cries personally despite knowing how irrational that was. There was no way she could have known or understood the events of the evening that led us here. Still, it was rare for me to encounter a problem that could not be overcome, and I huddled in the wagon holding the angry babe, refusing to meet the eyes of the other passengers. Tears of frustration brimmed my eyes. It was unfortunate that magic couldn't be worked on children.

The older woman across from us pursed her lips and edged closer, offering to take her. Without hesitation I thrust the ruddy-faced child at her. The woman sang a song like memory, soft and gentle, and soothing all around. The babe fussed a few moments more, her face still squalling-red, but slowly she quieted and stared up at the singer. There was a collective sigh amongst the group. Dirty glares vanished behind heavy eyelids as the wagon rolled on.

"What's her name?" The woman asked.

"Oerina," I said. A lie, but to tell the girl's real name would only invite death to all who heard. The girl did not know her name anyway or, if she did, she should best forget it soon enough.

The old woman smiled warmly as the girl reached one clumsy hand toward her face. I half wondered if I could hire the old woman for the remainder of our journey since she had a magic I could not replicate, and it would be worth all the money I had to keep the girl placated.

"Is she your first?" She asked between hums.

I nodded, spinning lies with truth. "I never even held a babe before this one."

She smiled. "Hm. Where's her mum?"

"Gone, I'm afraid." There was no need to elaborate, people always filled in their own stories.

The woman nodded, understanding. "I guess she's about ten months. A year, maybe?"

"You have an eye, madam. She'll be one turn next month." I studied her. "Do you have many children?"

Her gentle smile did not change, but her eyes dulled enough to let me know the rest.

"Aye. I had five. Though the gov took three of 'em before their thirteenth birthdays. They left me two to grow." She sighed. "Suppose I should be thankful they left me them."

I was quiet. They had also taken me during one of the collection times. I was sold from one noble house to the next until Master Ripiel recognized some small magic in me. I counted my stars lucky for that fateful intervention, his claiming of me saved my life. It had taken the slaughter of four noble houses during an uprising for child slavery to fall out of favor. But the king had never made it illegal, and now he never would. The old ways died hard.

I cleared my throat. "I haven't seen my parents since before my fourth birthday. Don't even know which region I hale from."

She shifted the babe to one arm and patted my knee. "But look how well you've turned out. With one of your own, and both of you looking so fine."

I swallowed uncomfortably while looking at the girl in her bejeweled slippers and satin gown. The garb would have been ridiculous even for a minor noble but especially on this wagon where any noble would not dare show face. Master Ripiel used to say that managing details whilst under stress was one of my biggest failings, and I had been under a considerable stress when I had taken the girl.

The woman coddled the babe for the rest of the night, even seeming to enjoy it. She cleaned her bottom and fed her a bit of the food from my bag and by the time the sun painted the sky in blues and oranges, the girl was deep asleep.

The roosters announced the morn as we drove into an old village where the structures leaned uniformly away from the mountains in the distance. The woman showed me a way to swath the baby around my chest and over one shoulder so I could bundle her whilst having use of both arms. Her eyes narrowed as she tsked at my ineptness.

"You need the help of an experienced person, son," she stated flatly. "For your sake and hers."

"I am heading to my sister's house just west of the border." I said, "She has agreed to take us in until we can make other arrangements."

"I thought you were collected. How is it you know your sister?" Suspicion ebbed behind her eyes.

"Sister from one of my former houses, not sister by blood, ma'am." I said too quickly.

"You're travelling very light, aren't you?" She asked.

The other travelers had already grabbed their bags as they departed the wagon, leaving it empty. I wore only a large satchel that held a book, parchment, some fair amount of coin, and some food scraps.

I coughed, hoping for her sake that she would let it go. "It's a fresh start, ma'am."

"Left in a hurry too, didn't you?" She asked.

I shifted from foot to foot as my jaw tightened. She was turning out to be more observant than was beneficial. I hated imparting folks when their names were not written in the book. The effects of death, even singular, always rippled toward more than intended. And this woman had already done us a great service.

Noticing the tension in my posture, she patted my arm. "It's all right, love. I won't tell anyone about you. But I suggest you both dress lower, just in case one of them irritated passengers noticed." She motioned toward a small storefront where gowns and frock coats were suspended in the single window. "Selia won't open until she's got the cows fed, maybe a couple more hours, but when she gets here, buy the plainest stuff you can. Get some better walking boots, too."

She motioned toward a tavern that leaned heavily to one side. "You can get decent food there and," she pointed toward a livery, "find further transportation there." She sniffed as her eyes grazed the length of me. "They sell horses, but don't let old Han's son swindle you. He has no fondness for strangers."

She stared another minute, chewing her words in her mouth before spitting them out. "As much as you might want to, renting a carriage will draw too much attention. And wagons going further west than here only come through once every two weeks. I'm sure that you're in a hurry to be off?"

I nodded, silently considering multiple ways to deal with this woman while listening to her talk and making a mental checklist. I couldn't afford the fatigue that would follow the heavier spells and wondered if we made too much of an impression to wipe the memory of us away.

She leaned closer and whispered conspiratorially, "The gov didn't leave me my last two children, I took them and ran. I once wore the same look that I see in your eyes." Her wrinkles deepened with empathy. "It took me a long time to lose it."

I breathed relief and reconsidered my options. "Thank you, ma'am. I don't know how to repay your kindness."

She shook her head. "Nothing to repay, lad. Someday you can help someone else when they need it."

My gaze slid down to the sleeping girl bundled against my chest.

"Best of luck to you both," the woman said and turned to leave.

My hand snaked out and lightly clasped her shoulder, holding her in place. I whispered only a few words in her ear before I let go and stepped back. When she turned around with wide, confused eyes, we were lost to her. Her gaze swept through the area twice before she shook her head and turned away, shuffling down the street. Even if they tracked us this far, I hoped the old woman wouldn't remember much about us. It was better this way.

My desperate belly overruled any fear of dysentery as we ate a hearty breakfast at the leaning inn. The girl fussed upon waking but took a few bites of the soft oats they served. I didn't know what babies ate so decided to stick with the simpler fare to avoid accidentally killing her. We traded our fine clothing for drab, homespun cloths in the small shop. In exchange for the satin shoes, Selia gave us a simple blanket and a large amount of cloth diapers. The babe had experienced nothing less than the finest fabrics against her privileged buttocks but when I changed her, she did not fuss at the lesser garments.

Han's son attempted to swindle me when I purchase a bay gelding, but he didn't know that my kind cannot be swindled. In the end, he gave us the horse, saddle, saddlebags, blanket, bridle, and feed for a third of what they were worth. I thought of making him give it to us for free but that would evoke too strong a memory to cover, and every spell took more energy than I could afford.

Each interaction drained me a bit, having to alter each memory was always tiring. They would remember an overweight man travelling alone, the outline of the swathed baby aided in contributing to the image and it would be difficult for them to recall anything else if they were questioned.

By mid-morning we were riding west with the bright sun upon our backs and the map in my hand.

Chaos would be descending upon the country, the likes of which couldn't be remembered, and I held the only heir to the throne against my chest.

The bodies would have been discovered by now. Three fresh names collected for the book in my bag, never mind the casualties of association—bringing my total to thirty-four. Three names a month had been Master Ripeil's price for living in luxury. He was one of the few people who had managed to maintain full possession of his powers without much oversight. Most folks found to have a bit of magic were used for entertainment, their lives ending when their magic ran out.

Three names a month hadn't seemed like much when I agreed to follow in Ripeil's footsteps. But as my score met double digits, I felt the weight of it upon my soul.

Ripeil had warned me that our magic was finite. It came with an unknown expiration and would cease working without warning. There was a day when we would be as powerless as everyone else, he said. But while I had it, I should use it to make a better life. Without hesitation, I added my name in service to the book and had been completing contracts ever since.

When a familiar name appeared in Master Ripeil's book he sighed heavily and shook his head. "This is why you should avoid making friends in high places. We are not allowed to put emotional investments before business. Remember that."

We planned everything out, as we usually did, and drove the carriage near to the man's manor, hiding deep in the woods to avoid notice. Assessing the rhythms and routines of visitors and servants, we tried to determine when our target would be alone. Unfortunately, he was a popular man prone to regular evening feasts and had at least one mistress, a common woman who sold goods to the manor. His wife was informed every time that lady stepped onto the premises. But the way he leered at the servants made me think that his interests were varied.

Ripeil clucked his tongue and sighed. "This fool married too far above his station. His wife is one of the queen's elder sisters and probably our contractor." He peered at me with arched eyebrows. "It would be a simple thing to have the queen add his name to the book. Honestly, with the lecherous behavior we've witnessed over these last few days, who could blame her?"

The following evening, we waited until the stars were clear before creeping into the house. Conveniently, the lady of the house had gone to visit her sister that morning, providing us with a rare opportunity. The manor had few guards, the lord believing that his popularity worked better than armed protections. I sent two of the guards into a deep slumber while Ripeil handled the others in a grislier way.

The candles still cast soft shadows when we entered the lord's antechamber. We froze upon hearing the distinct rhythmic grind of bed frame and floor as a low groan issued from the bedroom. Ripeil shook his head and motioned me into a shadowy corner until our intended target was alone. After half an hour, we finally heard a soft snore.

The floor creaked as tip-toeing steps moved toward the door. A thin girl, too young and too pale, opening the door just enough to ease herself through. She wore only a thin shift and carried the rest of her clothes bundled in her arms. She hurried out the chamber doors without noticing the forms in the shadows.

Ripeil entered the bedroom alone, as he had done a hundred times before. I had offered to do it myself, to spare him the murder of his former friend, but he had insisted.

It never took long. Just a hand placement and a couple of words. Once it is completed, you run before anyone discovers you. But after five minutes without the stir of magic, I knew Ripeil was spent.

An angry voice rose in the air, followed by a desperate whisper and a sickening, soft sound of metal entering flesh.

Master Ripeil's voice ordered me to run but I stayed and waited. Both our lives were forfeit if we failed to fulfil the contract. I slid deeper into the shadows as a large, naked man barreled through the doors. Ripeil was crumpled on the floor behind him, a pool of darkness spread from his chest as he moaned and writhed. But I could not help him.

The lord turned around, clutching a dagger in front of him. His belly jiggled low over his manhood as he spun and stepped with surprising agility.

"Where are you?" He hissed. "I know you're in here." He shuffled the dagger to his other hand nervously as he studied the room. With one hand he tore the curtains from the windows. Then he wildly thrust the blade beneath his desk, stabbing at nothing while simultaneously spilling a pitcher of water onto the floor.

Sipping in a slow breath of whispers I encouraged the water to spread across the floor and into his wandering path. His panic prevented him from noticing when the water morphed to oil and coated the boards with slickness. One foot slipped from beneath him, sending his large frame crashing. The man's leg bent at an unnatural position, pale bone jutting through ruddy flesh. He howled with a twisted face as blood swirled into the oil and the dagger skittered across the floor toward me.

Stepping into the dim light, I eased closer to him as the lord howled so viciously that spittle flew across the room. He threatened and cursed, thrashing against his pain as he attempted to reach me. His cheeks were ruddy and blotched and he watched with bulging eyes as I placed my toe upon the dagger and slid it back to him. It was too dangerous to get close to him.

As his fingers tightened on the dagger, he jabbed at me, but I was safely out of reach. I raised a hand and mimicked holding the dagger speaking a few words so that his arm followed my movement. Slowly, I drew my hand across my throat while the dagger in his hand did the same. Blood spilled onto the floor; his voice trapped beneath gurgles as his eyes widened in disbelief.

I waited until he'd ceased twitching before retrieving Ripeil's body. It had only taken a short dagger between his ribs to end him. Gently closing his eyes, I bent to lift the elder man but a soft cry from the antechamber stopped me.

The girl stood in shock inside the doorway. Having hastily donned the rest of her clothing, she carried a tray of biscuits and wine that threatened to topple from her trembling arms. She tried to scream, but the sound did not escape her lips. I felt the weight in my stomach then, the sigh of my soul, as I considered my options.

Usually, Ripeil would have handled these unfortunate events but now it was left to me. Memories could only be altered around seemingly unimportant things, but it was exceedingly difficult to erase trauma, and what she witnessed was traumatic. With a word, I caught the cry in her mouth and froze her where she stood, the tray stilled.

"I am so sorry, dear girl."

I brought Ripeil's body home with me. Although a barrel of coin awaited me the payment seemed a pittance compared to what I'd lost. I buried him between those two old sycamores he always favored, not too near the river. I mourned him deeply for as long as I dared, until another name appeared in the receiving book. Followed a week later by another. There were always contracts to be completed, and that is how I became King Frenhk's weapon.

I'd been fulfilling the book's obligations for close to a year, with none the wiser that I now acted as my Master. All was happening just the way Ripeil had prepared me for. When the names appeared in the book, I had four weeks to complete the tasks. After receiving the names, I studied the intended, created a plan, and executed then as quickly as I could. There was always plenty of coin waiting for me when I returned. Enough to pay for servants, wine, and sex.

Things were good until the wrong name appeared on those pages, followed in quick succession by two more wrong names. I was at a loss. The drying ink smeared on the pages of the dying book somewhere within the king's chambers before transferring its command onto my receiving book a county away. I stared at the script for a long while before putting it down and walking away, hoping that it would change. But the names remained fixed in messy black ink. Someone had stood before the dying book and written the names of the royal family, with one exception.

King Frenhk was hated for more than his consigning of children. He had a vicious temperament and had doled out quick punishments and unreasonable taxes for over forty years. Everyone waited for him to die, though those words were only whispered over a few pints in trusted company and isolated conversations. There was much doubt that his son, Alver, would prove any better a ruler. I had it from a reliable source that Alver's mother had died after the king had tired of her and written her name in the book.

The new queen was thirty years the king's junior and a quiet woman who avoided politics. They had a baby girl who was nearing her first turn.

I stared at the book for days not knowing who could have accessed it. The thought that I was being drawn into a coup, or that the book had fallen into the hands of a disgruntled servant made me equally uneasy. But the real issue that plagued me wasn't the killing of a tyrant and his family, it was trying to design how I was going to murder one—let alone three—members of the well-guarded royal family.

I did not know if the names were visible in the dying book until the contract was fulfilled, or if they vanished as soon as they transferred to my book, the receiving one. If they remained visible, then the king would know to expect me and the odds of completing this task were negligible.

According to my contract, I had four weeks to complete the assignments, and each day following that expiration extracted a price. At least that is what Ripeil had said, and I had no desire to discover what that price was. Using all Ripeil's old journals and texts as guides, I formed a desperate and foolish plan. If I failed in any of the three contracts, it was likely that I would die either way.

It took a week to secure a room in the village outside the castle walls. I dedicated the next week to studying the prince who, in all his arrogance and privilege, was easy to track. His day-to-day routine was predictably filled with hunting, fucking, and thwarting the efforts of anyone who tried to reign him in. He was better suited to studying sex and food than commerce and politics. It was useful that our preferences aligned.

On certain nights the young prince would sneak into the village searching for new exploits of either sex. It took three nights of lingering in his favorite pub for him to notice me. I flirted just enough to get his attention and disappeared before he could reach me. Offering the spoiled boy a toy before removing the offer only served to increase the value. It was an enjoyable dance and if he had been some minor noble, I might have made good on my offer. We were near the same age and the mutual attraction between us almost gave me pause.

While that dance continued in the evenings, I spent my days in stolen servants' clothes and slipped into the castle. The guards' memories were easy to obscure and by the average amount of them, I concluded the king was unaware that his name had been listed for execution. I studied Frenhk from a safe distance. The man was large and solidly built with a perpetual scowl etched to his features, but he proved to be just as predictable as his son in his interests.

The queen's movements hardly fluctuated from one day to the next as she was routinely encumbered with the babe and nanny. By all observation she was a doting mother. Every day she ate lunch with other noble ladies then took long walks in the maze-like gardens. She sat at her desk, wrote letters, and retired early each evening though often the lanterns in her chambers stayed lit until early in the morning. One of the greatest challenges would be that the nursery was adjacent to her own, and it was difficult to determine when the nanny was there or gone.

A simple poisoning would have been nice, do the lot of them and be done with it. But everyone knew the most dangerous job in the country was that of the king's taster and since the royal family were rarely in the same room together, they would have to be dealt with individually. The timing would be tricky since it would all have to be done in one night and I would have to be far away by the time the alarms were raised in the morning.

Three weeks after the royal names first appeared in the book, I was sitting in the pub, eyeing every lad who entered. Alver slipped through the doors wearing an elaborately beaded frock coat, which I assumed was the dullest thing he owned. In this environment, so close to the castle, seeing a young lord or lady trying to blend in and have some fun with the regulars was not unusual. It wasn't long before his gaze discovered me, the toy who had taken itself away, and sauntered over. He leaned against my table and made awkward small talk for which he had a lack of talent. But I suppose one didn't need too much skill at flirting when one had money and title. With his dark curls and wickedly boyish grin, he was appealing. I simpered to him and gave a bit of sauce back, which only furthered his advances.

He pressed to escape together to my rooms, but I just shook my head and told him that my bride was sleeping there. He raised his eyebrows, and I continued my lie, "We didn't have much choice in the arrangement, believe me."

"I have a similar fate awaiting me," Alver said before hinting at other places we could go. I claimed that there were too much family around and could not risk being seen.

"I suppose that it wasn't meant to be," I said, dropping a hint of longing as I cupped his cheek in my hand.

His eyes brightened with a look I'd seen him give right before he was going to do something troublesome. He smiled.

"How about an adventure?" He asked. "I know a secret way into the castle."

I chuckled as I tenderly tucked a dark curl behind his ear. "What if they catch us? The guards would kill us right away."

He flashed a broad grin. "Trust me."

We stumbled into the night; my arm wrapped around him for more than balance. He led me down a small footpath that wound through groves and brush toward the castle's back wall where the gardens were rimmed with thick, thorny hedges that were grown intentionally too dense to allow much in. However, there was just enough space between two offset hedges to squeeze through. Gripping my hand, he tugged me through, ducking down when the guards passed. Alver pulled me in for a swift kiss beneath the dark sky before we darted across the gardens and up a narrow staircase.

Rushing down winding halls and hiding in corners until more guards passed, we eventually entered his quarters through an unguarded small door. My awe at the ridiculous splendor on display in the prince's rooms was genuine. Rubies and emeralds glittered from the tapestries that adorned the walls, scattering fractals of light across the carpet as the lantern sconces flickered.

"Whose rooms are these?" I feigned caution and nervousness until he kissed my palm and insisted there was nothing to fear.

His kisses were filled with longing and desperation. When our lips parted there was a deep loneliness in his eyes that weakened my knees. It was best to be quick before I lose my resolve.

When Alver retrieved a jug and began to pour wine into two cups, I placed a hand on his wrist to stop him. Pulling him in for another kiss and stoking the fire between us, I took the wine from him and finished the pour. He did not notice the extra moment that my hand lingered over his cup while I plied him with questions and fawned over his taste.

I toasted to his health. It was cruel, I know.

When he tried to kiss me, I led him into the bedroom and made him recline. He was a handsome boy, and he might not have made a terrible king, but it was not his fate to ever find out. I smiled sadly as a sudden cough startled him. He made to rise but I pushed him back onto the plush blankets. Confusion flashed across his face as he struggled, but I whispered words that cemented him to the bed. He would not be able to cough up the poison that was already swimming through his blood.

I curled a lock of his hair between my fingers. "I've tried to make this easy on you."

His eyes widened as denial shifted to understanding.

"I am truly sorry, you don't seem like a bad sort. But once your name is in the book..." I sighed and kissed his brow. "If we were not who we are we, would have had a lovely time."

Death was swift, thankfully, and I hadn't used enough magic to tire me. Locking the small door that we'd entered through, I slipped down the quiet halls and headed toward the next name on the list.

The king's chambers sat in the highest corner of the castle and were well guarded, until I arrived. Those poor souls were left slumbering against each other. Come morning they would be labeled conspirators and executed without trial. I tried not to think of their families or the wide rippling waves of my actions.

Opening the door a fraction, I slid inside. Frenhk's rooms were surprisingly musty and more practically decorated than his son's had been. The king lay alone in his bed, a large form even from two rooms away. His tossing and grunting diminished any sound that might have reached him as I wriggled into a corner and waited for him to settle. But sleep would not take him.

Frenhk grunted and rose, dragging a robe around his shoulders. Muttering as he walked, he headed to a smaller door I had initially overlooked behind his desk. He stopped briefly to strike a match and light a lantern. His shoulders brushed the doorway as he disappeared through it, then returned a moment later carrying a familiar book. He placed it on a large desk and stood with his back to me, flipping through the pages and spitting curses.

What lay before the king was a forgery of the Dying book. It's mate, the Receiving book was well hidden beneath the flooring of Ripeil's quarters. The books were identical including the small, star shaped emblem at the top outer corner of each odd page. One could only see the star if they had a bit of magic in them. The book Frenhk stood over did not have that emblem. It was a gross oversight by the forger who didn't know of it. As I peered around him, I could see the names most recently written on the page, though they were not the names I had received.

I whispered, sealing him as tightly as the words would let me. There was no point in risking him bashing my head in with his fists. With a quick hiss, his lips fastened shut, his hands rooted to the desk, while the skin of his bare feet merged to the floor in fleshy tendrils.

"You lost it." I said lowly while moving to the other side of the desk. I pulled the book toward me and rifled through the pages of familiar names. Thousands of names littered across the pages, spanning decades and predating Frehnk's reign. The forger had done a good job after all.

Frehnk's face grew mottled and ruddy as he struggled to speak and move. But his words were muffled by the seal of his lips. His straining slid the desk a few inches, serving as a reminder that he was fully capable of snapping me like a twig if he'd been able to move.

Killing a king is an odd opportunity, it gives one pause to consider how that legacy will be written. What should I say to the man who tore apart families and condemned children to a lifetime of slavery?

I wanted to say, "I was a child stolen and sold. Lucky enough to be picked out by a broken man with bloody hands and a guilty conscience who trained me to follow in his footsteps. Unlike the other children who were worked to death, raped, or murdered. You thought nothing of using them and discarding them." But instead, I did not speak. He deserved no explanation even though I wanted to tell him that this job was personal, that I was glad to be the one to destroy him.

We stared at each other, while a vein bulged down the side of his temple.

I sighed. "I just want you to know that this situation—me in your rooms about to kill you—is an exact result of your own actions."

I closed the book and pushed it closer to him.

"I received three names in my book a month ago. Alver was the first. Your name, of course. And the queen's name." I said, leaning slightly closer to him. "I was surprised, but not displeased, to see your name written there. Though I wonder who is to thank for allowing me to provide a much-needed service to my country." I sighed, wondering why I was rambling and delaying. Perhaps I was enjoying it too much. But wasted time would only get me killed. "I am not sorry for what I am about to do."

His eyes bulged as my magic settled on his skin. His mouth sealed completely as his nostrils pinched tightly together, stealing his breath. He attempted to flail in his panic, moving enough to slide the heavy desk forward but still unable to move his feet or remove his hands from the desk. His skin ripped with his force scattering drops of blood across the wood. His bones cracked beneath his force as he squealed. Brown eyes bulged out as his face morphed to purple, then blue.

I counted the minutes that it took. Even though I tried not to enjoy my work, I found that I did not entirely hate it in that moment. As death took him, I released his feet and hands. His large form fell over the desk, on top of his false book. His muscles jerked as his bowels and bladder released.

The fatigue hit me like a punch to the stomach. I doubled over, grasping my dizzying head and attempting to fortify my will. There was only one name left.

Nausea unsettled me as I stood outside Queen Jormal's doors, not wanting to enter. The guards were curiously absent, and I toyed with the idea of leaving. If left alive, she would be queen regent, her daughter someday to be queen. She might even be a good queen, she had a grace and a kindness to her. If I killed Jormal, it would leave the princess alone in the world with only a nefarious aunt and too many advisors to raise her. A lamb alone in a house run by wolves. I would do to her what they had been done to me. I thought a hundred different ways but, in the end, the contract must be completed. It was the promise I made when I entered my name in the book. It was the queen's life or my own.

I entered the room slowly to find the queen sitting in a window seat, staring out into the dark gardens. Long dark hair cascaded around her shoulders. She did not turn when I entered.

"Is it done?" She asked quietly.

I froze before the closed door.

She turned to look at me and her youth startled me. She was younger than was rumored, closer to my age, maybe younger, closer to Alver's age. Tears stained her cheeks.

"Are they dead?" She asked, her tone elevating.

I nodded.

She looked down. "Only one name left. I hoped you might save me for last. Given the placement of the rooms and the easy exit from here. It is what I would have done had I been fortunate enough to be in your position."

I licked my lips, the urge to leave sliding over me again. "May I ask you a question?"

"You want to know why." She said and grew still and silent for a long minute before continuing. "I heard him talking about my daughter, our daughter, and what bargaining he could use her for when she was older. He spoke of how much money he could make from her. Of which country would be best to secure her to for his own interests. He didn't even pretend it was for the good of the country or our people. Just wanted to use her for his own gains." She sighed. "She's not a year old yet and he joked about making her a child bride if he had to, and his advisors laughed with him."

She stood and poured herself a glass of wine, the liquid danced through the glass.

"I never wanted to be queen." She glanced up. "Not if it meant being married to that horror parading as a man. I have a friend, a servant who was bought by my house from this one when she was but ten years old. She has been my companion and... more." She took another sip and gazed out the window. "She spoke of the things that happened here, about what the king had done to her and other children. I began to wonder what would happen to Rosalee if something were to happen to me?

"How far should a mother go to protect her child?" She dared me to answer, her eyes flashing. "He bragged about the book on our wedding night, a veiled threat if I should displease him. I know what happened to Alver's mother. It took some time and a lot of help, but we made a good replica of the book. Did we miss anything?"

My mouth was dry as I whispered, "The star." I stepped closer but she did not retreat. "Why your name? Why the prince's name?"

Her expression hardened briefly. "I saw enough of Alver to see his father in him His arrogance and refusal to be corrected, even when he knew he was in the wrong. Once, when he was drunk, he told me that once Frenhk died no one would ever hear from us again. It was the sincerest he had ever been with me."

"But why put your own name in the book?"

She pursed her lips. "Before I answer that I need you to make me a promise."

"What is it?" I asked.

"I need you to take Rosalee across the western border. I have a cousin, Oerina, who will take her and raise her in hiding. She will be safe there, which is all I want for her, to be safe and loved. I have a map to guide you." She retrieved a rolled piece of parchment and a large book from an armoire. "In exchange for your agreement, I offer you the Dying book." She placed it on the table, the roll of parchment with it. "Perhaps, you might find a bit of freedom for yourself."

The book's magic pulled at me.

"If Rosalee stays here, she will never be safe. If I leave with her, we will be hunted and they will kill me, leaving her vulnerable. If we stay, there will be rumors of a conspiracy to murder the king and they will execute me, leaving my child to be raised at the mercy of those who only seek to use her." She sighed, tapped the book with her fingers. "It is the best way to protect her."

The nanny lingered in the doorway of the nursery. She was older than Jormal, her clothing plain and demure. She held a squirming bundle in her arms, one hand reaching out as the babe struggled to see beyond the confines of the blanket.

I looked back to the queen. "There can be no witnesses."

"I know what needs to happen." The woman said with a clipped tone. "They'll kill me for surviving no matter where I go or what I say."

I sighed, knowing the truth of her words before returning to the queen. "I know nothing of children. Why me? There must be someone else you could trust with this?"

She smiled sadly. "You and Ripiel have been true to your word in the past. If you give it, then I might hope that my daughter may grow to a healthy age and, someday, become a benevolent queen. There is no one else I can trust, and no one more capable to complete this task than you."

I debated telling her that our words were bound only to the book. I had no obligation to the child or her wellbeing. But the weight on my soul grew heavier as I watched the women and the squirming babe.

"I will take her." I held one hand to my chest. "I swear that I will do all that I can to deliver her safely."

Tears brimmed the queen's eyes, pride holding them in her lashes before she gave a curt nod. "Thank you."

Jormal carried the girl into the nursery. The two women stood over the crib, their fingers intertwined, while speaking words of love. She sang a soft song over her daughter and while the women leaned against each other, I stood witness to what no one else had been allowed to see.

When they said their goodbyes and closed the nursery door softly behind them, I asked them to lie upon the bed. They held each other and, for all their controlled manners, I could taste fear in the air.

"I hope to make this as painless as possible." My eyes burned, my voice breaking upon the words. "May death be kinder to you than this life has been."

I steadied myself with a deep breath and said the words that dropped them to sleep, slowing their heart beats and breath in increments. I watched them still before placing my hands on their foreheads. I whispered a small blessing and paused, stumbling for a moment as the words turned to ash in my mouth. While my whisper still clung to the air, they were gone, and I was left to wipe wetness from my cheeks.

Time was pressing down as I swept into the nursery and filled a simple leather bag with the book, the map, two spare cloths, a large bag of coins that had been left out, and a few biscuits that remained on the queen's tray. I picked up the girl as gently as I could. She was heavier than she looked.

I slipped down those back stairs that Alver had introduced me to and rushed back to the village. If the girl cried, they would catch me since I would be unable to silence her. It was against the rules of magic to work a spell on children under twelve. Teenagers, as everyone knows, have their own rules.

There was a wagon passing through the village heading west. The driver agreed to let us on if I paid double, which I did.

It is likely someone will realize the true Dying book is missing. It is also likely that the Receiving book will be discovered at Ripeil's house, which is useless if no one writes in its sister book. The queen was right—so long as I held the book, I had my freedom.

Following the queen's map, Rosalee and I rode past the western border on a bay gelding, stopping only to eat and rest. I accomplished the heinous task of diaper changing and managed it better than I thought I could. The girl became a good traveler, as the simple magic of the swaying trees and flitting birds fascinated her. Her laugh was infectious.

I do not know what will happen once we reach Oerina's estate. I can only hope that she might consider keeping a former stolen child with a few spells left to watch over the girl.

CHAPTER FOUR

SONG ON THE AEGEAN

Based on a niche Greek legend.

The remains of the *Aspis* floated atop the water's surface. The rising sunlight illuminated her fractured cypress and pine boards as they drifted further away. It was a stark warning that the same fate would come to the crew of the *Danos* when the creature returned.

Captain Makris's voice was steady as we stared in shock at our sister ship's demise, his expression unreadable, but I noted a small flutter in his breath as he spoke. "Swallow your fear. Even mixed with the salt of the sea or your own tears, fear emits an odor that alerts predators of her prey's whereabouts. Whether those predators are aquatic or fantastic makes no difference. Fear has its own scent."

Makris's point—intended to strengthen our resolve or impart his wisdom—had worked for a while, even after the second song took half our crew. But now the stench of mounting trepidation sat upon the humid air, glowering like hungry gulls upon the mast.

With a dour expression, Makris examined the Aegean through the small lens he held to his eye. The myriad shades of blue-green sea dissolved into darker cobalt and sapphire as white caps formed occasionally atop too small ripples. For the last week, our yellowed sails had hung limp on the beams as the sun seared our skin. Without wind, there was no relief. Without rowers, we were adrift. And we had lost the rowers in the last two attacks.

Where once we were a crew of two ships and close to one hundred mates, I was one of only fifteen left hale. Seven others lay in the infirmary below, but without proper care, it was doubtful any of them would survive for more than another day or two. When the creature's cry had last lilted through the air, our physician had joined a dozen other men and leapt into the waters. He'd skinned and broken his hands to get through the ropes. As the water dropped like a shroud above his head, he hadn't even waved for aid. I had been tied tight to the boat and was reduced to watching him take my secret to a watery grave.

The creature's song was different for me. Her cry was haunting, sad even, but lacked the same hold over me as it did the men. That the captain noticed was a given, though he'd had the decency to not mentioned it yet. But Makris was too astute an observer to wonder why for long. I just hoped that he figured it out before the rest of the crew did.

Linus and Elias, two of the stronger crewmates, muttered that we'd somehow angered the sea goddess, but Makris shook his head.

"Perhaps a gorgon or a mermaid," he countered. His lips pursed into a thin line buried with in his obsidian beard. Curls of unruly black hair framed his cheeks. "Not a goddess."

"Mermaid? But the way she played with the *Aspis*, getting them to turn on each other..." Linus protested.

"A goddess would have killed us outright, in one large swell or storm. Perhaps a kraken. There'd be no lingering in her waters if she wanted us destroyed." Although he was only in his thirties, Makris's skin was weathered through years of sailing. Despite his demeanor, I saw the cracks forming in a face I had studied too adamantly. His jaw was too tense; his eyes were a bit too red, but his tone did not waver. Makris was sea born and raised. That fact alone should have been a comfort but, to anyone other than me, it was not. He searched each face until he found mine, then motioned me to follow him to his cabin.

I kept my curses to myself and held faith that he would not throw me overboard. He was too good for that and not easily swayed by superstition. Besides, with so few crew members left, he would need all hands available when the wind finally came.

The small cabin pressed us into close proximity, my heart ticked loud in my ears. Here there was no scent of fear, only the musk of labor paired with a covert look of concern. He dragged me into a stream of light, eyes narrowing as he studied my face and ran rough fingers over my smooth chin. I tried not to tremble, but my breath caught at the warmth of his skin against mine. He squeezed the muscles of my shoulders, grown strong under months of sailing, but he knew the differences between forms. His eyes travelled down, where the linen had gone thin enough to see the edges of the binding beneath.

Makris dropped his hands and stepped backward with a sharp inhale, and though I ached to follow, I stayed where I was.

"I brought you on thinking you were a scrawny boy with poor posture." He rubbed his eyes and sighed as if this were somehow a worse discovery than the creature that would certainly doom us. But he had trusted me, and I had betrayed that.

Shame prickled my skin. "I'm sorry," I whispered.

He shook his head. "This is why you don't hear her when she calls. While the others have been fighting and jumping to the waters at her first intonation, you have been the only one to show restraint." He stared at me, weighing the situation. "The others cannot know. It will only confirm to them that a woman onboard is bad luck. And they will blame you for our situation, whether or not you are responsible."

Having my thoughts reflected at me did nothing to quell my anxiety. "Yes, sir."

Makris rifled through a small trunk and handed me a shirt. "Put this on. What you are wearing is too thin."

I didn't wait for him to turn around before stripping the worn linen and tugging the shirt on overhead. Even with my breasts bound, I had nothing more to hide from him. And truth be told, I did not want to hide anything. Not from him.

"Alex?" He asked.

I shook my head. "Alexandra." The addition of that last part sounded foreign after months of not hearing it. Even the physician hadn't known my real name, not that I had done much good at hiding it.

"Didn't put much effort in, did you?" His smile was a slight thing meant to soften his next words. "You will leave when we make landfall. Until then, gods willing our survival, you must continue as you have been. Do you understand?"

My cheeks grew hot, eyes burned. I nodded. He watched my face until I looked away, studying the worn boards beneath our feet.

He cleared his throat awkwardly before asking. "Do you know why you can't hear it?"

Ever since the creature appeared before the *Aspis*, her cry too far away to affect our crew fully, I'd been pondering this. "I don't think she's looking for a woman, sir. I think she's searching for someone."

"A lover?"

I shook my head. The other men had already queried that guess, knowing so little of women that they couldn't imagine them wanting more than sex or revenge. But I'd remembered the legend my father used to tell me when I was young. "She's had ample supply of partners to choose from. I believe she's searching for someone specific. Have you noticed that her songs always sound like a question? And they repeat as if awaiting the right answer. I think the *Aspis* answered wrong and she punished them for it."

His tongue slid across parched lips. "When her voice comes, I go near as mad as the rest of them and then can't recall what happened afterward. Do you understand what she is saying?"

"No, it's just a feeling." I swallowed and watched his profile as he gazed out the small port side window. A small breeze rustled his hair as I debated for only a minute about mentioning the legend of Thessalonike. "Have you ever heard the tale about Alexander the Great's half-sister? Not the warrior, the one who had a city named for her?" The twitch of his eyebrow gave me the answer. His silence told me he was cautious about speaking her name. "In our small village the fishermen thought that she still searched for her brother, or for information about him."

His brows knit together thoughtfully. "It's been centuries. Surely, she'd have given up by now."

I shrugged. "Maybe I'm wrong." Our eyes met, and I was transfixed. In a compulsive moment of bravery and stupid desire for approval, I offered, "I could try to ask her since no one else can. It's been three days. She's due to return soon."

Makris hesitated, worry settling in the countenance of his jaw. "My job is to protect my crew and guide our way. You are still one of my men, even if you are not a man."

"You can't protect us if you're dead." I said, hoping he understood the feelings that motivated my actions. Even though I knew reciprocation was impossible to hope for. If we survived, I would return to my village and likely never see him again, consigned to work as my mother did, in some rich household until I died. A fate I had fought to transcend by lying my way onto the *Danos*. But the options for impoverished single women were either servant, wife, or whore. I'd always hoped for more.

Between hazy clouds, the moon cast silver light on the black water. The sea was flat, unmoving, as it had been the other times. Even the gulls had settled somewhere far from us. Makris tied the men to the ship, though he had left my bonds loose enough to slip through once the singing started. The crew would have questioned had I been left unbound.

The song came soft as dragonfly wings through the air, tickling our ears, before rising in pitch as it swept across the bow. Linus squirmed against the ropes. Elias squealed and groaned, as if being tortured. Makris stood rigid, leaning back against the masthead with closed eyes and clenched fists as sweat trickled down the side of his face. His bonds were not as tight as ours because of his limited ability to secure himself after the rest of us. It was sheer will that had kept him aboard the last few attacks, but the tremble of his shoulders was proof that his will was tiring.

I pulled my gaze away from the captain and searched the sea for the mermaid's form. Her tone lilted before starting again and, fixating on her voice, the words cleared in my head. Though sung in an old-fashioned tone with an unusual dialect, it reminded me of a song my mother sang when I was small.

"Does my king still live?" she asked.

Shimmying free from the ropes, I moved cautiously toward the prow. The song came again, and I waited for the slight pause in between questions to whisper with a shaking voice, "His legacy lives forever."

A figure glided through the water, circling once before floating beneath me. Huge black eyes, speckled with the star's reflection, took me in. Her features were an exaggeration of feminine—lashes too long, lips too full, face too angular—and decidedly no longer human. The alabaster of her skin blended with the moonlight on the water, dark salt-locks trailed over her shoulders and floated beside her. She cocked her head curiously.

"How is it so?" she asked. Her ethereal voice was edged with distrust.

I shivered. The stories said that was the correct answer, that she would depart after hearing that her brother's legacy still lived. But that ancient gaze lay me bare, as if it stripped away all disguises. My breath hitched. "I... I have his name."

Rows of pointed teeth gleamed in the moonlight in a threatening smile. Spindly fingers beckoned me as a tail skimmed the underside of the water. "Alexander?"

There was desperation in her voice, a wanting gone too long unfulfilled. Loneliness.

Behind me, Makris struggled against the ropes as they dug bloody trails around his arms. He cursed and moaned. A quick glance revealed his bonds had loosened at the strain. If he broke free, it would only be a few steps toward the rail and a short fall to the hungry waters below. The other men's grunts escalated in their toil, the mermaid's words ensnaring them seductively. They were each moving closer to doom.

I shook my head slowly, trying to quell my rising fear. "Alexandra. They named me after my father, who died in battle."

She cocked her head the other direction, eyes darting at the struggling figures behind me. "Are you trapped here?"

"No." Her question caught me off guard. "I am here to work."

She snorted. "You lie to yourself. I see it in your eyes."

I swallowed, glancing back at the crew. Makris pulled one arm from the ropes. In another moment, he'd be free.

"What do you see?" I asked.

Thessalonike's teeth gleamed again. "You're desperate for a life you can never have." My heart slowed beneath her discerning gaze as she continued. "Though you are surrounded by them, you are as lonely and different as I am."

The men's voices escalated, pulling me away from her cutting insight. "Please," I begged. "Please, let them go."

Her smile shimmered through the darkness, slithering dangerously as one eyebrow arched, as if knowing that every word she spoke was a spider's silk wrapping tighter around the men. "Join me, daughter of Alexander."

Elias's screams pitched higher; he'd break an arm soon trying to get to her.

"You'll drown me and then kill them too," I said, sure that she could smell my fear.

She shook her head slowly, her voice firm. "I will not kill you; I've searched a long time for a companion, and I swear these men shall live through these waters if you wish it." Long fingernails motioned me toward her.

Foam sputtered from Linus's mouth. His right arm had come free, his left soon to follow.

With a face reddened by strain, Makris stepped from the ropes. His eyes looked through me, glazed.

Salty tears crested my lashes as I scrambled over the rail and perched. Feet scrambled behind me as Makris' labored breath loomed closer. I inhaled, the thrum of my heart releasing my fingers upon the rail.

"Come, Alexandra. Let me free you from your bonds." Everything beyond the sound of her earnest voice vanished. Those words plucked a chord of longing in my chest that propelled me down into her open arms.

We dipped beneath the cool sea, breaking the surface just once, long enough for me to gasp air and glimpse the moon and stars above. Makris leaned over the *Danos's* rail, wide eyes fixed on me as her spell broke.

"Alex!" He shouted as the mermaid's embrace tugged me gently under.

Thessalonike has quieted since I joined her. Years have we spent swimming through passes, testing currents and tides of adjacent waters. We've dallied with whales, turtles, and dolphins, teasing the rays, and feasting upon tuna and mackerel. Watched mighty naval battles and bet upon their ships. She still laughs when men die. Yet somehow, we have returned to where my journey began.

The ship rocks beneath a full moon, its sun-bleached sails hang limp against the starlit sky. There is a familiarity to it that births an ache behind my breasts.

I know the man that leans over the rail, though his face is etched with time, his hair gone white. I've often remembered how the sun would catch the indigo highlights of his black curls or the ease of his smile when the sea was calm and the wind steady. The way his rich laughter warmed the air. What was his name?

"Makris."

His eyes glaze momentarily as my whisper skims across the water and enters his ears. He searches the water frantically, but I don't want to be seen, for what and who he remembers is gone forever.

Makris leans further over the rail, reaching a hand out. There is anguish in his voice. "Alexandra?"

The scent of salt and labor fills the air, but he is still without fear. My heart longs to answer. But knowing my words will drown him keeps me silent. I watch his features, etching them in my memory, for I know we shall not meet again. With a flick of my tail, I dive below the black water, back to where I belong.

CHAPTER FIVE

INSPIRATIONAL THEURGIST

Originally published in the 'Of Wizards and Wolves: Tales of Transformation' The David Farland Memorial Anthology with WordFire Press, February 2023. Edited by Lisa Mangum.

William spread a clean newspaper neatly over the grimy subway floor, sat down, and leaned against the yellowed wall. He scratched his chin beneath his gray-and-white beard as one train glided to a stop, the paper's curling edges lifting in the wind. A mass of bodies careened toward the stairs as he quietly pressed himself away from their hurried shoes and analyzed each wave of energy with keen interest.

One man tossed a few coins at the elderly man, who pulled his long, tattered coat around his chin. A woman paused, and William shifted his foot, his toe peeking between the sole and the

upper part of his worn shoe. She retrieved a five-dollar bill from her bag, but William didn't have a cup set out to receive such offerings, so she placed it atop his hands before rushing away.

William caught a hint of an energetic tug, but it was stale and quickly lost in the hustle of the commuters. He sighed and watched the crowd change as one train departed, and another took its place.

People walked by filled with purpose and goals, their eyes locked on their phones or staring numbly ahead. Their voices struck him like blunted arrows, easily deflected with practiced defense. The years he'd spent searching for an anomalous soul had made him patient, and he no longer resented the time he waited.

His transition was looming, as evidenced by last night's shimmers that had wafted down his arms. His fingers had trembled and gone translucent; he'd lost his grip on the mug, which landed with a thud on the bar. Thankfully, his fingers quickly solidified again. It was the third time in as many months.

There.

He caught a hint of bright yellow in an otherwise black-and-gray palette and struggled to his feet as the pull called to him. His hips and knees protested, groaning under the sudden unauthorized demand. Leaning against the wall to steady himself, he spied the boy. Black curls, acne, with recently sprouted sparse hair braving his upper lip. The boy adjusted his backpack while throwing his shoulder against the crowd.

Painter.

William huffed, tucking the five dollars into his pocket before loping after him. The crowd parted thoughtlessly around the old man, neither cursing nor grumbling as they also tightened around the boy and slowed his pace. It was a subtle shift of energy that none but the truly aware could feel. And the boy was unaware of much, other than his hormones and newly complex emotions.

The energy connected William to the boy, and for a moment, the old man could sense the world as if through a new lens.

He felt the boy—Zack—grip his pack tighter and struggle like a salmon swimming against the current toward the train. With a collective sigh, the pack of bodies scattered from his path one second before the subway doors slid shut. The train darted away without him.

William was close enough to both feel and hear Zack curse.

The old man placed his hand on the boy's shoulder, which strengthened the energy passing between them. The energy was subtle at first, the giving of it happening at a molecular level and growing larger. William felt the magic fill Zack's arm before wriggling simultaneously into his neck and down into his torso.

Zack spun defensively, slapping the old man's arm away. The physical connection was broken, but the energy still flowed. "A gift," William whispered, lifting his thick white brows, a smile on his thin, haggard face.

The arrival of another train kicked dirt into the air as it shuddered to a stop. Zack closed his eyes, and William slipped away into the crowd.

Still linked through the shared energy, William watched Zack claim a seat on the subway, briefly scanning the other passenger's faces. A moment later, the train jerked forward, and a surge of creativity sparked through the energy bridge like fire.

Zack pulled a sketch pad from beneath five cans of spray paint in his backpack. As he began to cover the paper with new ideas, William withdrew the connection—and smiled.

'Of all the comrades that e'er I had
They're sorry for my going away

And all the sweethearts that e'er I had

They'd wish me one more day to stay'

The words drifted through the thick tavern air as drunken men and women sang in fractured unison. William wondered if they were still called taverns. It certainly felt like a tavern. But that could just be the alcohol and questionable decisions being made that gave it that air. He blended in with the crowd, his beard neatly trimmed, his clothing comfortably middle-class.

People saw what they expected to see, and unless he magicked otherwise, he changed accordingly. He warmed his hands in the pockets of his leather coat and reclined against the wall as he listened. The energy pull ebbed stronger, like a thread tugged taut. It had potential. Hidden behind five overly confident and mostly off-tune men, a woman sang shyly near the bar. Mary's voice lilted toward him with a rosy hue. He felt her desire to be heard contrasted with self-limiting fear.

Musician.

The inebriated people swayed apart easily as he strolled across the room. He brushed gently against Mary's arm in passing and felt her shiver. The sudden connection forced her voice to rise in volume, and when the moment ended, she did not readjust her voice.

Faces turned to her with new appreciation as she hit each note with a richness and raw emotion that overrode better tone or pitch. People lowered their voices to give space for hers. William saw a man in tears, his lip trembling as the golden energy of Mary's voice resonated inside him.

'By a time to rise and a time to fall

Come, fill to me the parting glass

Good night and joy be with you all'

Connected as he was to Mary, William could easily imagine her later, sitting at her table and filling old music paper with new notes and clefs. Tomorrow she would restring and tune her father's dusty old guitar, too long abandoned in a closet. With Mary's passion reignited, she would not question the new uptick in inspiration. She would not remember the well-dressed man who brushed into her at the bar.

William reclined on a park bench beneath the warming spring sun as the newly returned robins sang amorous pleas. He sipped his coffee, paid for by the generosity of a passerby in the subway.

The warmth oozing from the cup eased the nagging of his arthritic fingers. He sighed, enjoying this simple pleasure his younger self would not have understood. But it had been such a long life, and it was nearing its end. Two painters, a sculptor, a poet, an actor, and a handful of musicians. It was a good haul for one night's work.

Unfortunately, none of them had been the one he sought. The artists he had touched were too full of other goals and familial obligations, things they could not put down with good conscience. Things that interfered with their ability to focus on creating.

He needed someone who had no such ties, but with the constant demands and impatience of this world, it had become like searching for a hint of ultramarine blue in a pre-1500s painting. Impossible. So, he simply gave each artist enough magic to inspire and rekindle their creative energies, to keep them going as he continued his search.

"Someday, you will have to choose wisely, too." That was what David, his mentor, had said before he transitioned. Back then, William had not understood what could happen. He thought that David's peaceful transition to an onyx-black raven that roosted in the Rockies was a lovely standard.

It hadn't been until his brother-in-service, Giotto, had failed to secure an adequate successor that William understood how dire the situation could be. Giotto's arrogant protégé had abandoned him before finalizing her commitment. She had taken most of his energy and inspiration and become famous, with no thought or intention of ever helping others.

When Giotto's last moment came, it was William who held his hand as he vanished into a long exposition of fusion jazz that filled a New York club for the better part of a night. When the music faded, several patrons had saved Giotto among four digital recordings that were never listened to again.

William shivered; it was the worst kind of ending after a life spent inspiring others. Worse, he knew how much Giotto hated jazz.

How well William chose his successor would determine his own last form. He didn't want to be a breath of wind that wafted through an orchestral pit. Nor did he want to be the worn sole of a ballerina's shoe. William wanted something more substantial, something that would linger and last. But after witnessing Giotto's end, it was hard to hope for an end like David's, and William found himself afraid to commit to anyone.

He closed his eyes and tilted his head back as the sun pierced the thin skin of his eyelids and turned his interior world shades of muted gold and amber. William thought of the boy from yesterday—Zack. He reminded

William of himself when he had been a youth. But the artist was too young. He hadn't lived enough yet. And Mary, the soulful soprano, had recently taken on the role of defense attorney. She had too many distractions with a big trial coming up.

"Excuse me."

A woman's voice jerked him out of his musings. His coffee sputtered through its lid and onto his hand.

"I'm so sorry. I wasn't trying to startle you." She was a familiar, forty-ish-year-old woman with strands of silver highlighting her brown hair at her temples. She was well-dressed in a simple business suit, but the designer bag on her shoulder was fraying and worn at its edges. Her brown eyes were warm with concern.

He transferred his cup to the other hand while wiping the coffee onto his tattered coat. "It's alright, miss."

She fretted, pulling a wadded napkin from her purse before shoving it at him.

William eyed her thoughtfully as a subtle, energetic tug drew his attention. There was an emptiness about her, a void that had been filled with more than she allowed herself to have now.

William remembered a similar hollowness back when he was struggling to create. But that had been a long time ago.

"Did you need something?" he asked.

She thrust a five-dollar bill at him with hands he remembered glimpsing the day before. "I was going to leave it on your lap but didn't want to startle you. I suppose I did, anyway."

William glanced down; his leather jacket had transformed into a tattered woolen coat. The toes of his right foot chilled as a breeze wafted through the split sole of his shoe. She must have recognized him from the subway yesterday.

"Can I get you another cup of coffee?" she asked. She clutched her purse awkwardly, and he suspected the five had been the last of her bills.

He waved her away. "No, thank you. I appreciate the offer, though."

William glanced around, noticing the other park benches were full of couples or families. He scooted to the edge of the bench, leaving enough space for her to sit a comfortable distance away. The sun was bright; more office types would be coming out to enjoy their lunch breaks on a day like today.

"What's your name?" he asked.

"Tamara." She cleared her throat as he slurped the spilled coffee from its lid.

"William."

He waited for her to settle into a comfortable space without attempting the immediate small talk that might send her scurrying away. She wasn't timid, he thought. She was drained. Her energy was barely reaching for him. "You must work around here."

She nodded toward 47th Street.

"Lawyer?"

"Paralegal."

He grunted before taking another sip of his drink.

"And you?" Tamara asked. "You must have done some work ..." She trailed off as her cheeks flushed pink.

William gave her a small smile. "Artistic Inspirational Theurgist, wizard class," he replied. No one had asked in a long time and, whether or not she went running, he enjoyed being able to say it.

Her posture stiffened, but she didn't move to leave. "Artistic theurgist …? Oh. That's nice. And, um, wizard class, you say?"

She dug through her bag, eventually pulling out a sandwich in a zippered silicone bag. "That must have taken a lot of work."

"Four hundred years, give or take."

Her eyebrows raised as she glanced sideways at him, as if his answers were not wholly unexpected. "Well, you look awfully good for your age, William." She took a bite of her sandwich.

William watched her with increasing interest. "Any hobbies? You seem like the sort who might be good at a lot of things."

She covered her mouth, chuckling as she swallowed. "Nah. I used to be, you know, when I was younger."

"Musician?"

She shook her head, smiling. "Can't carry a tune to save my life. I'm the black sheep of my family. Everyone else plays instruments or sings."

He rubbed his beard, trying to determine how to categorize her. "Painter?"

"Only walls, and I still make a mess." Tamara sighed as she leaned back against the bench. "How about you, theologist? Any hobbies?"

"Theurgist. I used to be a writer, but that was a long time ago."

A spark lit behind her eyes. "I did a little writing back in high school."

"What made you stop?" William leaned toward her, attempting to reel in the energetic line that was spooling tentatively outward.

Her shoulders sagged slightly. "My folks died young, and I had to look after my younger brother and sister." She shrugged. Her voice held no self-pity. "You know how it goes. Life is messy and busy, and it has a way of turning out different than you thought it would." Her gaze shifted guiltily to his tattered coat and worn shoes. "I'm sorry. I should have filtered that before it left my mouth."

He smiled. "No offense taken. I'm curious though—why don't you write now?"

She half shrugged and did not reply.

"Would you if you could?" He tugged gently on an ink-black thread that spun from her chest, giving it a thimbleful of energy. With a gentle nudge, that creative line hummed to life.

"I'm too old for that now," she replied, but there was still that light in her eyes.

It was William's turn to chuckle. "It is never too late to start again, Tamara."

Tucking her empty sandwich bag into her purse, she narrowed her eyes thoughtfully. "Been nice talking with you, William. Hope to see you again."

He nodded, studying her as she hurried away.

Maybe he should revisit Zack. The boy had potential. William felt strongly that whoever his replacement would be should dive into the work with passion.

A middle-aged man scurried past while quietly reciting lines that William knew too well.

"Our doubts are traitors and make us lose the good we oft might win by fearing to attempt."

Actor.

It was easy to place a small stone in the man's way that slowed him down, and equally easy to keep the man from tripping as William imparted a bit of magic into him. A little inspiration improved every performance.

A week later, he saw Tamara sitting outside a café on a Sunday morning. She was sipping black coffee while typing one-handed on her laptop. William watched as she set the coffee down and attacked the keyboard with the full focus and fury of both hands.

"William?"

He turned to see a petite woman with black hair pulled into a neat bun behind him. "Jane, I didn't expect to see you again."

"I thought I might have missed you," she said, giving him a quick peck on the cheek. "I wondered if you had transitioned already."

"Soon, I think," he mumbled in a low voice. "Just some loose ends to take care of."

She nodded, catching the implication. "Have you finally found your successor?"

"Remains to be seen. There are several with potential." His eyes slid back to Tamara as she continued typing.

"Don't dawdle, William. You are running out of time, and I know how indecisive you can be." Jane said it with a smile, but her tone was serious.

She patted his shoulder. "Just pick one, and let the cards fall where they may."

There was a yell behind them from the café, followed by a crash of dishes. A woman screamed as her companion, a short, round man, attempted to cough and could not. His face morphed into shades of maroon as he clutched his throat.

Tamara darted from three tables away. She wrapped her arms under the man's, hoisting him to his feet. Clasping her hands at the top of his abdomen, she made sharp thrusts upward. A chunk of barely chewed apple flew from his mouth.

The man leaned onto the table as Tamara released him. The man's companion embraced her, crying. They tried to repay her, offering to buy her another meal, but she declined. Gathering her computer and jacket, she hastened away with flushed cheeks.

"Huh." Jane cocked her head like a curious dog. "Writer?"

William nodded.

"Of course." She clucked her tongue. "Likes the action but not the attention. Just like someone else I know."

"I was thinking about someone else, actually. There is a young man who—"

"A young man? Are you joking?" Her look stung his pride.

"He has a lot of potential," William said.

"All young people are full of potential, William. You need someone who enjoys the process. Someone who wants to help others. Someone who has lived a little." Jane tapped her shoe on the concrete.

"But Zack seems like a good kid."

"A kid." She glared at him. "Should I remind you about what happened to the last good kid? Should we talk about Giotto?"

He scowled and bit his lip. His vision suddenly darkened, as if his eyelids had closed and refused to open. He swayed gently on his feet.

"William?" Jane's voice rose in concern.

Her worried face greeted him when he opened his eyes again.

She shook her head slowly.

"You shimmered for a moment." She swallowed nervously. "Like sunlight moving through morning lake mist."

He sighed, wondering if that might not be such a bad ending. They parted, and William felt the quiet pain of knowing they would not meet again in this realm.

William spent the better part of the next two days following Zack through crowded subway tunnels, down dark alleyways, and, eventually, to a small gallery in Soho. After the boy was removed by security, he graffitied a large, colorful phallus on the side of the building.

William tried to intervene, telling Zack about the life of an Artistic Inspirational Theurgist, but when the boy's eyes glazed, he switched to saying wizard. He bought the young man's time with food from a street vendor, but when the last of the jalapeño-and-shrimp tortillas disappeared down the boy's throat, he hurried away without a backward glance.

When William pursued, Zack threatened to hurt him. William resigned himself begrudgingly to the thought that Jane had been right.

He spent the next week watching Mary's trial, which was almost over. But on the weekend, she met someone while singing another Irish tune. He played the fiddle and sang in a bass that complimented her soprano. William had to admit they made wonderful music together.

The shimmerings were happening more frequently, sometimes three to four times a day, and William worried that each one would be his last.

He was afraid of transitioning alone.

Sitting and leaning against the subway wall, he closed his eyes. The noise did not stifle his thoughts. He hoped he wouldn't get stuck down here as a worn-out harmonica tune, or worse, a reedy treble note of an abused accordion. Depending on the words, graffitied poetry might not be so bad. Until someone scrubbed it off.

"How are you doing, William?" Tamara wore a pleasant smile and offered him a small cup of still-steaming coffee. "Thought you might want this."

William lumbered to his feet and nodded his appreciation before taking a long swallow.

"I've been looking for you for a couple of days, actually," she said.

"You have?" He frowned at the strong energetic tug that drew him toward her. She was different. The void he had detected when they first met was gone.

Writer.

He smiled.

"I wanted to thank you," she said, standing her ground as people jostled against her.

A tingle worked its way up William's spine, and the hair on his neck bristled with an electric surge. "I'll walk with you."

They headed up the stairs and made their way out into the morning light. William shimmered for a moment but returned before Tamara noticed. He walked beside her, his knees aching at the brisk pace she set.

"Our little talk that day in the park really inspired me. I've sold a poem and written a couple of short stories," Tamara said.

"Already? That was fast." He tried not to let her see him struggling to keep up.

She glanced at him and slowed her pace. "It doesn't matter if I'm late for work today." Her smile widened. "Today is my last day."

William paused. The crowd around them thickened and stopped. "What?"

"I quit my job."

"What are you doing now?"

She laughed delightedly. "I don't really know. Take a couple of months off. Figure out what I want to do."

He examined the multicolored energy line coming from her. "What do you want to do?"

"Help people. I just don't know how, yet."

The crowd moved again, but they stood staring at each other. William swallowed. "I think you would make an excellent Artistic Inspirational Theurgist, wizard class," he said impulsively.

She shook her head and laughed. "What kind of job is that?"

He shoved his coffee cup into her hands. "Just watch."

Pulling at the collar of his shabby coat, he tugged at the thinning line of magic within him. His clothing glistened, morphing into a tuxedo with a black overcoat. His beard sparkled and vanished, along with twenty years of wrinkles. A black oak cane materialized in his hand. People paused and gasped at the transformation, offering a round of applause.

"See?"

She shook her head, handing his coffee back to him. "Not really. Being a street performer doesn't appeal to me."

They walked slower up the street toward her office.

"I just inspired two poets and an artist to create something today. An actor will think about my showmanship when he steps on Broadway tonight. A dancer will—"

"Uh-huh." Her tone was skeptical.

William moved in front of her and blocked her path. "This is what I do. I inspire people—people like yourself who have lost their passion. People who think they are not good enough or who just need a nudge to focus on a canvas and paint for an hour. Or pick up a musical instrument. Or sing loudly at karaoke. Or even write something buried inside them."

Her eyes narrowed, but he continued, undaunted.

"The stress of the world makes it difficult for people to find their own inspiration, so I give them some of mine. Where would societies be without its artists and visionaries?" He licked his lips, hoping she would understand. "Art gets us through the difficult times, and everyone is an artist, Tamara. My job is to find out what that means to them and how to coax its growth. Then hope that they feel called to pass that inspiration on to others."

He felt a shimmer ripple through him; his magical display had taken too much from him. His vision clouded as a moment of panic took hold. He had waited too long.

Tamara's warm hand rested on his arm. The energetic line inside her reached into him, winding around his frayed thread without hesitation and making William solid again.

She sighed, studying the lines of his face. She removed her hand a minute later. "Inspirational wizard, huh? Tell me more."

He cleared his throat. "Theurgist." But he smiled as he spoke.

"Is it time?" she asked. Sadness deepened her voice as they sat beneath the full moon on their park bench.

William nodded slowly. His hand trembled. "I'm afraid, Tamara. What if I don't ...?" His voice trailed off in a whisper.

She squeezed his hand. "I got you. You don't have to worry." She wrapped an arm around his shoulders. He had grown thin over the last months. "If you turn into a string of music, I will record it and put it on repeat forever."

William laughed, which seemed a strange thing to do in his last moments. But it felt good too. "Even if it's jazz?"

"Yes, William. Even then." Her arms were warm around him. "I love jazz."

He leaned against her and closed his eyes. With a long, soft sigh that rustled the leaves like wind, William let go of all that he'd been.

The caw from the bird that roosted in the branches above was muffled by the late-spring snowfall, but it still pulled him from his slumber.

William stood and stretched. He sniffed the air, appreciating the scent of pine and juniper and catching the more intriguing smells of other animals.

Other animals.

He stood tall on four legs and paws. His gray-and-black fur was thick and warm. A full tail swished the snow behind him.

"Morning, William."

An onyx-black raven watched him with sharp eyes while shuffling from foot to foot and ruffling its wings.

"David, is that you?" William's words came out as a soulful howl.

The bird cocked its head as a hawk landed on another branch. The surrounding bushes rustled and parted as a black bear waddled forward. A moment later, a white-tailed deer sauntered into the circle.

The raven landed softly before him. "I'm so glad you made it, William. We've been waiting for you."

CHAPTER SIX

HERE TO STAY

Snow flitted past the familiar figure who stood in my doorway. Though sage had settled at the corner of his eyes, Danford still wore his traditional leather uniform and thick wool cloak with grace. His breath fogged in the frigid air, cheeks reddened from the wind, yet his eyes held that familiar warmth. That he had been the one to deliver the Senate's orders for my mother's execution made everything worse.

I'd known the sentence was coming. Maja was one of the most powerful mages in a century, but she had crossed lines that could no longer be ignored. Her erratic behavior had been a growing concern for the Senate for the last eight years. Unfortunately, she was still physically hale, but her sense of reason had twisted with the cognitive decline that occasionally came after too many years of magic. If the Senate had ever bothered to look closer, they would have seen the signs of my mother's true nature long ago. But they rarely did anything that didn't serve their own purposes.

That I should be the one to carry out the execution spoke more of the Senate's fear of my mother than any faith they had in her offspring. And until she was dealt with, Maja would continue to be a festering wound. A thing that hadn't yet managed to heal, even after years of work.

My hands stopped shaking on the third read-through of the order. I couldn't be sure if my anxiety was because of the writ or the man who delivered it. Danford sat silently by the fire sipping his tea while avoiding eye contact. His presence brought equal parts comfort and embarrassment. After the years we'd spent together it had been a great defeat to finally admit that I couldn't remove my emotional armor, not even with him. Though I was the one who left, it hurt me just as much as it hurt him. It had been years since we'd talked and I had denied how deeply I'd missed him until he was sitting in my home. Regret ached in my chest every time I looked at him.

I cleared my throat. "Did you know what it said when you agreed to carry it?" My voice was loud in the stillness of the room.

Danford took a slow sip before answering. "I suspected. I knew how difficult this would be." He shrugged slightly. "I didn't want you to receive it alone."

The firelight revealed the streaks of silver laced through his dark beard and thinning hair. It was fond memories that still drew me to him, I knew that. Our time had passed, and it was my own doing. I'd failed him time and again by disappearing when things got hard. But I always wondered if he held as much regret at the loss as I did. If he still cared as deeply as I did. If we could try again. I'd known enough of regret to recognize when my bad habits rose during hard moments, and I didn't avoid problems like I used to. I had tried to become a person worthy of him, even though I'd never hoped for another chance. Maybe that was why he'd come. But that thought felt too hopeful, too dangerous.

If I disappeared with Danford, the conundrum regarding my mother would return to the hands of the Senate. Let them deal with the consequences of empowering Maja and using her children in their political games. If it weren't for them, my siblings' hands wouldn't have been coated in blood when they were still young. Maybe their trauma would have been lessened. Maybe we would still speak to each other.

But the truth was, Maja had cultivated her children's mutual animosity like a gardener tending poisonous flowers. Pruning any potential connection as it arose while sharpening their thorns. Our mother had scarred us each in ways we'd been forced to handle alone.

"You can't avoid this, Lara," Danford said, his gaze meeting mine. The timbre of his voice settled in my chest. "Your siblings and their messengers should be here soon. I delivered yours last."

My mouth went dry. "What? They'd never—"

The door shook beneath a firm knock. My stomach dropped. I hadn't seen Charls in seven years and Talis had been hiding away for over a decade. Charls might heed the orders—he'd always been the most compliant of us—but Talis had sworn she'd never see our mother again.

Charls appeared in the doorway, his burly frame blocking out most of the light. His thick fur cloak was drawn up to his neck, blending in with his unkempt beard. A snow-covered hat rested on his head, catching any flakes before they could melt on his skin. His smile was small and thin. A young soldier shivered behind him.

I let them in. We didn't embrace—to assume that familiarity would have felt forced after so much time. Instead, we gave a small, polite nod. Charls removed his hat and shook out his knotted hair before leaning his staff against the stone hearth.

"You didn't have to knock," I mumbled awkwardly.

Charls glanced at Danford. "It's been a long time. It would have been presumptuous to assume your door would remain open for me."

We sunk into fractured small talk. Charls sipped his tea and chatted about his journey. They'd come by corvid. The two giant birds were covered beneath heavy blankets, their large woven carrying baskets left tilted to provide them shelter from the mounting snow. Though we didn't speak of Maja, her presence hung over us like a heavy cloud.

"Do you think Talis will come?" Charls asked.

"She doesn't have a choice. None of you do." Danford said.

A knock sounded at the door a moment before Talis burst in. She was bundled in thick red wool, with only her traditional fur hat standing out. She breezed past me and hung her cloak away from the others. Her features had sharpened over time and her brown-and-gray hair was braided into a style reminiscent of her youth in battle. Time had intensified the resemblance between Talis and our mother, but no one would be foolish to say that aloud. Talis wrinkled her nose at the scent of the tea and took a seat equidistant from Charls and I without uttering a greeting. Her soldier companion entered shortly after, shaking off the cold and giving a polite nod to everyone in the room.

"Let's just get this over with," Talis said curtly.

"You haven't changed," Charls said. Talis scowled in response.

I warmed my hands on my cup and stifled a sigh. I had almost hoped that old bitterness would be forgotten, but deep down knew it wasn't possible.

After all, the only things the three of us had in common were our absent fathers, Maja's hazel eyes, and a mutual resentment. Realizing that peace between us wasn't likely led me to agree with my sister's sentiment.

Danford spoke abruptly, as if remembering why he had come. "The Senate requests that you three carry out the execution of Maja."

Talis snorted. "If it were merely a request, I wouldn't be here. Demanded, you mean. Under threat."

Charls stared down at the table's uneven grooves, his hands clenched around the cup of tea which had begun to boil. "If something must be done about her, why are we expected to bear the brunt of it? We haven't seen her in years. If the Senate wants her dead, they can handle it themselves."

Danford's expression was grim. "They've already tried. Hundreds have died at the border in the last week."

The room fell silent, except for the crackling fire. After a few minutes, the three of us exchanged glances.

"Shit," Charls grumbled. "I always knew she'd torment us one more time. There's no way she'd die without turning a final screw."

"Mother always said she'd not go gently into retirement. I guess this was what she meant," Talis said.

I didn't speak. There was no point to it. I had sent ravens to them both over the years to let them know what Maja was doing, asking for advice or support but neither of them ever responded. Eventually, I gave up. Their actions or reactions weren't my responsibility. Nor was the brokenness of our relationship entirely my fault. Their forced presence now brought me no satisfaction.

Charls shifted in his seat and set the steaming cup on the table. Talis's drink had formed a thin coat of ice on top. My hands were empty. The sudden swell in emotions had sent the cup somewhere far away, maybe to the obsidian cave that I used to hide in. Danford's eyes moved from my hands to my face with a look of quiet understanding.

"I don't hear much up north," Charls said. "Guess I've been cut off for too long." Guilt weighed the edges of his words.

Danford spoke again. "Maja has been trying to cross the northwest border for two weeks. If she succeeds—"

"Let her go," Talis interrupted sharply. "Good riddance. Our neighbors can deal with her."

"That would be equivalent to declaring war," my voice was small in comparison to the others. My sibling's presence had triggered old habits from those formative years of neglect and survival - to fade into the background when tensions rose. To hide or disappear. It had taken many years for me to find my own voice, but now I found myself slipping back into old patterns. I cleared my throat and sat straighter.

"We've kept her from crossing the Diamsk bridge so far, but we can't take many more casualties." Danford said.

"What about the mages?" Talis asked.

Danford shrugged. "They only send the younger, less experienced ones against her. The rest are cowards. But the three of you together..."

The burden of our mother draped around our shoulders with a collective exhalation.

"I guess it was always going to be our lot to deal with her." Charls drained the rest of his cup, wincing as it burned his throat.

Talis stood by the fire, rubbing her hands together as mist flitted from her fingers into the air.

I rubbed my eyes again. "It doesn't matter. She's a storm that we must reckon with."

Charls' eyes narrowed on me. "But why send you? You've never—"

Danford interrupted before Charls could finish his thought. "We should leave before the weather gets worse."

I met his gaze with a grateful smile.

My boots broke the hard crust atop refrozen snow, sinking down into the powdery drift beneath. The sound of our feet reverberated in the thin mountain air as we trudged in silence towards the smoky plumes that wisped from the horizon. Charls, Talis, and I kept our eyes fixed ahead as we pressed on, each breath weighed equally with umbrage and caution.

Danford held me back, his expression filled with deep concern as my siblings moved ahead. He gently tucked a lock of hair behind my ear. My heart tugged and the urge to flee with him was nearly overwhelming. We could hide from my mother and the Senate. I didn't owe them anything. The words were forming on my tongue when he spoke.

"I'll wait for you."

I swallowed hard. "You'll wait?"

"For you? Always."

I glanced up the hill to the giant birds still harnessed to the baskets that had dragged us miles from their homes. One corvid cawed softly, rasping out a thin line in the frigid air. It shivered, wings settling to its sides as it snuggled against its mate. I nodded slowly and squeezed his hand before trudging away.

Charls and Talis stood at the crest of the hill, gazing down the long, steep slope. Their gasps still hung in the cold air as I caught up to them. In the valley below, ten pyres burned with bodies while four more awaited their turn. Only a small group of soldiers remained on the bridge separating the two countries. Maja stood alone, her deep indigo cape flapping in the icy wind.

Charls cursed through his frost-tipped beard as his wooden staff turned in his gloved hands. Talis's expression was like a battered shield.

Disgust burned my throat. "I wonder if she knows we're here."

A spell flew from Maja's hands and engulfed another stack of bodies in flames. Smoke swirled red and black against the dull grey sky. A man screamed from inside a pyre. His hand flailed from under his companion's remains, but no one could save him.

Maja turned slightly towards the hill, just enough for her sharp cheekbone to be seen as she angled her head in acknowledgment.

"She knows," Talis said.

We sighed. One in resignation, one in contempt, and the last with the forlorn weight of correctly anticipated disappointment.

"Talis and I spent years fighting beside our mother in battle," Charls said to me. "You'll stay behind while we take care of her. The Senate had no business sending you in the first place – your magic is too weak."

I ignored the unintentional insult and continued walking. Our journey down the hill was hindered by the weight of snow that caught our feet. My magic came well after my brother had gone. Charls and Talis had been nearly grown when I was born and had struck out on their own when they were sixteen and fifteen, respectively. They knew nearly nothing about me. Today, that seemed like it was about to change.

Suddenly, Talis stopped in her tracks with a stricken expression. Her cheeks were flushed. "I shouldn't have to do this, not after everything she did to me. Not after..." Her voice shook with the pain of old wounds reopening. Then she stiffened her shoulders and said simply, "Mother couldn't wait to be rid of me."

I let out a soft snort. "You couldn't wait to leave us either." My voice had a hard edge that startled them.

Talis rested a hand on her hip. "You were the only child she wanted. She said as much. I was just a tool for her to use," she said bitterly.

I shook my head, my hands clenched my cloak. "That was one of the lies she told you to make you leave. If you believed that, after all the other lies she told you, that's on you. But whatever you assumed wasn't the fault of the eight-year-old girl that couldn't leave. I did my best to survive after that and I don't owe you anything. So you can take your anger and misery and—"

Another pyre burst into flames, cutting off my words.

I swallowed, feeling a fool at letting my emotions get the better of me and a little proud that I'd kept my voice from trembling. Charls and Talis stared at me as if seeing me for the first time. My position atop the hill allowed me to look them in the eyes.

"Maja never wanted to be a mother. After you both left, I was nothing more than a confidant and servant. Certainly not the favored daughter you accuse me of being." Talis bit down hard on her lip, but I continued. "Did neither of you question why she drove you away so early? She was terrified that you wouldn't need her. That you'd outshine her. You were a potential threat to her power. Once you'd gained some proficiency, she put you in situations that she didn't bother to prepare you for. Then she humiliated you for failing." I shrugged. "You were too hurt to recognize what she was doing or why."

Talis crossed her arms. "She wasn't threatened. She's always been stronger than either of us."

"That's what she wanted you to believe. The only thing that truly worried her was being made inconsequential or losing control." I looked at them with fresh eyes. How had they never realized what I'd seen so clearly? Our mother had always been irreparably broken and couldn't tolerate those who tried to be whole, so she broke her children's spirits one at a time. Hurting others made her feel powerful.

Maja resumed her assault on the bridge. Shards of ice burst from her hands and punctured through a woman's chest. Dying shrieks reverberated up the hillside while the remaining defenders ran for cover behind their dented shields.

"I'll draw her attention," Talis said. "Combat her fires. There are certainly enough resources to work with." A few flurries landed on her eyelashes. "And more on the way, it seems."

Charls stared at the bridge below as another soldier fell. "I can handle her ice."

"I'll take care of the rest," I said.

"No," Talis quickly interjected. "I agree with Charls. You're not strong enough."

My laughter was brittle. "Why would you think that? Because I was always the quiet one? The nice one? I kept my head down and learned from your mistakes." I cursed and shook my head. "I'm the one who lasted the longest and I know her best. While you were busy licking your wounds, I was watching. And that has made me better equipped for this job than either of you."

"But your magic—" Talis's cheeks flushed.

"Is none of your starred business. Just like the rest of my life that neither of you has been in. When the day is over though, I imagine you will understand me better," I said. I took a deep breath. I'd spent years practicing these words and yet saying them brought no satisfaction. There was hurt and shame on both of their faces and I swallowed the sudden urge to apologize. Instead, I said, "If I can get close to her, then I can end this miserable reunion and we can all go home."

Talis and Charls parted as I swept past them. They caught up easily, though the tension between us had fractured slightly. My breath steamed in the air.

"I'm sorry I never answered the ravens," Charls muttered.

"Me too," said Talis. "I just..." She bit her lower lip and paused. Conflicting emotions drifted across her face. "I have to think of my family." Charls and I stopped, turning to her in surprise as she continued. "Evelyn and I adopted twins three years ago. They'll be six next month." Another blast from the bridge drew our attention as she continued. "I've been so afraid that I'd end up like her. I thought it'd be best to cut everyone off, but now I think maybe my reasons were more cowardly."

My chest tightened. "I know something of cowardice." My hand quivered above my sister's shoulder, though I didn't touch her. I couldn't yet. My emotions were whirling inside me, preparing to send the next thing I touched far away. I glanced at Charls. "Maybe we all do. We did what we needed to survive. I'm glad you've made a better life for yourself." Talis's eyes were glassy. "I mean that. None of us deserved what we got. You, especially."

Talis wiped her eyes and looked away. We were almost within range of Maja's magic, she would act before we could reach her. Talis and I took a couple of steps but stopped when Charls remained still. He ran a gloved hand across his face and sighed heavily.

"My partner, Miesha, has been sick for a few years. She won't make it through the winter. A healer is with her, but nothing can be done. It's simply a matter of time until..." His eyes watered, though the tears evaporated when they reached his lashes. "I only want to be with her when it happens."

Talis patted his arm. My throat constricted. The moment between us was thin and fragile as glass, broken when Charls' eyes widened.

Maja let out a piercing scream, her arm shot up towards the sky. A horse's smoldering corpse rose from a pyre behind her, flames dancing along its body as it hurtled directly towards me.

I dove sideways. Charls dropped his staff and rushed in front of me. His gloves burned away as flames burst from his palms. He moved forward, throwing a spell at the missile. The horse burned bright, winking like a blinding star, before shriveling and falling to a charred, smoldering husk in the snow.

Talis tugged her gloves off, summoning snow from the ground and surrounding air. It condensed and hardened into a large ball of ice. With a burst of power, Talis hurled it at Maja. It shot through the air until it was met with one of Maja's fiery blasts. Our mother laughed as the wind picked up the horse's ashes and swirled them into our faces.

"Bitch." Talis spat.

I climbed to my feet. That both Charls and Talis had reacted showed Maja that I could be used as a liability if necessary. Or, by directly assaulting me, she'd tried to force me to use my magic instinctively. But I knew better than that.

In my final years with Maja, I was subjected to her sometimes brutal attempts at eliciting a magical response. I kept tight control over my magic for many reasons - one being that my mother's ignorance allowed me to exist with less overt abuse than my siblings. Or maybe I just learned to absorb it better. Another reason was that I feared being placed in the same category as my mother - too powerful to live peacefully. Only Danford ever knew the truth about my magic. I turned slightly to catch his form atop the hill. Hope blossomed behind my ribs. Maybe there was still a future worth fighting for.

As Maja cackled, she turned her attention back to the soldiers. Their arrows were reduced to ashes before reaching her.

Talis and Charls slowed their pace to walk beside me. "Why would she target you?" Talis sounded almost offended. I could only shrug.

Charls had been obedient until Maja's demands went too far. Talis had pushed back on our mother's orders since she could talk. But growing up with someone who demanded to be the center of everything taught me it was best to go unnoticed. I spent my childhood hiding in books, pretending I didn't exist because it felt safer than the world around me. My magic manifested as an escape mechanism in response. Everything was a competition to Maja, and both Charls and Talis's magic made them threats to her. I never wanted to be on the receiving end of our mother's animosity and, if she'd known what I could do, I doubted I would have survived in that house.

When my magic bloomed, it was never little Lara who was blamed for things going missing. Maja was too fixated on Talis to see what was happening with her youngest child and never wondered where I went for long hours. I still felt guilty for adding to the weight Talis shouldered, so I'd hid my magic from everyone. Until Danford.

We reached the base of the hill, where the snowy landscape was covered in blackened gore and pale, misshapen bones. The gently falling snow gave an innocent disguise to the gruesome scene.

Maja gestured dramatically to the remaining soldiers cowering behind their shields. "Just look at my beautiful children! All grown up and thinking they can do as they please."

"She'll use old wounds and try to cut where she knows we've bled before," I said.

Three burning bodies lifted into the air, arms flailing like fiery wings as they soared towards us under Maja's magic. Talis flicked her hand, causing two of them to freeze and drop twenty feet away from us. Charls huffed as the third body exploded into larger chunks of burning flesh.

"We know what she's like," he said.

Talis turned to me. "What can you do?"

I hesitated before answering. The truth was that I owed her apologies too. Our attempts at survival had caused us each to do things we might have regretted. "Remember what happened to the pigs before you left?"

Confusion flashed across her face. "The ones that mother accused me of somehow drowning in the barn?"

"I did that."

Talis startled. "What? How?"

Charls's shoulder brushed mine as his hands flamed again. I flinched away. Everything was too close now and I didn't want to risk another accidental teleportation like the teacup in the cabin. Maja was raising more bodies, coating them in ice and twisting them into grotesque, contorted figures.

"I can transpose things," I said.

"But the pigs—"

"It was an accident. I tried to bring them back. Sometimes I can, but things don't usually come back the same. Sometimes saturated. Other times frozen, fractured, or shattered. Once I brought back a silver candelabra in the middle of melting."

Charls's fire melted one of the frozen bodies as it sailed toward them. It fell to the ground, limbs splaying with a sickening thud. Talis shifted the ice on the other body toward its feet while simultaneously raising a wall of hardened snow before them. The corpse's skull crashed against the barrier.

"Where do things go?" Charls asked.

I shrugged. "It depends on what I'm sending. It could be the bottom of the ocean, or the moon, or an active volcano. I don't know unless I go with them, only then can I direct it."

Talis placed a hand against the icy wall. It hardened beneath her palm. "Does mother know?"

"Stars no. You think I'd be standing here if she did?"

"Do you have a place in mind?" Charls's voice hinted at disbelief.

"Yes."

"You've done this before?" Talis looked more curious than disturbed by the notion.

"Yes," I said, lowering my voice.

"How many—"

"Later," I said. "I have to reach her to make it happen."

"How close?" Charls asked.

"Contact, if possible."

"I'll go first," Talis said, dashing around the wall.

With an expletive under his breath, Charls gripped his staff and jumped over the wall, leaving me alone. I tried to calm myself as I heard Maja's voice echo across the landscape. After a deep breath, I sprinted from the wall and ran toward a group of undamaged conifers. I stumbled and slid on the icy ground.

"You're still useless, Talis!" Maja yelled, melting Talis's icy projectiles with ease. "I thought you'd have improved by now. You promised I'd never see you again." She sneered before launching another barrage of flames. Talis's eyes narrowed, but she remained silent. "Always were a liar."

A wall of ice barely shielded Talis from the onslaught. She ducked down, but not before the flames singed her hat. With one hand, she extinguished the fur with a blast of ice. Her breath shuddered in the air.

A burst of fire caught Maja off-guard. She sidestepped Charls's attack and launched one back at him. Although he had higher ground, his feet slid backward under the force of her power.

"Why don't you scamper away again, boy? Might be the only thing you were ever good at," Maja said.

I slid behind the wide pine branches. Maja was only fifty feet away. A handful of remaining soldiers on the bridge nocked their arrows.

Talis stood and drew the snow from the ground before spinning it toward Maja. The woman countered quickly, using the same fire that she fought Charls with.

Though our mother still wore a toothy grin, her voice was strained at the effort. She squinted slightly as she searched the landscape. "Now, if only my other daughter would join us."

Maja clapped her flaming hands together before spreading them out while she spun. A wave of fire fanned outward, knocking Talis to the ground as her shield broke. Charls stumbled and fell atop his staff.

The soldiers wailed, caught by surprise. Their exposed flesh seared while a portion of the bridge caught fire. One arrow sailed from its bow but was burnt crisp before it could strike.

The tree beside me ignited in flames, but I opened my arms and embraced my mother's fury. The fire vanished into me. Maja faltered. Her spell sputtered and died. She stared in shock before a smile broke across her face.

"I knew you had power!" she yelled. "No child of—"

An icy ball slammed into Maja's chest. She flew sideways, landing on the slushy snow with a gasp. Talis ran toward her, forming another, larger ball in her hands.

But Maja was already recovering. An ice spear formed beneath her hand. As Talis threw the ball, Maja's spear sailed through the air. It splintered the ball into large shards and continued. Charls hurled a line of fire at the spear, but it was too slow. The spear pierced Talis's side and jutted from her back. She fell with a sharp cry.

"No!" I screamed, dashing forward.

Charls yelled. His staff ignited and he launched it with an angry growl.

Maja jerked sideways as the staff impaled the ground. She hauled it into her hands.

I yelled for Charls to run, willing him to be anywhere other than where he stood. The staff's flames died, replaced with an icy sheath that sparkled diamond-hard in the light. Maja, flung it toward him.

I ran toward her, breath heaving, as Charls's flames rose to meet her assault. The staff stabbed downward, aimed at his chest.

I wrapped my arms around my mother and let my emotions transport us away.

We stumbled into a room made of sharp black glass beneath a dormant volcano. A room I'd known too well over the years, though I hadn't visited it in a long time.

I pushed Maja away and leaned over, gripping my knees to catch my breath. She stumbled into the wall and hissed. Blood dripped onto the ground from a fresh cut on her hand.

"Where are we?" Her voice was hoarse and confused as she wiped her hand on her cloak and noted the small pile of children's books in one corner and a broken doll in another. An empty teacup sat beside it.

"Somewhere you can't hurt anyone." My words echoed around the chamber. "You've caused enough damage."

Maja squinted at me and licked her teeth behind her lips. "Do you really think this will hold me?"

"It will." Sadness filled my voice. I'd never wanted to do this, not really. I'd only ever wanted her to change, even though I knew she never could. But I guess every child clung to that hope, no matter how improbable it was.

My mother frowned. "I knew the Senate would drag all of you out of your little lives to attack me." She looked at me with an odd expression. If I didn't know her better, I might have thought it was regret. "I didn't want to hurt them."

"You've always hurt your children, mother. And all you had to do was make better choices."

Her expression hardened. "I did what I thought was best."

I shook my head in disbelief. "You're a bigger liar than your children ever were."

"Except for you."

I took a deep breath. "Maybe. But there's something you don't know yet."

A small flame glowed atop her fingertip, its light reflecting off the cold walls. "What? That you're a transposer? Do you think that's impressive?"

It was. I knew it was, but I refused to let her goad me. "No, I'm not talking about that."

"What then?"

"You'll die alone here." I said. "No one will grieve you or bury your bones."

My mother paled. "Listen, Lara. You can't just leave me. I tried to be a good mother to you. Better than to the others. I know I made mistakes, but I loved you." Her words were coated in honey as she stepped forward, extending an imploring hand out. "You were always my favorite. Are my favorite. My sweet, quiet girl. Always so good to me. Let's go home together."

"That's not possible."

Fire shot from her hand, and, with a wince, I allowed it to strike my chest. The flames licked across my skin before snuffing out.

I shook my head in disappointment. "I told you. You can't hurt anyone anymore. I should have done this years ago, but I'd always hoped that you'd do better." I wiped my eyes and slowly brought my hands together. When I pulled them apart a field of bloodied snow appeared between them. Talis and Charls needed me. "I have to go now."

Maja stumbled forward, reaching desperately. "Lara, don't—"

The cold burned my lungs as I stepped back into the spot before the bridge. Smoke blackened the sky and the stench of death wafted toward me with the shifting breeze. Two soldiers leaned over Talis, obscuring her from my view.

Charls was propped upright with his eyes closed. He spoke with another soldier, whose hands gripped the spear that jutted from his shoulder. With a jerk, the soldier yanked the spear out. Charls screamed as his opposite hand moved to the wound. That cry intensified as he cauterized his flesh. His scream died when he lost consciousness. The soldier dotted Charls' brow with a damp cloth and rolled him onto his side before covering him with a blanket. His breath was steady. He'd hold Miesha's hand again.

As I approached Talis, one soldier met my gaze. "She needs a healer," he said.

I swallowed. "Tell Danford to take her by corvid."

The ground surrounding her was stained red. Talis's eyes opened as I knelt beside her.

"Mother...?" Talis whispered.

"Gone."

"Good... good." Her words rattled in her chest. "We can go home."

"Evelyn will be waiting for you."

"Lara?" Her eyes closed; the lids fluttered but didn't reopen.

"Yes?"

"I'm so sorry...."

I brushed the hair from Talis's brow. I kissed her forehead. "So am I."

Several soldiers hoisted Talis and Charls onto makeshift gurneys and carted them up the hill toward the corvids. I sat on the ground until a thin blanket of snow lay across my lap and the sky had turned a darker shade of grey. Tears stung my eyes when I saw the birds fly away.

The quiet was disturbed by a familiar rhythm of footsteps. Danford knelt beside me and brushed a lock of hair from my eyes.

"Are you alright?"

I didn't have to answer. He gave me a sad smile and helped me to my feet before wrapping his arms around me. The shoulder of his cloak was wet when I pulled away and studied his face. He brought my hands to his lips and breathed warmth onto my fingertips.

"You waited," I whispered.

He nodded, eyes glassy. "A long time. Longer if you need me to." He said it like a question.

I leaned into his chest with a sigh. "No. No more waiting." He kissed the top of my head as I took a shaky breath. "I'm here to stay."

CHAPTER SEVEN

THE STEALING BONES

Originally published in Night Shift Radio's Storyteller Series Podcast - Print Edition. Edited by Mike Wyant Jr.

Isa sat beside the stone fountain, stealing sips of water as the noonday starling light beat down. Half of the liquid evaporated from his hands before it met those parched lips, but he dared not take more lest the guards see.

The sacred fountain was not meant for the likes of him and his brother. Though he wondered why those without status were unclean when they harvested the food and serviced the homes of the elite. He thought, if anything, the situation should be reversed. But no one sought the opinions of a street urchin, so Isa kept his thoughts to himself. An old thorn bush once protected the fountain, but that had mysteriously vanished two years ago.

Noori ceased spinning and, spying the wetness on his brother's lips, dashed to the fountain. Isa reached to stop him, but the older boy's hands submerged fully into the water and rose to splash his face. A guard shouted as well-dressed women clamored their offence. Noori's hands dipped again, scooping cool water to his mouth. He smiled at the smaller boy, who gripped his arm and dragged him down the uneven cobble streets. They darted through the crowded market and into an alleyway, hiding beneath a discarded awning and protected from the guards who ran past.

Isa panted, still clutched his brother's hand. He whispered with a firmness reserved for these situations. "You *can't* do that. What if they caught us? We could lose our hands."

Noori curled in on himself. Tears leaked from his tightly shut eyes. He wagged an accusing finger at Isa before his hand formed a fist and he struck the side of his head. His cries edged on screeches that would draw unwanted attention.

Isa shushed him, wrapping thin arms around his larger frame, hoping that the deep pressure would calm him. "I'll get water, just be quiet. I'll get us water."

The boy rocked despite the embrace of his smaller brother, but eventually he settled.

Isa's heart pounded in rhythm with the thump of boots that echoed toward them and moved away. Noori continued to sniffle. He wiped his snotty nose down a grimy sleeve.

Isa caught his brother's eye—it only lasted for a second—and felt better. "It's okay. We're okay."

Noori's gaze travelled above to the awning, then down at the cobbles, anywhere but at Isa. His fingers worked into words that only he and Isa knew. 'Cause you saved us again. The guards are stupid.'

Isa smiled and shook his head.

A scuff of shoes came from back down the alley. Recognizing the sound of sandals, he placed a hand on Noori to quiet him.

"I am looking for the spell seer." The voice was like a dry cough, hoarse and old. "Which one of you has the sight?"

Isa froze. Noori shoved the canvas from atop them and pointed at his brother with an awkward smile.

Isa rose hesitantly to his feet.

The lines on the old man's face etched deeper as cloudy eyes narrowed in study of the boys. "Is it you?"

"What do you want?" Isa asked.

Noori rocked from one foot to the other upon hearing the hesitance in his brother's voice.

The old man held up a calloused hand from inside his yellowed robes. His sandals—once fine—were aged and worn, his white hair and beard were yellowed in places. "I'm not here for trouble. I need help."

Isa stepped back, pulling his brother behind him. "I don't help strangers," he said, moving toward the street.

"I can pay you."

Isa stopped as Noori stumbled into him. They turned slowly. The man hefted a leather pouch, moving it enough to jingle the coins inside. Isa forced a dry swallow as Noori laughed.

"It would get you off the streets for a while. Perhaps pay for some training for a job." He arched a gray eyebrow. "Will you hear me?"

The boy bit his lip, chewing on caution, while boots paused down the street.

The old man edged past them, blocking a pair of lightly armed men, donned in fabric too dark for the midday heat.

"Step aside, old man. Are those the boys who defiled the fountain?"

He brought a weathered hand to his chest, his voice smooth. Even Isa felt the pull of the man's spell. "My grandsons have been helping me all morning."

The guards swayed like men too deep in their cups with pockets easy to pick.

"No. It couldn't be these boys," the younger guard said. "Sorry to disturb you, sahib."

"Do not worry yourself, young man."

The men walked away in dreamy slowness as the old man turned to the boys, blocking their escape.

"Now, will you hear my offer?"

Noori rocked again, heel to toe, tucking a fist under his chin in a familiar fashion. Isa hesitated; he'd kept them safe for years by exercising caution.

The old man smiled broadly, false ivory teeth set too white against his yellowed ones. "I have water and food. There is a bath and some linen that I have no use for." He glanced at their thin sandals. "My son's old sandals might fit you."

'Water!' Noori signed quickly. 'You said you would get us water.'

Isa sighed and gripped his brother's sleeve. "Fine. I'll hear you. But don't think of trying those spells on us."

He petted his beard with a look of satisfaction. "I wouldn't dream of it, my boy."

He led them to a middle-class home of mud and brick near the eastern edge of the borough. It had been a fine neighborhood, but time and the once bustling economy had moved past it. Three servants greeted them, a mother and daughter dressed in pale rose robes, and a muscular middle-aged man with hollowed cheeks and empty eyes donned in brown. They gave low bows as the old man entered.

"Master Leil," the older woman began. She glanced at the boys, while the girl wrinkled her nose at the smell that trailed in with them. "How may we serve you and your... guests?"

Leil chuckled, giving them instructions as he herded the boys to a garden at the back of the house. Purple plum trees grew alongside date and olive trees while bright butterflies flew gracefully through the enclosure. The scent of jasmine drifted in the air.

"I am blessed to have a natural spring below this land," Leil explained. "It provides more than enough food. Eat whatever you find."

Noori zipped from one tree to another, gulping down plums in two bites while juice trickled down his chin. Isa tried to subdue him, but it was no use.

"He is safe here," Leil said. The women set out soft pillows and blankets to settle on under the shade of a tree and poured fresh water into wooden cups.

Isa settled on a pillow and sipped his cup, while keeping a cautious eye on Noori. He wanted to gulp the water but forced himself to savor it like a delicacy. He knew he was being measured, felt the scales behind the old man's eyes taking his weight and substance.

Leil grabbed Isa's chin and frowned, noting a fading bruise. "Does he hit you?"

Isa pushed him away and shrugged. "No. Never. He hits himself." He rubbed his chin, still sore from Noori's fist. "I just get in the way sometimes trying to stop him."

"How long has he been like this?"

Isa shrugged again, as adolescent boys are prone to do.

The man clucked his tongue while the woman and girl served heaping plates of roasted lamb and baladi, goat cheese, olives, and dates. Isa stared at the sliced meat and swallowed his saliva, then downed the rest of his cup.

Leil piled food high onto a wooden plate, then handed it to Isa. The boy hesitated, but the emptiness of his stomach won out and he snatched the plate. He only choked once while stuffing the food into his mouth.

The man made himself a modest plate as Noori continued to tug plums from the trees, oblivious to the better food that awaited him.

"How long have you been taking care of him?"

Isa decided the man had bought a few answers by filling their bellies. "Three years."

He raised an eyebrow. "On the street that whole time? Where are your parents?"

Isa swallowed a bite of lamb before asking, "What do you want?"

Leil smiled. "Straight to business. I appreciate your directness." He wiped his hands on the napkin. "I lost something in the desert when the city of Granam fell. Do you know it?"

Isa purposefully watched Noori rock back and forth across the gardens. Granam had fallen before the last plague, long before he was born. Maybe before his parents were born, but he wasn't sure. That city's tale was deemed too frightening to teach children, according to one of his old teachers. But Isa lingered in the corners of drinking houses and underneath the windows of gambling dens. When people drank, they talked about many inappropriate things, and Isa listened.

"What did you lose?" The boy asked.

"My wife," Leil said, forcing the boy to look at him. "I want to give her bones a proper burial before I die."

Isa bit his lip, shifted on his sudden desire to get away, but his compassionate heart held him against his instincts. "Why didn't you go back sooner?"

The old man gave a listless sigh. "I tried when I was younger, but I lost the way. The spells that killed that place turned me around and sent me home repeatedly. I hired other men to find it, but each one failed—if they returned at all. Eventually, I gave up."

"Why now? Why me?" Isa knew the answer, but still wanted to hear it.

"I heard of a boy who can see through spells. Maybe even undo them. They say he can slip into places he should not be." Leil's eyes flicked across the garden as his tone darkened. "I heard he has a brother that needs care."

The hollow-faced servant stood behind Noori, clasping a blade that glinted in starling's golden rays. He spoke a few words to Noori, but the boy didn't look at him.

Isa jumped to his feet and called his brother's name. Noori loped toward them as the servant reached into a tree. He cut down a black plum, following the boy with his eyes.

Noori dropped to the ground, ignoring the pillows and plates, and stuffed handfuls of lamb and cheese into his mouth, followed by cupsful of water. Isa met the old man's eyes.

"I hope we can reach an arrangement," Leil said, biting into a plum.

The burro began another sandy circle in the same stubborn pattern, trying to turn around as the simple spell confounded her. Isa jumped down. Jini, the donkey, couldn't see the way like the boy could and Isa had hoped that the beast would mind him. But Jini would not obey twelve-year-old boys, especially those who did not yet know how to command respect.

He pulled his pack from the donkey's back and slung it over his shoulder. He would have to drag the beast forward. Leaving her in the desert was wishing death upon her and trying to return home without her was wishing death upon himself. Pulling the white linen over his head to protect from the heat, he tugged Jini forward as she fought and bit at him with each earned step.

Isa saw spells like thick shadows. Granam's first spell appeared as a thirty-foot-tall wall of thorns and weeping poison vines that extended to either horizon. As they drew closer, small shades of vipers slithered out, offering flicking tongues and soft hisses. They lunged as Isa pushed past, causing him to startle even though he could see through them. Jini stomped her feet and tugged her head away until Isa's hands were raw from gripping the rope bridle. Beyond the spell, Jini walked calmly behind him, as if she'd known that there was nothing there.

Isa scowled at her. "Stupid moke, you shouldn't have gotten all worked up."

Jini snorted as he pulled her onward.

Stone walls and buildings rose in the distance while blackened trees reached empty branches to the sky. One hundred feet from the city gates, the dust swirled around them in widening circles. Isa tossed a light blanket over Jini's head before she could react—whether or not the dust devils were real, she'd be calm and protected. Drawing the linen around his face, he edged cautiously forward.

The dust hovered just above the ground, dancing around their feet as they passed, as if deciding what to do with the boy.

Beyond the dust, under the hazy starling light, they paused at a pair of stone gates. One side was nearly ten feet tall, with a carved lion that stared down upon them while the other side had toppled in half. Its matching lion lay face down and submerged in sand. One iron door hung on crumbling hinges, while the other was missing.

Nothing moved beyond the gates. No cacti grew, nor lizards crawled; there were no beetles or birds. Granam was lifeless, except for the pair that now entered.

Isa had heard dozens of accounts about Granam's tragedy. Those stories issued in hushed, drunken voices late at night with occasional arguing over which account was true. It was all conjecture, of course, for no one had survived the city's destruction. One day it was a thriving halfway point for trade between Minnent, his home, and Kabril. The next day, no one could find it. The spells had locked it away and left no one to tell its tale.

Isa did not consider the source of the curse. He figured it had run its course, and its purpose completed since everyone was dead. He was more afraid of Minnent's fate if he failed to return than he was of these half dead spells.

A foot of sand lay atop Granam, ebbing against the walls of empty bee-hive homes, dipping in places to reveal chipped mosaic entrances. Dozens of empty buildings stood proudly in the withering heat. They needed care but seemed habitable. Isa peered inside a few doors but dared not enter.

Retrieving the map that Leil had drawn, he followed it to the center of town. Passing the covered well, a single home stood free of dust, as if ignored by time. The door swung open under Isa's hand. A gust of stale air smelling of sandalwood and decay escaped the cool room.

He tied Jini to a post and pulled the linen over his nose before stepping inside. The home had a welcoming chill. The dome shape with the small opening at the apex allowed the warm air to escape while keeping the room twenty degrees cooler than outside. He wandered into the center of the home, eyeing the clean chairs and table.

The door slammed shut behind him, accompanied by a snort. An aged feminine voice spoke, "Took him long enough."

Isa jumped. An old woman, face as dried and shriveled as the dates he enjoyed, stood at the door. White hair snaked in knotted tendrils from under a faded orange headscarf. Her eyes were as orange as the scarf, though sharp and unyielding. She stood strong and straight, bearing good posture for her age.

At least that was the spell she wove, the image she wanted Isa to see. But, unfortunately for him, he saw beyond the glaze of lies that encapsulated her. Beneath the faded linen, under the time-eaten locks of white hair, was a faceless skull without expression. Because bones are just bones, Isa reasoned. Her eyes glowed like bitter embers in a midnight fire.

The illusion snorted again as the bones idled toward a chair. She gestured to an identical one across from her. Outside, Jini grunted.

"Bring it in if you want, won't make any difference in here. And it might help the burro some; nothing outside survives come nightfall," she said.

Isa stared as the mandible did not move. There were no tongue or vocal cords to create a voice, yet he heard her words as clear as Jini's protests.

The bones sighed, sending a gust of damp air to Isa's face ten feet away, and prodding him into motion. Outside, the starling dried the air as the boy untied the burro. Jini startled at the old woman, her nostrils flaring at the odd contrast of odor and image.

Isa led the beast in and wiped her down. He pulled a treat from his pack, which Jini quickly devoured. The ember eyes pressed into his back, but he was in no hurry to meet them.

"Do you speak?" Her voice was thick with time, yet hollow of substance.

Isa considered that her voice must be in his head, a thought that did not endear her to him. He turned, frowning as he struggled to see the illusion, but the realness of animated bones was far brighter than the spell. He sat in the chair as it creaked under the unfamiliar weight.

"You must be her," Isa said.

The illusion scowled while the bones did nothing. "How is Leil?" She asked.

"He wants to see you."

"Did he send you to bring me out of here?"

Isa frowned, refusing to look at her. There was a knot in his stomach as he thought of the spells he had encountered. The confounding and pushing away spell, the thorn-wall and vipers, the dust devils, and even the bones before him unraveled slowly to reveal their truths.

"Do you want to go?" Isa asked, glancing around. He spied a withered hand sticking out from under a pile of blankets along a far wall. He sighed, fighting a fear that wet his skin, and feigned ease. "It seems like someone has made a lot of effort to keep anyone from going or coming."

The illusion smiled and clucked her absent tongue. "You are a clever one, aren't you? Better than the other ones that made it this far. Where'd old Leil find you?"

"How long have you been here?" Isa asked. "You've been dead a long time already."

The eyebrows shot up as he considered the effort it took to maintain her illusion. The image gave a broad, gap tooth smile. "Who are you?"

"No one. Just a boy."

"A talented boy, I'd wager. And how did Leil convince you to come?"

Isa looked up at her, fiery eyes boring into his for a long moment before he looked away.

"He holds something dear of yours, eh? That's what he does," she breathed, her tone changed. "He steals what we love and uses it as leverage."

He studied the floor. "He said you were his wife."

There was a cruel sound in his brain while the bones laughed. The illusion did not laugh. Those cracked lips remained pursed together. The conflicting images hurt Isa's eyes.

"I suppose that is one way to sway a sympathetic heart," she said. "*Not his wife. Not even a friend.*" The bones were still as the illusion spoke. "We were siblings, and rivals. He was jealous of my talent."

Jini's ears perked toward them, brown eyes lazing under heavy lids as she listened and shifted from one hoof to the other, snorting occasionally.

Isa coughed, pulling the stopper from his flask and swigging back water before he looked at the bones. "He's your brother?"

Her eyes sizzled. "Was my brother. I'm dead, remember?"

An image of Noori flashed through his mind. His brother's wide eyes and self-injurious head strikes at his leaving. Noori crying after him as he rode Jini away from Leil's house as the man servant restrained him. Isa had promised to return soon, that he would be okay, but his brother could hear his concern. Noori had talents easily overlooked by those that did not see beneath the obvious. Those talents were best kept hidden from those like Leil. If the old man or his servant hurt Noori... Isa drew his thoughts away from possible outcomes and back to the bones.

The smell of sandalwood ebbed through the room as a narrow beam of light focused through the dome top. Isa saw the spell she was weaving and wondered aloud, "How do you still have power if you are dead?"

"It's the bones, boy." She gestured to the dried hand that reached out from beneath the blankets. "These old bones can keep going if there is life to feed them." She rolled up the illusory sleeves of her robes. "I suppose that is why he sent you to me."

Isa scratched his head. "I figured as much."

"And you came anyway?"

"He has my brother," he said. There was a press on his skin, as if he were being wound in a spider's cocoon. The room lost its refreshing coolness, but Isa remained calm. Life had taught him how to get out of worse traps than this. "And he wants your bones. It may have been a gamble on his part. How did he trap you here?"

"We sought the same thing, and when I won out, he used nearly all his power to send a violent storm." She clucked her tongue again; her eyes had diminished to a reminiscent glow. "It was too late by then; I already had the power we both wanted. Spun it to my soul and bones, but not my flesh—a novice mistake. You mispronounce one word in a spell and..." she huffed. "He killed everyone here instead. My husband and children, my neighbors, and friends. Those who survived the storm starved and withered. And I could only feed on the living and hope for revenge."

A sigh rattled her bones, sending deep shivers across the table to Isa. "The spells are to keep him out. I have no doubt that he still wants immortality, would love nothing more than to grind my bones and eat them, but he is too weak to get past the spells. So, he finds others with some power and sends them to their doom." The illusion raised its eyebrows at him.

Isa bit his lip. "You said you wanted revenge."

"And you think you can give me that? Rescue me from this prison and do what, exactly?"

The threads pulled tighter around him as Jini brayed at the odd sensations creeping up her legs. But Isa could see where the spells could be undone.

"If Leil has not seen you in fifty years, why would he believe that you still live? He sent me to collect your bones, not your soul." Isa shrugged. "What if I deliver you to him as you are? Then you can do whatever you want with him."

The illusory eyes narrowed. "No one can get out of here. I made the spells unbreakable, even by me."

Isa huffed and plucked at a place on his shoulder, then another on his knee. The invisible webbing that she had been silently spinning fell away from him and Jini.

"Every spell has a weak spot." He smiled sheepishly. "And each one can be undone."

The bones slapped their knees, howling at his display. She stared at him with renewed interest. "What's your name, boy?"

He stuck out a hand. "Isa."

Her finger bones cracked as she took it, freezing his hand.

"Qadira. I'll give you five days to get us out of here, little spell breaker," she said. "After that, I'll steal your flesh and your donkey to feed my bones."

Leil had given him eight days to return, and that was two days ago. He'd promised Noori to be back before that in order to soothe him, and knew his brother counted the days. "I'll get it done in four."

By the time starling set, Isa had dismantled the dust devils. It was simple enough once he realized that, although they formed and ended in different places, the dust devils paused in a twenty-by-twenty-foot area south of the falling gates. The spell was woven together in long spirals of magic which the boy had undone by unhooking four points. It had looked more complicated than it was. He hoped the rest were the same. Qadira was unimpressed with this accomplishment.

"They've been faulty for years. I'm not surprised they didn't rise against you." She huffed, having not bothered to watch him work. Isa wondered if seeing her years of labor and spells undone by a boy irritated her, but he didn't dwell on it. He kept his thoughts on getting back to Minnent.

That night, Jini and Isa stayed inside Qadira's home. She insisted it was unsafe to stay elsewhere. There were creatures that slithered and crept through the walls of the other homes. She denied they were her making. But there was no sleeping while she watched him. He could not trust her hunger for revenge to outweigh her hunger for sustenance, and he still searched for a way to undo her, if necessary.

Qadira offered him water, but it smelled putrid, and Isa saw the rot of the food she offered under an illusion of goodness. He thanked her and ate from his rations. The portions he had taken from Leil's home were more generous than he was used to, so it was no brilliant feat to divide what he had into even portions.

He left with the starlingrise and, taking Jini with him, headed past the gates to the spells beyond. Jini stayed near him while he examined the thorny wall, the lunging vipers, and the poison-weeping vines. Even though it was all an illusion to him, the spell's resistance was genuine enough. He felt the hard backward press of it on his lungs. The spells worked like one-way valves, snapping closed to refuse exit. Isa stepped back. He could only take the pressure of the combined spells for a minute or two at a time before his lungs clamored for breath.

Walking the perimeter of the wall at a five-foot distance was safe enough and allowed him to study the spell's intricacies.

It was a three-dimensional puzzle, and he hoped that undoing one spell would weaken the others, but first he had to find a loose thread. By noon, he had walked the enclosure three times, tugging the linen over his head to protect from starling's heat, and was no closer to dismantling it.

Jini followed, nudging him for food or water, or simply for her own amusement. The boy leaned on the donkey, sharing carrots and turnips until she turned and walked the other direction. He watched her, catching a shimmer in the viper spell, while four lunged in sequence at Jini as she passed. There was one that posed in stillness, its tongue barely flicking.

The surrounding vipers hissed and lunged; one even spitting the illusion of venom at Isa as he approached. The repulsion of the spell was strong, as if giant hands were squeezing the air from his lungs. But the one snake did not move. Here was the ending thread that was pulled too tight. A slip knot held the viper spell together.

Isa smiled, despite his lack of air, and yanked the viper from the thorny wall. The vipers flailed and spit before dissipating in a curtain of cold mist. He stepped away, taking deep breaths and congratulating himself. But there were still two more known spells, and the ones Qadira insisted were not hers.

The rest of the day passed in tedious frustration. He would find a vine that didn't weep, or a dulled thorn, but they would not be undone. The vines and thorns were entwined, but they were not the same. It was a clever spell, Isa had to admit and said as much to Qadira that night while she offered him rotting food and attempted to plie him with sour water. Her illusion seemed thinner, the bones gleamed whiter, though Isa couldn't be sure.

He was too tired to dwell on it. Curling along the edge of the room, he wrapped his dirty linens about him and stayed near the donkey. He slept, despite the bones watching him, and dreamed of Noori's tear-streaked face.

It was not the scratching of sharp claws on the outside wall, but Jini's shrill bray that woke Isa hours later. Qadira's bones sat in their usual seat, eyes aglow as they simultaneously watched the rattling door. Over the last few years, he and Noori had grown accustomed to the scratching of rodents and nocturnal pests, so he pulled the blanket around him and attempted to sleep again. But Jini would have none of it. She brayed loudly and stomped a hoof too near his leg.

Grumbling, Isa stood and leaned against the wall as the burro eyed him nervously. He ran a calming hand over her back and down her haunches as the scuttles outside continued. Shimmers of magic slipped under the door, only to retract suddenly.

"What are they?"

Qadira huffed. "I told you it's not my magic."

"But it is magic, and you've had years to investigate it." The boy turned to her. "Whereas I've only had two nights."

She crossed bony arms over her chest. "They came after I created the barriers, back when there were still people and animals left. They grew into the large lizard-like things they are now. I would wake in the morning to discover the eaten carcass of a goat or a pig on my doorstep and then the remains of an old friend or neighbor. But they never came in my door, always leaving the remains like a prize for me." Her hoarse voice slipped to a whisper. "There has been no one left in many years, but they still prowl."

Isa wrapped the blanket tighter. "After the barriers? Then it can't have been Leil's magic."

"No," she agreed.

Isa turned a thought in his head. "Your children died here?"

"My entire family, save for a sister in Minnent, but I suspect she is dead by now, too."

"Did any of them have your skill?" He asked, thinking of his own family who had an array of practical talent before they disappeared.

"My son, but he died protecting everyone, moving townspeople inside and rounding up the livestock. He even covered the well before the lightning took him," she said.

"Leil did that?"

"Yes, but it was my greed that brought it. I knew what Leil was capable of. If I had let it go, they would still live."

A bit of spell-thread slipped from her sleeve as she spoke, wrapping itself tightly around the two bones of her lower arm before weaving itself into an intricate pattern and pulling itself so taut it was barely visible. Isa noted for the first time the silvery threads that wrapped each finger bone, each neck bone, and even around each rib that he could see.

Isa knew that people often couldn't see the results of their own actions, least of all how it affected their immediate world. The creatures were born of her own guilt. The fact that she was unaware of the spell's casting would make dismantling it that much harder.

"How do I dismantle the push spell?" He asked, changing topics.

She clucked her tongue. "Back to business, eh?"

"The vines and thorns will take patience, but I am good with puzzles."

Glowing eyes narrowed through the illusion of an offended elderly woman's face. "What will you do if Leil hurts your brother? What if he kills him?"

Isa frowned, thinking of Minnent, the kindness of the unclean folks that lived there, the thieves and vagabonds that occasionally took them in or fed them. The bakers who made extra bread just to give away to those who could not pay. The guards who were patient with Noori or looked the other way when they caught them stealing. It was not Noori that he worried about, but what might happen to those people if he did not return. Leil didn't know it, but he threatened more than his brother.

Keeping these thoughts to himself, Isa asked, "You don't know where the push spell begins and ends, do you?"

She shrugged. "It has been a long time, boy."

Bright morning rays of starling chased away the creatures and found Isa and Jini back at the thorns. He plucked and twisted at them before having to step away because of the pushing on his lungs, then moved to a new section. Five hours later, Isa baked beneath the star, frustrated, and tugging at every memory he had of thorns in an effort to see the truth behind the spell. He recalled the thorn bush that had once guarded the sacred fountain.

'Why thorns, Isa?' Noori asked, tears shining in his eyes. Isa had washed the blood from his cut after removing the thick barb and wrapped it in a piece of linen torn from his shirttail.

'To protect itself. It didn't want to hurt us; it just wants to live without being hurt.'

Noori sniffed. The larger boy took either everything, or nothing, personally. Any physical pain to either of them was always taken personally. 'Like us, Isa.'

The boy nodded while he bled through the linen. It had taken a trip to the local physician to staunch the bleeding while Isa kept Noori calm. For weeks after, the guards and the townspeople pondered what had become of the three-hundred-year-old thorn bush that surrounded the sacred fountain. One morning it had been there, and by afternoon it was gone. No one could explain it, but its disappearance opened the fountain for stolen drinks from vagrant children.

Blood. The answer to the thorns was blood. Would you be willing to bleed on them to survive? Are you willing to hurt as much as the person who made it?

Isa pulled a paring knife from his bag and stood before the thorns. He held his breath from the pressure of the pushing spell, bringing the point of the blade down on his thumb, and winced at the pain as blood oozed to the surface.

Jini idled away, watching quietly as Isa let three large drops fall onto a thick thorn. Isa considered he was wrong, that the blood would fall to the ground below and he would be stuck again. But the liquid sat on the thorn, suspended for long seconds before vanishing into it. The thorn trembled, that tremble reaching out in a slow rumble to the surrounding ones as they crumbled to sand and fell to the ground.

Isa jumped, whooping, and punched the sky before sucking his thumb and wiping it on his shirt. Jini snorted.

"Like you could do better, moke," he said but scratched her ears and neck.

Three spells down. Most spells were built with purpose and planning, driven by clear thoughts and motivation toward a specific end. When those thoughts were muddled, or spells woven with too much emotion, it became a more complex task. Finding the beginning or end of the spell was like looking for a mirror in a pool of water. Isa had learned the hard way that some of those emotional spells could never be undone.

As starling sank toward the horizon, Isa had dispelled half of the vines. It took several hours to realize that the vines comprised four lower and upper quadrants set at equal intervals. Isa stood upon the disrespectful donkey's back as the air was pressed from their lungs, whilst Isa reached up to the midway point of the vines. He counted himself lucky that he only fell twelve times and that Jini only kicked him twice. He thought only one of those kicks was intentional.

They slunk back to Qadira's beehive home. Isa's water was getting low, but his food rations were holding for both him and Jini. He asked about the well that her son had died protecting, but she was quiet this night. She did not offer him the rotting food, nor the foul water.

Isa savored a plum, squashed from the journey, and asked, "Does it hurt when the spells fall?"

Qadira's icy breath brushed his cheeks. "Not exactly. I feel myself disappearing one unravelling at a time. I sit here alone all day, with nothing but memories that play havoc on me." She stood, grabbing one of his empty water flasks and heading toward the door. "It isn't pain, but the grief of five thousand lives, three children, and a beloved husband."

She opened the door and made to step out into the darkness. Isa ran to stop her as the hiss and scratch of large claws echoed off the walls of abandoned homes. He grabbed at her robe, but his hand slipped through the illusion. His fingers iced as they brushed her undead bones.

"They don't want me," she whispered. "I'll get you water from the well."

Isa allowed the lie to settle and wondered if she knew it was a lie. "Should I go with you?"

"No, boy. At least let me protect you." The door shut behind her.

Isa peeked out the window, watching large, spiked lizards with red eyes trail behind her down the dusty street. They shone of a thousand silver skeins tied to the walking bones. Those skeins snaked under Qadira's garments, slowing her steps as she ambled away. Isa spied a large web above her, spreading out to cover the city. Qadira was a spider caught in a web she could not see. A web that she had spun herself.

The vines fell the next morning, though they resisted Isa's efforts at every turn and Jini amused herself by nudging him further into the pushing spell and watching him gasp for breath as he stumbled backward.

"I'll leave you tied inside with Qadira if you keep it up." He warned, but ran a gentle hand over her back.

Jini nudged him again, lips pulled away from her teeth and he felt the familiar pushing away but realized it was more of a pulling toward. He squinted his eyes in the midday light and saw a wall of spidery thread previously hidden by the vines. Above his head were thousands of lines leading into the town, drawn to a single point. He followed the lines, Jini trailing behind.

The threads swayed gently as Qadira hefted a leaking bucket into her arms and filled two water jugs. Long lines of webbing spun out from under the sleeves and neck of her illusory clothing. Isa saw her opalescent bones clearly for the first time in the bright light. Each bone encased with spell thread, like a puppet and not the master.

"I hear you, boy." Qadira said, offering a flask of water to him and settling a filled pot on the ground for Jini.

He sipped the water but did not pull his eyes from her or the strings as he spoke. "There are only two spells left to break. The pushing spell that keeps us from leaving, and the creatures that haunt the night. I think they are connected."

"And you think I should know how they were made?"

Isa shrugged, studying the boney toes that sunk into the sand. "Are you afraid of being alone?"

The illusion was nearly translucent beneath starling, but he could see her scoff. "I've been alone for fifty years, other than the occasional dinner that wanders in. Loneliness and I are old friends."

Isa plucked at one thread in the air, saw it tug at her shoulder, startling her. He asked. "Then are you afraid of leaving?"

The jaw hung open for a second too long, before Qadira marched away. The boy and donkey followed at a safe distance.

He trailed her into the house as she stormed from one end to the other, which was not far at all, until she sat down in her chair. She stared at him with murderous eyes, but Isa stared calmly back.

Fifteen minutes passed with Jini snorting and stamping at the tension while the boy and the bones observed each other. Finally, Qadira uncrossed her arms and tapped the tips of her phalanges on the table.

"Why would I be afraid of leaving?" She asked.

Isa cautiously sat in the opposite chair, resting his hand near hers. He swallowed, considering the weight of his words. "I figure everything you ever loved, and all that is left of them, is here. So, leaving might feel like a betrayal. These last two spells are born from your guilt and pain." Isa bit his lip. The only way to escape here was to have her do some work, but this work was different. He could dispel the pulling threads, but the creatures she would have to undo herself. "Leil may have committed the crime, but you willingly spun yourself into this prison."

Bones should neither cry, nor breathe, nor move. Bones should be dead and still when they are no longer covered with flesh, but Qadira's bones had cursed themselves with a bitter eternity and the only way out was for her to sit with her sorrow. Her illusion was barely a shimmer, but it wept while ember eyes dulled behind her tears.

She turned away. "Do you know what will happen when you dispel my magic?"

Isa was quiet. He had been preparing for the possibilities since the day they met. He knew what her stealing bones would do, but he did not waver. Noori waited for him.

"In order for us to leave here, you must sit with those creatures. Listen to them. When you have made your peace, I can undo the last spell," he said. "But there isn't much time left. If I don't return as expected, bad things will happen in Minnent."

Qadira regarded him curiously. "I thought Leil only threatened your brother."

Isa shrugged. "My brother would only be the beginning." It was a lie made of truth.

When the skittering claws came to the door that night, Qadira wrapped her rotting robe around her and stepped out to meet them. Her sobs and whispers crept under the door and through the cracks around the window. Occasionally she would say someone's name. Sometimes her voice broke and racked Isa's insides. Grief was a companion he had known for too long, though not as long as Qadira. He had sat with it long enough to understand it, and certainly enough to recognize it when it raged, or cowered, or crumbled before him. Sometimes grief needed to consume us so that we might let it go.

Isa wound linens around each arm and leg and covered his head and his face. He wrapped his hands, leaving the fingers out for easy use because magic, much like grief, can alter people and he knew Qadira would not come back the same.

She returned as the day dawned; her illusion erased along with the lower threads that had bound her to the creatures. The bones of Qadira stumbled inside, searching for the boy. The sustenance needed to keep her last spell alive stood before her as an underfed and unarmed adolescent.

Gone was the voice in Isa's head. Gone was the elderly woman, replaced by something that should not be. Was this the spell of immortality that she and Leil had fought and killed for?

Its bony maw gaped open, rotting breath fouled the air in a silent scream. Qadira lunged at Isa while Jini brayed and stomped from a safe distance.

The boy stepped out of reach. Those hands would freeze and rend him if they could. He danced around the room, lunging, ducking, and falling back. There was no point in speaking. Her ability to negotiate was lost under instinctual survival, and her last spell was worth more to her than her revenge or his life.

Jini's braying grew louder and Qadira turned on her with a silent hiss, stealing across the room. The donkey was a simpler target, though it was turning toward the door, angling its rear toward the attacker. A boney hand reached for the beast, fingers curling in sharp points. But Isa was there. He wrapped bundled arms around her midsection to hold her back and kept his head low.

Jini's weight shifted onto her front legs, kicking both hind legs out. The hooves met Qadira's skull as Isa leapt back. She fell to the floor in a hard crash. A stream of morning light issuing in from the roof's hole landed on Isa's back as he jumped atop her.

He tugged the robes away from her chest while she was momentarily dazed, though the spell threads attempted to bind him. Isa's nimble fingers searched for the knot of the spell tied around her bones, as the binds entwined his arms.

Qadira's icy fingers gripped his arms, the cold working its way through the layers of linen. Her eyes were on fire as her mouth opened in silent protest.

Isa jumped back, pulling away from her grip as the cold seeped up his limbs. Qadira clambered to her feet, robes gaping open to reveal her sternum and ribs. Behind the left side of her chest, a knotted thread shimmered in the starling light.

She stepped forward and Isa stepped to meet her. He held his breath, the threads on him loosening, as he wrapped his arms around her. Qadira froze, surprised, as her cold worked into the boy's frame. She dropped her arms to embrace him and Isa would later wonder if, underneath the horror, she knew what he was doing. As her mouth opened wide, teeth preparing to taste his neck, she paused.

Isa looked into her eyes before yanking his arms away. A trail of silvery thread wrapped around his hand. Qadira reached out, but she was already crumbling to the ground. The bones had come undone, but there was a fire in the eye sockets that regarded him with a new respect.

He gasped for air, rubbing his arms vigorously to return the warmth to them. He grabbed a large blanket and scooped up the bones, tying the ends together to make a package. Isa stepped outside into the bright day, unwinding the linen and basking in the warmth for several minutes. Above, the webs had fallen.

Jini snorted as Isa secured the bag to her back and climbed astride her. They hastened away from Granam, the donkey requiring no encouragement to move. When night inched across the sand two hours later, Isa tossed a light blanket over he and Jini and drifted into slumber.

In his dreams, Qadira was made of flesh and blood. Her skin smoothed into a younger version than the illusion he had known.

'Give me the bones of your donkey so that I might live. She will not suffer for it.' Qadira's voice wormed into his brain.

'She isn't mine to give,' he replied.

The woman smiled seductively, leaning closer to him. *'Give me the bones of your brother, then. Let me relieve you of your burden.'*

Isa's heart grew heavy with her words.

'Your life could be so much simpler, so much happier, if he did not exist.'

He felt the temptation, and the rush of guilt that followed, then shook

his head. *'I'll give you something better.'*

Leil waited for them in the garden. His glee threatened to break the crevices

in his face when he saw them approach.

Isa searched for his brother, opening his mouth to ask when Noori

dashed from the house, laughing with excitement at seeing him. He rocked

from his heels to his toes, making rare squealing noises while clapping his

hands.

Isa slid from Jini's back, smiling at his brother while quickly assessing his

state. Noori was clean, dressed in fresh clothing with newer sandals. His

cheeks were a fraction fuller, and Isa thought he looked taller. He sighed

in relief; he had feared the old man would not be true to his word.

Noori patted Isa's shoulders awkwardly while he embraced him. Jini

snorted and swayed behind them, nudging Isa's back with her nose. Isa

untied the pack and removed the blanket before the girl led the donkey

away.

Leil's eyes gleamed. He rubbed his hands together, reaching for the pack.

"Did you find the bones?"

Isa stepped back smoothly. "How many others were sent to retrieve your

'wife'?"

His eyes narrowed. "I sent many men over the years, but you are the first

to return."

"Where is my payment?" Isa clutched the bag, waiting until Leil produced the large pouch of coins while the bones inside the pack chilled Isa's hands. The boy who could break spells knew enough to put them back together if he wanted. Once he saw how something was undone, he could retrace the knots and ties to work it in reverse order again. After Isa had rewoven half the spell, the bones of Qadira were sewn together, waiting.

Leil frowned, watching the boy squirm. Isa placed the package on the ground, the bones inside stilling as the old man stepped forward. Isa drew Noori back with him.

Leil's knobby fingers worked to untie the blanket. As the knot loosened, the package burst open. Sharp, bony fingers gripped Leil's throat, shoving him backward as it rose and stepped from the cloth.

Isa could not hear the words Qadira put in Leil's head, nor did he wish to. He pulled Noori behind him, his shrieks turned to cries.

Qadira lifted the old man while his sandals flailed for purchase on the ground. Leil's eyes bulged as his fingers clawed at the bones. His cheeks hollowed as his skin became parched and dark, as all life was sucked from him.

The old man weakened as the skeleton's jaw opened wide and bit into his neck, tearing flesh as blood splattered below.

Noori tried to run, but Isa held his hand and whispered, calmly explaining his plan. The older boy gulped fear, but nodded in understanding.

Leil ceased writhing, his arms limp at his side as the stealing bones took another bite of him.

Still holding the end of the spell thread, Isa tugged. Qadira jerked backward, dropping her prize. She turned, opening her mouth in anger, and lunged at him. Isa shoved Noori away as boney fingers gripped his arm. He yanked harder on the thread, seeing her jerk again. But the bones were strong, and his world grew dim as he struggled against the cold that engulfed him.

He yelled at his brother to run as Leil's servant ran into the garden.

Noori barreled into the bones, tumbling with her on top of Leil's drained corpse. Isa dropped to the ground, shivering. The older boy's face was pent with fury as he struck Qadira with bare fists, unbothered by the cold. Isa struggled to his feet as Noori shook the bones and screamed silently.

The hollow-eyed servant rushed toward them, raising his knife. But he didn't make it.

Qadira's eyes flared bright, the bones shone iridescent, and then she, the servant with the knife, and Leil's corpse, were gone. They disappeared into one of Noori's undoable spells, perhaps to the same place the thorn bush had gone after it had stabbed Isa those years ago.

Isa wrapped Noori in his arms as he continued striking the empty ground. Several bushes and trees around them vanished.

"I'm okay. It's okay," he said. "You saved me, Noori. It's okay."

Noori gulped air, his limbs taking a few minutes to settle. His cheeks were wet as he rocked and settled back on his heels.

'No one hurts Isa,' he signed finally.

Isa tugged Noori to his feet and secured the money to his belt. Noori wiped a hand across his nose and gave a semi-smile.

Isa took his hand and led him from the gardens toward the stables. Jini brayed from inside.

"I'm glad we're brothers," Isa said.

Noori patted Isa's back before signing. 'We save each other.'

CHAPTER EIGHT

SILENT SPELLS

It started with an unfair promise, that the older child would care for the younger. The promise sowed resentment that was neither child's fault. It was that same resentment that pulled Minh's hand from his sister's while they stood over their father's grave. His hands were raw and blistered from cutting into the frozen ground, a broken shovel proof of his labor, but it was not pain that drew him from her. It was the weight of a promise demanding fulfillment.

They'd buried father next to a grave as old as the girl. They sang songs of sorrow and called the spirits to guide their parents to each other. Ciandra wept, bluebells springing through the ground where her tears landed. She was a ray of warmth, but the delicate flowers would freeze when she moved away, and that warmth never reached her brother.

Minh stared at the graves a moment longer before turning away. There was no time to settle in grief. "Enough of this. We should be ready if they come back tonight." He did not spare a glance for his sister as he moved toward the house.

Ciandra touched her lips with small fingers, then placed her hand on the space between the graves. Her lips moved, but no sound escaped. She was content knowing that a pair of saplings would root soon, and, someday, wave their limbs to the mountains and that foreign land where they'd come from.

Minh watched her from the door before closing out the winter air. He was a lanky boy of fifteen, straddling the space between adulthood and childhood, and if she had been the elder, their safety would have been assured. Father would still be alive. Ciandra had been given the gift, while Minh had been given too many words and nothing of the silent spells.

The bit of protection that lingered from father's spells was already withering and rotting with his body. When the scrimmagers returned for the girl, there would be little left to shield them. They spent the day tending to the cows and pigs, placing long spikes around the barn's perimeter. But Minh knew it was futile. Escape would be their only hope of survival, but the winter storms through the mountain pass would kill them just as surely as the monstrous creatures that had taken father.

Not long after they'd settled together on the floor and drifted to sleep before the fire, the scuttle of claws across the roof woke them. Minh's thoughts turned to escape, or, to his shame, giving them what they wanted. But he stayed huddled beneath their shared blanket, wondering what would be left of their home when the creatures were done. Desperate wails from the barn issued through the night until, one by one, each cry was silenced.

Ciandra peered out from under the blanket, watching the boy for reassurance. The fire burned low, reflecting off her ruddy cheeks and black glass hair as she trembled. One tear rolled down her cheek as she clutched her stomach in agony. Minh offered no words of comfort, tucking the blanket tight, and rolling away from her. The girl scooted close, laying one arm across his back, which he did not push away.

They pretended to sleep until dawn, as the world outside grew quiet with death. Morning light chased the scrimmagers away, leaving long claw marks across the roof. The eastern part of the porch swayed in the gentle breeze. The bulk of their grain storages were strewn across the fields and stamped into the ground while the spikes Minh had arranged lay haphazardly in contempt. Tears stained Ciandra's face as she pointed towards the barn.

The pigs were scattered throughout the pen, rib cages splayed open in gore. What remained of the cows was put on graphic display, soft brown eyes staring at them from the top of spikes. Thick tongues lolling out in grimaces.

Minh held back tears, disappearing into the house until he recovered. Father would be disappointed in his weakness, but father was always disappointed in him. The destruction had destroyed any hope of lasting through the winter without aid, and the neighbors would not offer it. The scrimager's actions were under the command of the Gray Shaman, and no one, other than their parents, resisted her.

"We must leave." Minh said, voice cutting through the quiet.

Ciandra's eyes were wide with questions. Minh pointed to the white-capped mountains on the horizon, a sliver of pass barely visible in the haze of distant snow.

"To the Gowun territory. Uncle will help us." Minh kept his eyes trained on the pass, ignoring the tremble of his sister's lip. "There's no other way."

They bundled under layers of heavy coats, packing small bags with rice biscuits, bread, and water. Minh sighed as Ciandra struggled to lift a pack onto her small shoulders but refrained from calling her a burden. He was ordinary, untalented, with no spells and too many words. The shaman only wanted his silent sister. But the promise he'd made was all that was left of father, and he wouldn't meet his parents again if he dishonored it.

Minh set the structures afire, saying a small prayer for the animals as they burned. It was all he could do. The flames leapt up the walls and over the roofs, consuming everything of their childhoods. Gripping father's staff in one hand and Ciandra's wrapped fingers in the other, he pulled her down the road. They turned back every so often to watch the smoke blacken the sky. It was a hundred miles to Uncle Yue's, and they'd be hard pressed to make fifteen miles a day if the weather was good, which it never was this time of year. If he were traveling alone, he could make twice the time, but he brushed that thought away.

Ciandra did not complain, even when at the end of the day saw her limping behind with chapped cheeks and lips so raw they bled. They sheltered within a grove of trees, burying into the warm ground with the small trowels they'd brought to cover their leavings hoping to decrease their scent. As the temperatures dipped, they huddled together, shivering, and swallowing unspoken sorrow.

In the morning, Minh wrapped the girl's feet to prevent further blistering. He bundled her hands and face, drawing the cloth over her nose and cheeks before they started the steep path that lay between mountainous peaks. The wind whipped snow into their eyes as the air thinned. His skull throbbed with each upward step, feet slipping repeatedly, despite father's staff and they were forced to rest after only a few hours.

The boy cradled his head, steeling himself to continue despite aching muscles and muddled thoughts. Ciandra sat before him, staring with their mother's gentle eyes, and unwrapped one of her hands. She placed cool fingers on his forehead, easing the throb and removing the pain. Minh released a long exhale at the relief.

"Thank you." He said, despite knowing that she shouldn't use her powers.

Flashing a crooked smile, she re-wrapped her hand and tugged him to his feet. The snow mounted as they trudged along the pass, slowing their steps until the sky darkened. Ciandra discovered a small crevice to shelter in, protected from the wind and snow. They leaned together, eating dry bread and hard cheese, until they drifted to restless sleep. Minh prayed they wouldn't freeze in the night.

The morning welcomed them with bright light and crisp air. The snow had stopped, leaving the world in brilliant white. Stumbling from the shelter on sluggish legs, they continued up the mountainside. It was miles later when Minh noticed the loss of one of their food bags, left to freeze in the small crevice.

His words were angry and hurtful, sputtering in the thin air and, though he knew he should have checked before they left, he couldn't admit the blame was shared. He let Ciandra cry for a long moment, but finding only wretchedness from the sound, he shook his head.

"It's fine." His tone softened by a throat thick with guilt. "We'll find food when we get to the valley."

She wiped her red nose with the back of her sleeve, staring at him. Quickly unwrapping her hands, she spoke in her special way. 'I can make food.'

He shook his head. "It's too dangerous."

Her brows knit together in frustration as she glared at him, fingers dancing so quickly her brother had difficulty keeping up. 'What good am I if I can't make food? You should let me help when I can. You don't have to do everything by yourself."

"Wrap your hands before you lose them." He snapped, setting his jaw as he looked back down the mountain. "We need to keep moving."

Her face fell, but she complied, and they marched on.

They reached the summit near starlingset, the beauty of golden rays sparkling on snow was lost as windy gusts attempted to toss them from their feet. They clutched trees and held each other as each step stole their breath and burned their skin. Ciandra turned to her brother, questioning, but he shook his head.

Camping under the wide, sweeping branches of a tall tree, they found warm ground amidst the fallen needles and leaves. The small birds that called it home protested until Ciandra offered them crumbs from her small meal, then they nestled in close to her. The branches protected from the icy wind that raged around them.

The howl came in the middle of the night, echoing through the pass. The creatures had discovered the lost pack and would be on them within a day or two, though Minh didn't say it. He pulled his trembling sister close as the birds cooed softly, seeking to comfort her.

"We'll move faster down the mountain than we did coming up," he whispered, ignoring the doubt in her eyes. "They can't hunt during the day. We will be okay." Though even he could hear his lies.

Ciandra looked back at the way they'd come and shivered. Descending the shorter side of the mountain was treacherous in the dark, but by the time starlinglight struck the snow, they were half-way down. In their haste and growing fear, Minh struggled to cover their tracks, slipping and stumbling while relying on the staff to avoid falling. Ciandra moved gracefully down the slippery inclines. Each step surefooted, often waiting for him when she had gone too far ahead. The boy's face flushed at her competence, and he wondered if he was holding her back. He wondered if he was becoming her burden, but there was only softness in her eyes as she watched him.

By the time the moon rose, they had reached the plateau and nestled in a group of winter bushes adorned with sharp, green leaves and poisonous berries. There was a dusting of snow here, but the southerly wind warmed them as they nibbled on the remains of their food.

Ciandra asked him to speak of their mother and things father would never tell her. Though she'd never known their mother, the resemblance grew stronger every year. Remembering the past saddened Minh, but he finally relented. He couldn't tell her all. There would be time in years to come for that.

Minh was an only child for 7 years when Ciandra arrived a month earlier than expected. The doula sent the boy outside to wait under a warm solstice moon while mother silently birthed the girl. But the process took the last of her. The doula's face was sad and swollen when she exited the house, and she did not speak to him as she passed. The flowers beneath the porch wilted while the cows lamented in the barn, and he knew that mother was no more. Two days later, his father received a writ from the Gray Shaman, the woman who ruled the province. Father's face, still turgid from grief, went red, and he burned the letter in the fire.

"Just let her try," he'd said and held Ciandra closer.

From then on, father took the children everywhere with him. They were in the fields when he plowed, and the barn when he doctored the livestock. He carted them to town to make trades and receive news. He trusted no one to watch them, especially not the neighbors who fawned too much over the girl, while ignoring the boy entirely. They called Ciandra a straw in the wind, but father spat on the ground when Minh questioned its meaning.

Ciandra was quiet and rarely fussed, watching the world with large black eyes, and absorbing all that she saw. But, even so, Minh struggled to love her. She had killed his mother. Father's attempts to tender the boy's heart towards her had only deepened the resentment.

The years that followed were hard in every way. Mother always gave them good crops and healthy animals, but with her passing, everything failed. The crops died; the livestock sickened. It had never been a good place for a farm, father said, but mother had insisted because she liked the view of the mountains, and she could make anything good.

As Ciandra grew, the land grew hearty again, more bountiful each year. Her presence was enough to bring life and abundance back to the land. Even the livestock mated again, and the cows and pigs grew healthy.

She always had a kinship with the animals, mouthing strange words, and laughing soundlessly with them while they were drawn to her warmth.

When Minh was twelve, he caught a fever for a week and nearly died. Their father worried and prayed over his son with tears in his eyes. One night, Ciandra crawled into his sick bed, curling around him while he slept. In the morning, the fever was gone and within a day he was well again. Father thanked her, though she didn't understand what she had done.

Each year on the eve of her birth, another writ would arrive from the Shaman. And each year, father would watch it burn. He would not discuss what it said, though as time passed, he became increasingly nervous.

"If anything happens to me, you will need to protect her," he said. "The Shaman would take her, if she could. She can feel her power growing." He stared into the other room, where Ciandra slept. "Soon, she'll be beyond crops and simple healing. But she will need someone to love and protect her. And she will need to love in order to understand her power fully."

Minh had argued with his father, not understanding why they should disobey the Shaman. Their neighbors called them fools and said their disobedience would get them all killed. It was the only time father raised a hand to him and there was a look of regret that immediately crossed his face.

"The Shaman is merciless, caring naught for anyone but herself. She could make the land bountiful for all, yet she only does it for her own gain. If she takes Ciandra, she'd use her to no good end, and if she can't use her, then she will kill her."

That is when Minh had made the promise to protect his sister with his life.

By the time he finished speaking, Ciandra's eyes flickered beneath their closed lids. A smile teased the corners of her lips as she dreamed. She looked like any other girl, but, unlike other girls, small buds of yellow flowers poked through the ground around her. The leaves on the bushes thickened, the berries ripened from poisonous to edible. He let her sleep past starlingrise before rousing her, then buried any signs of their presence while she stuffed the berries into their bags.

Traveling through the flatlands was easier, warmer temperatures and signs of life jutted through the ground. Minh estimated they were halfway to Uncle's home, but still not beyond the Shaman's territory. They'd need to continue walking after starlingset to stay ahead of the scrimmagers. Once the monsters reached the flatlands, they would easily outpace them.

The scrimmagers had sleek bodies that gleamed like lava glass, with narrow, feline faces. It was their long claws and sharp teeth that allowed them to easily climb walls or rend flesh. They were the Gray Shaman's spies and minions and had been haunting the children's homeland since Ciandra's first birthday. A likely response to the unanswered writs.

When Ciandra turned two, father heard the creatures scuttling outside and had gone to meet them with his staff, leaving Minh to watch the sleeping girl. But he'd listened at the door instead, unaware that one creature slipped in through a window. When he caught it perched atop the edge of her crib, he screamed. It replied with a shrill sound, lunging for his face with its talons. Father burst through the door, bringing the sharp end of his staff down upon the creature in midair. Minh still remembered the sickening spray of yellow blood as the body thudded to the floor. Ciandra sat in her crib, unharmed and unafraid.

The next day and every few days after, father cast meager spells to keep the beasts away. His magic differed from mother's, leaving him worn and tired. The spells faded quickly, if they took at all. Mother's spells lasted her whole life and seemed to energize her when she made them. Like Ciandra, she was born to the voiceless magic. It flowed through her, connecting her to the silent places in everything. Too many words, father said, dampened the magic in everyone else. That is why people who talk too much have no magic. They spend it every time they speak without purpose. Father told Minh that it was better to have fewer words and a little magic when you needed it.

Minh had always wished for magic, but even when he practiced being quiet for weeks on end, none came. He only had father's staff and a voiceless sister too young to be useful. Ciandra took his hand, giving him a weak smile, before he tugged it away.

They found more berries and rough vegetation along the road. Ciandra wanted to provide more, but it was still too dangerous. Magic was a beacon to the scrimmagers. There would be no escaping if she were so brazen about using it.

He offered to kill a rabbit they came across, but the girl protested. When the animals near her suffered, she felt it too. That was why they raised animals, but never ate them. They would sell them to neighbors or villagers but, even when they were miles away, she suffered when they were slaughtered.

They ate what they could forage and plodded onward, even when the starling dipped towards the horizon. With little coverage in the flatlands, they were vulnerable and exposed. As the darkness closed in, the boy imagined the creatures stalking them, their claws scraping the ground, their mouths open to feast upon his bones. But as starling light came the next morning and his vision cleared, he saw no evidence of his imagination.

While they slept for a few hours in the morning starling, Ciandra's magic grew plants and fruit foreign to this side of the mountains. They ate the bounty, but the boy worried this would draw the scrimmagers faster.

The warming temperatures allowed them to dispose of their heavier clothing and unwrap their hands. They napped in the late afternoon and slept too long, a week of fatigue taking its toll. As the sky settled into shades of hazy blues and pinks, Ciandra shook her brother awake. They hastened down the road with urgency, understanding the danger that loomed somewhere in the darkness.

A long rallying cry cut through the night, signaling the creature's proximity. Too close.

Minh gripped Ciandra's hand and ran, dragging her when she struggled to keep pace. They ran until their lungs burned and their legs trembled. Until she stumbled and fell.

His breath was short and labored. Minh's heart thudded in his ears as he dropped the packs. He drew Ciandra across his back and, maintaining a tight grip on the staff, ran on. But the lanky boy couldn't maintain that pace for long. After a hundred yards, he faltered and dropped Ciandra to the ground.

Minh doubled over, gasping. They couldn't run any further and they were exposed under a waning moon and starry sky.

The shrill cry moved closer. The sound made him wince. Minh stood protectively in front of Ciandra, gripping the staff with both hands.

Panic threatened to consume Minh. The scrimmagers didn't want him. He was unimportant. She was everything.

Ciandra placed a hand on his arm. Her dark eyes, so much like their mother's, were filled with faith. Minh steadied himself. He wouldn't let them take her without a fight.

She crouched behind, waiting, as shadows whispered. The tall grass swayed, rippling as the beasts slinked toward them. Minh trembled as a scrimmager came into view. It looked beyond him, to the quiet girl hidden behind his legs. His knuckles blanched on the staff, though it trembled in his hands.

The boy was an obstacle between the creature and his prey. It slinked from one side to the other, with narrowed eyes. The scream pierced his skull, warning Minh to move away. Seven others surrounded them and joined in chorus. Minh held his ground, knowing he'd be shown no mercy and preparing to do the same.

Ciandra tugged at his sleeve, speaking with her hands, but Minh couldn't look away from the predator. The girl persisted, her movements frantic. When he glanced at her, the creature leapt.

Minh's staff cracked across its jaw. It landed, shaking its head before it pounced again. It knocked him backwards, snarling and snapping. Its claws gripped the staff. The boy wrenched the staff away. His next spin struck the creature's ribs. Talons lashed out, stripping the skin from Minh's knuckles as he yelled.

"Run, Ciandra!"

Sleek, black bodies moved closer. They watched the struggle, waiting to strike. The scrimmager's claws slashed Minh's gut. The extra layers of clothing saved him from a fatal wound, but the gash was long. He stumbled and fell while blood dripped to the ground.

The scrimmager stood over him. Its angry cries loosed spittle into Minh's face as its claws frantically tore at him. As wicked eyes watched him hungrily from the grass, he yelled for Ciandra to run again.

Ciandra appeared beside her brother, holding out a shaking hand to the creature. She snapped her fingers to draw its attention as her lips moved in soundlessly. Transfixed, the scrimmager released the staff and slipped toward her.

The howls faded. One by one, each scrimmager came forward, entranced by the gentle sway of her hands. She reached one hand out to stroke its angular head. It leaned into her palm, purring a small thrum of pleasure. She greeted them as they vied for her attention. Minh rolled to his side, still clutching the staff as he struggled to find his feet.

When Ciandra had stroked each of their heads, she stood as tall as she could. The dark figures stared at her. A knot of worry issued between her brows as she took a deep breath. Holding her small arms wide, she closed her eyes. The scrimmagers waited in stillness.

In a swift movement, Ciandra clenched her hands and drove her arms to her sides. A chorus of crunches sounded as each creature toppled to the ground with bulging, empty eyes. Their limbs twitched as life left them.

The girl dropped to her knees, clutching her stomach. Tears stained her cheeks. Minh scurried over the bodies and scooped her into his arms. Her mouth hung open in soundless agony. He ignored the pain and blood that dripped from his hands and stomach. Minh carried her away from the carnage, whispering words of consolation in her ear. The same way father used to.

Minh covered her with a blanket and sang her favorite song. She cried, whether because of her actions or the pain that it had brought, he didn't know. Ciandra had always been a gentle soul, and Minh realized he'd been a fool for thinking kindness equated to weakness.

They built a fire, no longer worrying about those who might hunt them. As the girl rested, Minh dragged the broken bodies away from the road into the tall grass. He wondered if the Shaman felt their deaths the way Ciandra did. He hoped so. When he returned to the fire, Ciandra was roasting the sweet potatoes she had grown. Her eyes were still swollen from tears, though she gave him a reassuring smile.

Minh studied his sister, perhaps for the first time. Ciandra had more than their mother's eyes. She had her crooked smile and soundless spells. But, more importantly, she had the same strong heart full of love.

He smiled back at her, grateful for a promise he'd never wanted to make.

CHAPTER NINE

BENEATH THE GLASS DARK

Originally published in the 'From the Depths' Anthology, Wyldblood Press, January, 2023 and was written during deepest grief after my dearest friend left this world far too soon. Edited by Mark Bilsborough.

Isla's smiles were always brightest following weeks of submerged isolation. Her dark hair would cast a greenish, algae-infused hue as it caught the sun's first rays and dripped rivulets of stale water down her back. She would be pale and thin from lack of nourishment and sunlight, and you would fret over her as her feet stumbled. But she would insist that your worries were unfounded because she was never truly alone down there, and she promised to always return.

Those first few days after returning, she would speak enthusiastically about the clumsy turtles and curious fish. She would hint about the eels, but never say too much, hoping to spare you more worry. Then she would inquire about your parents, your brother, and your neighbors. But her words would fade over weeks or months, and the shine in her eyes would dim. Then she would disappear into the lake again and you would sit upon the same pier that you sit at now. But true to her word, she would eventually reach a hand from the water, and you would pull her up every time.

You knot the rope around your ankles with bone-sore fingers while considering, 'Is this the only way to avoid those who appear daily on your doorstep, armed with the best of intentions and unflinching opinions?'

Their intrusions have been undaunted by your retreats or your animosity, and they cannot seem to fathom that all you really want is silence.

The edges of the stone blocks scrape across the planks as you pull them an inch closer to the edge of the pier. You know that this is the one place where they won't follow, because they can't. The place where Isla would go when she needed to escape this world, back before she escaped it for good.

The ropes burn the thin flesh of your ankles as you tug them gently to ensure that they will hold tight. Your neighbors' voices creep from their open windows through the night air and when one of them laughs with full belly relief, it cuts you with a sharpness that emphasizes how separate you are. You do not remember the last time you laughed, nor the last time you wanted to enjoy anyone else's.

Small lines of blood seep through the cracks in your parched knuckles as you struggle to drag the stones the final three inches. Your limbs tremble, but you are sure that it is due to fatigue. Your breath labors too, but that is because you spent long winter months sitting beside the fire watching Isla's eyes dim their shine. Then more months of sitting alone.

Inactivity has made you weak, you tell yourself. But you were always a good liar. Especially to yourself.

Your heavy feet stumble backward, teetering on the edge for a moment before regaining your balance. Isla would chide you for that. She had always made this look easy, but this is your first time. You sit cross-legged on the rough, scarred boards and watch the lanterns cast flickering light from distant neighboring windows.

Only an empty house will keep them from coming. Perhaps tomorrow the herbalist will stop appearing with their wares of oils, dried weeds, and nature-sharpened stones—in which they insist there is magic. But you felt no magic from any of their herbs or tinctures, and all the rocks ever did was cast blinding prisms across the floor in the afternoon sunlight. How you resented them more for their well-meaning, but false, promises.

They never understood the quiet magic that filled your sister's being, that stuff that kept her strong longer than she ought to have been. And since they did not understand that, they have no right to know about her parting gift to you. There is some magic that can only be passed through sadness and only used to satisfy a deep longing for solitude.

You will not miss the faith-driven neighbors who profess hallowed words and prayers full of inexperience and discomfort. They know nothing about life or death, hiding behind their biased and unproven prayers with resolve that has never been tested. They cling to their faith like handfuls of straw, and you hope for a strong wind to twist it from their grasp and scatter it so that they might understand the true frailty of existence.

There are the neighbors who express concern by coming to your door with single-bowl food creations full of pity. But you know they return to their homes and talk in hushed tones about your sorrow and anger, so you never answer the door. Instead, you let their food rot on the doorstep until they return and collect their putrid efforts. You hope their bowls are ruined, and they might not save them. You hope they grow to understand loss. To have it shake and rend them to their cores so that you can bring them a piteous casserole with too much salt and no flavor. You hope that...

No.

It's another lie you tell yourself as you swing your thin legs above the glassy dark water. You would not wish this hollow ache on any of them. But you wish they could understand, even if you're unsure that you do.

Still, they shouldn't try to force you from your sorrow. These people don't know that when grief is all you have left of someone, you will fight to hold on to it.

Your toes dip into the cool water, and a shiver wriggles up your legs. The rope strains against your calves and grows taut around the blocks that sit beside you. The moonlight streaks through wispy clouds, spotting the skin of the water like soundless rain on a forest floor.

It's okay, though you know nothing is okay. It's just another lie.

Your sigh lingers, hanging in the air for a moment as you stare down into the still depths beneath your feet. As you wonder about the catfish and the smallmouth bass that might be erratically swimming below, a chorus of toads begins their lover's calls.

Isla loved those throaty cries. Every spring she would reemerge from the water and trudge into the house, dripping puddles behind her. She would wring out her algae-spattered hair entwined with hydrillas and wrap her lake-chilled arms around you. You would complain that she stank of fish and rotten eggs as you pushed her away. Then she would smile as if the weeks under water had reminded her of all that she loved.

When you were younger, you didn't understand why she needed to go away. It always felt personal, though Isla insisted it was not. But how could she claim to love you and also need to be away from you?

Now you know that it was never about you at all.

You take a breath to hold faith in the magic she imparted as she lay dying. Then you push the stones over the edge. They crash through the water's surface as you follow them gracelessly, leaving ripples spiraling in your wake.

The frigid water shocks, stealing your breath and locking your muscles tight. But there is no need for air since you haven't been able to breathe in months. Not since she died and left you hollow.

The stones sink for a long time, and you close your eyes as they drag you away from the streams of moonlight into the darkness. Isla insisted that there was nothing dangerous in this lake, nothing that could hurt you unless you let it. But your heart flutters at all that you cannot see.

When the stones settle upon the murky floor, the weight of the water squeezes the last of the air from you. The final bubbles exit your mouth and dart upward, disappearing, but you are unafraid. You have Isla's breathless magic to keep you here as long as you like, and finally, the environment reflects you.

You are alone in silence and darkness.

A day passes. You know this because golden rays illuminate the tendrils of the hydrillas and curly leaf pondweeds that sway in the water beside you. When the catfish nibble your toes, you kick them away but know they will return to bother you, just like a cat. Shadows appear above as people stare down into the water, wondering where you have gone. But you are quiet, anchored by the stones as you sway in the drift.

Did Isla feel alone down here? Or at peace? You don't notice when the water licks the tears from your eyes and carries them away.

By the third day, the catfish has claimed you as a point of interest and gathers friends to nip at your hair and your nails. They seem to enjoy the game of you pushing them away only for them to return. They disappear at night when something sleek and dark lingers nearby, assessing your presence.

When most of the shadows above have returned to their lives, only one remains. That person lingers, sitting on the edge of the pier and occasionally blocking the sun's rays as it travels across the sky behind them. They sit exactly where you spent long days waiting for your sister to reemerge from her self-imposed isolation.

That person sees you. They know you are hiding in the waters with your silence and your sorrow. But they do not bother you, and by the sixth day, you find comfort in their consistent presence.

As the sun sets on the eve of the eighth day, casting you in near-total darkness, an eel brushes your hair and hisses in your ear, 'Give up your magic and join us.'

But you do not reply. Your sister warned you not to trust the eels. They can't hurt you unless you reply, and this one's words feel too desperate with want.

The next day, a snapping turtle is swallowing its wriggling meal through the strips of light when the person above shifts and stands. With a splash that sends the fish darting in calmer directions, he swims toward you. The water distorts and widens his face, making him pale and wan. He reminds you of Isla. Why have you not thought of him these last few months?

He keeps a safe distance, but mumbles through the water with his little air. "Do you need anything?"

You shake your head and his lips purse in concern.

With the last of his breath, he says, "I will be here when you are ready." He kicks his legs to return to the surface and climbs out. A minute later, his shadow resumes its post.

It is strange to be valued when you are a broken thing. Loss has fragmented your ability to think, speak, or care about yourself or others. It is curious, then, that he returns each day knowing that you are damaged.

With some shame at the slowness of your realization, you understand he is probably shattered, too. Perhaps he does not need to be alone in the darkness like you do. He might have taken the advice of the faithful, or the weeds of the herbalists, or the meals of the gossiping neighbors and you decide that, if he did, you will not resent him for it. You would rather he had those tools than the anger that had taken hold of your father during Isla's illness. Or the bottle that mother sank in to and had yet to climb out of.

The eel taunts you nightly, brushing your limbs with its slick body and leaving you no peace. It plays with your hair and eats its meals before your eyes so that bits of fish and frog float in front of your face, drifting toward your nostrils, while it gnashes its small sharp teeth.

'There is nothing for you up there,' it whispers. 'You belong with me in the darkness. I have tasted the salt of your tears. If you wish to give them up completely, all you need to do is speak and you will never feel sorrow again.' It curls around your waist, caressing you through the fraying fabric of your nightgown. 'Here we do not linger on what is lost. Your sister knew this. She knew that you would belong with us.'

You shiver for the first time since you dropped to the lake's floor. But your lips remain tightly sealed. To speak to the eel is to resign yourself to staying in the darkness forever and there is comfort knowing that someone waits for you above.

Days and nights slip past, and you lose track of how long you have been under these waters. You don't remember the last time you felt the breath of wind against your cheeks or saw the flutter of wings in a blue sky or felt the warmth of the sun upon your naked skin.

The blossoming ache for these images overwhelms you. Your heart quickens as you consider the neighbors who would bombard you with questions. Are you capable of forming a reply yet? You haven't formed a complete sentence in months. So, you stay with the catfish and the curly leaf pondweeds and the hydrillas and watch the day turn to night from twenty feet below the water's surface knowing that, up there, life goes on without you.

When the eel dons the illusion of your sister's features, with grey eyes and dark hair hovering around her oval face, you know it is not her. No matter how much you wish it to be.

'Stay with me,' it begs. 'They do not know you as I know you,'

The eel lies so easily, and you remember that Isla would have understood why you hide, but she would not want you hidden forever.

'I am lost and alone without you,' it says as it encircles you. 'I need you.'

Words have power. Yet, so does silence, and when the darkness lies to you, it is fine to offer nothing in return.

When the shadow wafts across the water the next day, you think of words to speak. You want to tell him about the eel and its lies, though you will never speak of the longing the eel grows in your breast. He should know why Isla hid down here so often before she became physically ill. Why it wasn't until the throes of her sickness and struggle that she gave up her isolation and clung to the warmth of others.

Isla must have come to the same conclusion that you reach now. You both could handle the darkness and the whispers of the eel alone. That is easy. But when Isla was dying and knew that she would disappear, she needed the love of others to help her live.

Her last months were full of well-intentioned neighbors bringing their one pot dishes and garden flowers. The herbalists brought tinctures to stave off the pain that gripped her bones, while the faithful whispered prayers over her. She knew that there was nothing they could do, but perhaps it was that outpouring of care that sustained her longer than she ought to have lived. Perhaps that is a magic you still don't quite understand.

You wave to the figure overhead. There are things you are ready to say, and he has been waiting patiently to hear your voice.

He dives into the water, like you used to do for Isla, and pulls out a knife from its sheath. The eel slithers around your feet while the catfish boldly swims back and forth before you, trying to lay claim to you. They hiss and chatter as he nears, but you shove them away.

As the blade saws through the first rope, he is already losing breath. He didn't get the same magic from Isla. You take the knife, and he darts upward as you sever the last bond.

'Don't leave me,' the eel cries, his words making you pause as your stomach wrenches.

These are the same words you whispered to Isla as she lay dying. You cannot speak to the eel and reassure it, but, if you could, you would tell it you will return when the world overwhelms you again.

For now, you must live where the sun can warm your cheeks and the sound of the toads fill the night air. You must eat warm bread and wrap lake-chilled arms around those you love. You must remember to comb your hair, change your clothes, and be gentle with your words that, too often, have cut like glass.

With tendrils of hydrillas twisting in your hair, you rise through sun-glittered water and break the bright surface. Sharp light blinds you as strong hands wrest you up and on to the old pier where you flop like a gasping, graceless fish.

A breath—your first in months—makes you cough.

"Sis?" He says.

The warm timbre of his voice hurts ears that have grown accustomed to quiet, but you wrap your arms around him. He does not complain about your stench as he hugs you back. The sun kisses your cheeks while the wind brushes your skin. You breathe together while a toad calls from the shore. Your brother listens as strained words tumble from your lips, softly at first, then hurrying with their need. He helps you toward the warmth of the house where fresh flowers and rich foods await.

You take tender steps forward and do not glance back, while far beneath the glass dark surface an eel awaits your return.

CHAPTER TEN

A FATHERING OF BEARS

athan rubbed a calloused hand across his brow and once again considered killing the lanky boy sprawled across the tavern table in front of him. Kuma's face was partially covered by his black curls. His mouth hung open, a thin stream of saliva strung between the boy's lips and the aged table beneath him.

The tavern had quieted when Mathan's mountainous figure stepped through the door. Several patrons had quickly sobered and scurried out after he'd passed them by with the heavy thumps of his footsteps. Only Vera, the barkeep, approached without hesitation. Though they looked of a similar age, Mathan's grizzled face and gruffer manner gave the impression that he'd lived much longer and had angrily resisted the sourness of aging. In contrast, Vera wore the acceptance of time like a fading flower.

She glanced at her companion before tossing a towel over one shoulder and nodded at the boy. "Thought you'd want to know."

His jaw flexed beneath the coarse beard. Frustration and disappointment ebbed from him like a parent staring at an empty cupboard. Or like a father judging a son. He sighed. "Maybe I should leave him."

"Oh no. He's not my problem. I'll set him on the street if you don't take him. Let the watch cart him away." Vera said, though her voice lacked conviction. She had a fondness for the boy that, even though he'd shown more attitude than sense these last few years, hadn't completely diminished yet. Kuma had been one of several youths who'd helped rebuild the establishment after the fire.

Mathan grunted. Waking up in a filthy cell might do the boy some good. Spirits knew he didn't know what else to do with Kuma. Lately, the boy pushed him beyond reason. Their recent stream of arguments and matching tempers had escalated to a dangerous level. Mathan saw it for what it was, though. His son's physical growth was not matched by emotional maturity. Kuma's challenges would be worse than his peers, though. More feral and dangerous. For Mathan, that awareness brought the unspoken fear of losing his son to adulthood and being alone again. He scooped the boy under one arm and hefted him to his feet with a disgruntled sigh.

Kuma moaned. The stench of digesting fermentation rose from his breath. Black eyes, barely open, found Mathan's face. A wide grin spread across Kuma's face as he chuckled. Mathan considered dropping him. Let the boy wallow on the floor and awaken in his own vomit. Instead, he readjusted his arm around Kuma's torso and, with a brief nod to Vera, headed toward the door.

"Patience, Mathan," Vera said. "Frida was a pain in the ass for nearly four years. Practically drove me mad and after the incident with the fire, I'd be a liar if I said I didn't consider sending her to my parents for more than a season. But I can tell you, now that she's grown, I would have missed a lot if I hadn't held on to her. No matter how much she pushed me away."

Mathan's lips drew thin. His gaze lingered on her long enough to see her flush uncomfortably before he looked away. Vera, like everyone else in this town, saw what was before her and nothing more. He didn't know how much longer that would last. Here, the Ayi was just a long-lost fairy tale. Mathan, Kuma, and all their kind were lesser-known creatures of myth and fireside stories, too strange to be as feared as the creatures that turned to wolves on the full moon.

Many of the favored stories told by passing minstrels were the ones where the last great southern sleuths had been burned by hunters. The stories didn't tell of how the cubs had screamed or how only a few Ayi had taken to the woods and survived.

No one spoke seriously about the Ayi, the bear people, anymore. It was best that way.

Though Kuma had grown since they'd been here, it was only a matter of time until someone noticed it wasn't at the same rate as his peers and there was still another few years before he'd be considered fully grown. Mathan had already noted the shifting looks of more discerning men and women. How many more new moons would come before people grew more curious than fearful of the beasts that bellowed in the darkest of nights?

They'd lasted here five years, three years more than Mathan had expected, and longer than he'd ever lived anywhere outside of a sleuth. The stability had allowed Kuma to have friends and receive close to a proper education. It was more than Mathan had ever been given and, where other parents might have felt resentment, he had nothing but gratitude for the home he'd been able to provide. He'd hoped to give a sense of stability rather than the chaotic relocations he'd known. But Kuma didn't appreciate Mathan's efforts, no matter what he did.

He dragged the boy into the brisk autumn air. The closed tavern door muffled the voluminous swell of the remaining patron's excited chatting about the entertainment that the awkward boy and his strange, terrifying father had provided. Flickering firelights slipped around the edges of tired doors and shuttered windows onto the stoney street as they walked. Rich aromas of warming stews and yeasty breads filled the air. These scents were pleasing, but inspired no craving.

Above, a waning crescent moon traversed across the star littered sky. Two days until the new moon and then they'd have to wear the chains for a night.

Kuma mumbled, stringing a name into more syllables than was ever intended. "Alisom."

Mathan shook his head. Given their situation, he'd discouraged Kuma's attachment to any girl, but that one in particular was too dangerous. The mayor's daughter was prettier than she'd ever be kind, and her sneering glance had ensnared many boys who believed their future lay entwined with her good opinion. He'd said as much to Kuma, but the boy had re-acted angrily. Hearing the name leave his drunken lips again only strength-ened Mathan's resolve. They'd have to leave before the situation escalated.

It was five miles to their dark cabin sheltered deep in the woods. Mathan had smothered the fire before leaving in search of the boy. It was dumb luck that Frida had found him at the edge of town after he'd searched some of the surrounding thickets and favored hunting grounds.

The cabin's interior still held the pungent odor of hormonal youth and no matter how often the windows and doors were opened, there'd been no diffusing it. There was a deeper smell there too, but it was too much of Mathan for him to detect. It whispered of deepest forests, thick fur, and heady musk. Both scents were equally feral and distinct, clashing with each other in a way that gave all animals in the area a sharp warning: come no nearer or be caught in the conflict.

Mathan dropped Kuma onto his cot. The boy groaned and rolled onto his side before drawing a blanket over his head. The thought that the boy would have a nasty headache in the morning brought Mathan some small satisfaction. Until he remembered that Kuma would be even more disagreeable than usual.

He lit a lantern, not bothering to relight the fire. It was cool, but not uncomfortable, and the fading heat of the day still clung to the cabin's wooden frame. Plus, Kuma would adapt to the chillier air soon enough. Mathan had already noticed the hair thickening across the boy's chest. Soon it would creep up his neck to his chin. Kuma would spend the rest of his life deciding if he'd let it grow wild, as was his nature, or tackle the daily battle of trimming it back. The boy's coat was darkening with each turn, nearly as dark as Mathan's own. As much as they both hated to acknowledge it, they were more alike than they were different.

A stick snapped, breaking the silence of the woods outside. Mathan stiffened. The sound might have come from one of the overgrown deer paths, but the continued movement didn't sound like prey. He slipped toward the door, pupils dilated, breathing deep. A metallic scent flooded his nostrils. Blood and something familiar. No, someone. His stomach sank with dread.

He pulled the axe from the wall and stepped outside. Thyra would be a fool to come here. There had been no sorrow in their parting, and he'd never regretted it. She'd been a terrible mother. Kuma was a toddler of scratched skin and thin bones when Mathan had met them. After travelling for a year together, she'd given him up with barely a sigh. No tears had left her eyes. She'd given no words to speak to the boy as he grew. She'd only asked that Mathan never speak badly of her. In fact, he'd rarely spoken of her at all. For all Kuma knew, the mother who'd birthed him had perished not long after he'd been born and Mathan had taken him in.

She met him at the edge of the cleared yard. Thyra's dangerous beauty had thinned and worn, and Mathan wished that one of his lies had been true. It would have been simpler if she had died. Her large black eyes speared him in the sliver of moonlight. In her arms, she offered the mangled torso of a doe. She kept her voice low, closer to a purr than a growl. "I mean no harm."

Mathan stood ten feet before her, patting the axe with one hand, and doubting her words. Thyra had never been an honorable Ayi, and he was loath to doubt that people changed without great effort. Thyra had never struck him as the studious or remorseful type. The deer's blood dripped to the ground; the iron scent made him salivate.

"Why are you here?" He asked.

She took a hesitant step forward. Dried leaves shifted beneath the toe of her boot. A spattering of blood followed. "I need to see him."

A fist squeezed his heart. "It's too late."

"Please, Mathan." The fluttering of her voice was desperate. "Let me see my son."

He closed his eyes with a labored sigh. The darkness would be across them all in two more nights, and he wanted her far away by then. Thyra had never been willing to wear the chains when the turn came, preferring to hunt wild and fill the countryside with terror. Once, he'd woken to the slaughter of half a herd of cows. Her naked skin painted with their blood, muscle and tendon still strung beneath her sharp nails. But she'd brought back no scraps for the boy. It was Kuma's constant wailing that had convinced Mathan to take the boy and leave before her neglect killed him or made him more beast than man.

Mathan had raised the boy as his own. Perhaps the last years had been challenging, but he'd been worse than Kuma at that same age. The boy was more his than any blood could have made him. And he'd protect him with his dying breath.

"No, you've no right to him." He said. Her eyes narrowed. That she'd thought to sway him so easily nipped at his pride.

"He's my son." She hissed between her teeth, breath white in the darkness.

His grip on the axe's handle tightened. He stared through her. "Leave before my tolerance wanes."

The subtle tilt of her head caused a prickle across his skin. Thyra was as lethal as she'd ever been, but Mathan had a half century more of experience and was more seasoned at keeping his emotions controlled. He'd been wild too once, but he'd spent years learning to collar himself. That control resulted in a repressed seething that filled any room with warnings of danger.

"You won't hurt me." She said. Her voice had turned. Gone was the false sorrow, leaving only a hard edge of contempt in its place. "You can't keep him from me."

"Why did you come?" he asked. "It's not for love or regret. What do you think he can do for you?"

Thyra didn't flinch at the honesty of his words. "I have a proposition for him."

Mathan licked his teeth. His instinct had been right. "What sort of proposition?"

"That's between me and my son."

The entitlement in her tone, as if Mathan had been nothing more than a nanny over the years, brought a low rumble to his throat. Thyra's eyes flashed as he spoke. "You've been no mother to him."

She lowered the doe to the ground and looked up at him. It looked initially like a submissive position, but as her toes dug into the earth, the tension in her limbs revealed a readiness to attack. The air thickened around them, collecting in the dewy air like a fog. Her eyes flicked to the cabin where Kuma's lumbering shape cast shadows against the thin curtains. Thyra relaxed, face softening. "What does he know of me?"

"You died giving him life. You loved him," Mathan said. "In other words, he knows nothing about who you really are."

She wiped her hands on her dark pants. It blended with the stains. "Tell him I want to meet him." She caught the look in Mathan's eyes and continued. "Tell him or I will spin a different tale. One that might not put you in as good a light."

His voice was a low, dangerous growl. "Thyra…"

She snorted softly, then turned and trekked back into the woods so stealthily he only knew which direction she was going by the scent of her in the air.

"Father?" Kuma leaned against the doorway, gripping the frame tightly. "What're you doing out here?"

Mathan's gaze lingered on the woods before he turned to the boy. "Getting some fresh air."

Kuma sniffed, his nose and chin jutting upward. "Fresh kill?" He stepped forward, swaying slightly. His words slurred. "Spirits, I am starving."

The usual dramatic tone often made Mathan smile, but his good humor had withered. He scooped the deer from the ground and ushered Kuma inside.

Worry woke Mathan too early. When he saw that Kuma had picked the deer's ribs clean and left the carcass on the table to fester, his anger surged. He considered shaking the boy awake. To howl at him about hygiene and cleaning up after himself. He'd come close to calling the boy an annoyance lately, but those words once unleashed couldn't be recalled. The man knew that from experience. His own father had often called him a burden, and it was soon after maturing that he'd left their small sleuth for good. A few years later, Mathan had heard that the hunters had slaughtered everyone, including his father. He wouldn't replay that anger or loss with Kuma.

He threw the curtains back and opened the windows. Morning light flooded the room. With the fall harvest, there'd be no school for Kuma to attend for another two weeks. Time enough to move. If they hustled, they could make it to one of the ocean side counties before classes resumed. That adventure might placate Kuma. He'd always wanted to see the ocean.

Thyra's appearance caused a relentless pressure to bloom behind his eyes that no amount of rubbing diminished. Mathan spent an hour searching the perimeter of their territory for any sign of her and found none. Instead of bringing relief, her absence only intensified his worry. She would not be dissuaded so easily. She'd always enjoyed the chase more than the kill. In her mind, Kuma was now a prize to be won, a prey to be corralled. Mathan would have to tell the boy something or watch her twist the truth.

When he returned to the cabin, Kuma was holding his head at the edge of his bed. The boy groaned when the door slammed. Mathan smirked and waited for Kuma to complain, but the boy said nothing.

After a minute, Kuma managed the few steps to the table and poured a glass of water from the pitcher. He took a long gulp, a stream of water trickled down his throat to his collar, then lay his head upon the table. Kuma sniffed and lifted his head, eyes narrowing at the clean surface.

"Did you finish the deer?" His voice was a whining accusation, filled with the haughty entitlement of the overindulged. Mathan prickled, but he had no one to blame but himself. He should have left it for the boy to take care of.

"You picked the bones clean with your greedy, drunk fingers last night after I carried you home," he said. "Least you could have done was toss it out. Now you accuse me?"

Kuma's cheeks flushed. He sucked his lower lip and looked guilty. Mathan could sense the apology on the boy's tongue, could see it working around his mouth, but it did not enter the air. It was one of the moments that Mathan quietly pined for the gentle and reasonable child Kuma had been only a few short years ago.

With a huff, Kuma pushed away from the table and stood. His jaw was offset, his gaze on the door. "I'm heading to Jake's. We're going—"

"No." Mathan's voice was thick and stern. He saw the boy tense. Rebellion scratched beneath his skin. "We need to talk."

Kuma sighed with elevated drama. "Shit. I'm sorry about last night, alright? I'll—"

"Do not think yourself grown enough to curse in front of me yet. Sit." The edge to Mathan's voice was sharper than Kuma was used to. It startled him and, with his head hung low, Kuma slid back into the chair.

Mathan's thick hands rubbed together, sounding like strips of dried parchment in the thick silence. Kuma shifted awkwardly in his seat, and Mathan noticed a spattering of dark hair across his upper lip. He didn't think it had been there last week.

"I need to tell you something," Mathan said. His deep brown eyes met the boy's black ones. "It's about your mother."

The color faded from Kuma's cheeks. Confusion swept across him. "My mother? I don't understand."

"She came here last night," Mathan spoke slowly, softening his voice as much in embarrassment at a lifetime's worth of lies as to lessen the sting of them. "She wants to see you."

Kuma studied Mathan's gnarled hands as they continued to rub aimlessly together. The boy was quiet for a long time. They'd left Thyra before Kuma's third birthday. It wasn't likely the boy remembered anything of her. Mathan expected anger at the deception. It had been Kuma's favorite response lately, but what came instead was something wary, tentative, and tinged with hope. And, somehow, that was worse.

Kuma cleared his throat before asking, "What does she want?" He showed no surprise that his mother still lived.

Mathan stared at him as if a veil had partially lifted. He wondered if Kuma had always known that Thyra had abandoned him, that Mathan had lied to him all this time. He looked away to hide his shame. "I don't know. She wouldn't tell me."

Neither of them moved, frozen between fight or flight, which had been an increasing part of their daily dynamic. This was different, though. They walked a spider's silk of caution with their words. Kuma's face had fallen into shadows, a heaviness draped across him, and he seemed suddenly older. "What if I don't want to see her?"

"She'll insist on hearing that from you."

He sniffed. "What can she do about it? She's certainly no match for you."

Mathan wiped a hand across his face. "It won't matter."

Kuma sat upright. "What?"

"She's always been an expert at sniffing out weaknesses. She'd go for those first."

Thoughts flicked rapidly across Kuma's face. The boy was an open book, and Mathan realized not teaching him to guard his emotions well might have been a failing. A stubborn pride rose as Kuma spoke. "What weaknesses? We don't have any—"

"Your friends. That girl, Alisom. Vera's tavern," Mathan said curtly. "Thyra will sniff them out unless you meet with her."

He'd gone pale in the warm sunlit room. "You could chase her off. You could…"

Mathan shook his head. "We *both* have weaknesses and she'll know how to use them."

Kuma didn't ask what Mathan's weaknesses were. Maybe he already knew. His voice was strained. "I didn't think I'd ever see her again."

"You knew she lived?"

He nodded. "I remember her scent, the shape of her eyes. I just knew that one day she was gone and you weren't, and everything was better. But I never remembered missing her."

Mathan released a heavy sigh. His vision went glassy, but he didn't wipe his eyes. "I'm sorry. I didn't know what else to say when you asked."

Kuma nodded, pouring another glass of water, and setting it before Mathan. "As much as I want to believe she's returned for me, I don't dare. From what the minstrels say, Ayi mothers aren't prone to sentimentality."

Mathan stiffened. "Don't mind those damned minstrels. They know nothing of us. Most Ayi women are fierce mothers, putting others to shame. Thyra was just born different. It happens with humans, too. Not everyone is meant to parent."

The boy's lips pressed thin. His cheeks flushed. "What do you think she wants? You knew her once, I'm sure you can guess."

Mathan didn't want to speak ill of Thyra to her son, but he deserved some honest warning. "She looks lean. Time hasn't been kind to her. With the loss of hunting grounds, she might look for a partner, one more compliant to her will. Someone better surviving in the world of men. Or she may have some scheme to use you for. I don't know for sure, and my opinions of her are biased."

Kuma nodded and stood. "I promised to help Jake with their harvest. His dad's illness has worsened, and the younger kids are too small to be helpful."

Mathan thought to stop him but didn't. Kuma helping his friend was a testament to his nature. "Be careful."

Kuma nodded once, then disappeared into the autumn day. Mathan sat at the table, spinning the cup in his hand before downing it. Thyra would hunt him like a young deer. By the end of the day, she'd know everywhere Kuma went. Each house he visited. Each place his gaze lingered a little too long, and she'd use the good people of this place to gain leverage over him.

Mathan followed Kuma at a safe distance to Jake's home. There were twin girl toddlers playing in the yard wearing matching dresses. A boy of around eight and a girl not much older tended the chickens and twins. The girl watched Kuma and Jake with obvious envy as they carried dual sickles into the tall rows of wheat that spread toward the horizon.

Jake's father leaned in the doorway, a sickly shade of green marring his complexion. He looked frail. His wife came up beside him, skirt swaying around her full hips, and ushered him back inside. She said something sharp to the children before closing the door.

There was no scent of Thyra. There was some truth to what Kuma had said about the Ayi. Typically, the maternal instinct wasn't as strong as the father's. The males tended the cubs for a longer time, and sometimes the females left. Mathan had never asked Thyra who Kuma's father was. It had never mattered to him.

He sat in the woods for a long time, inhaling the hearty scents of the home and autumnal air. The sun's warmth was soothing as it travelled across his back. It was late in the day when Thyra came. The boys were glistening with labor, laughing the way good friends do, as they lumbered toward the cabin. The eldest girl still stood in the yard, watching them with large dark eyes. Their voices drifted in the air.

"...Alisom invited us. She mentioned you by name. You *have* to come," Jake said.

Kuma held back his smile, though the desire was plain on his face. "We'll see. Father needs..." Kuma's step hitched. He inhaled sharply. Tension rippled through each of his tired muscles.

Jake's manners didn't change. Even when a strange woman appeared ten feet behind his sister, he didn't know to be afraid of her. The long braids Thyra wore were matted. Her dark leather clothes were stained with dirt and blood. Her skin was as pale as milk, those two black eyes darker than coal.

Before Jake could say anything, Kuma had rushed forward and placed himself between his mother and the girl. From the bushes Mathan tensed, but he resisted the urge to intervene. Now that they'd met, this was a battle Kuma would have to navigate as best he could.

Taking Kuma's cue, Jake drew his sister toward him.

"Tell your mother I'll take that dinner tomorrow," Kuma said.

Jake's eyes flicked from Thyra to Kuma. Kuma took a small step forward. "I'll see you later." Jake and the girl stood in the cabin doorway, hesitating before going inside.

A grin tugged at Thyra's lips. Her voice was sickly sweet with forced warmth. "You've grown so well. You're nearly as handsome as your father."

Mathan's hands clenched. Of course, she'd start with the reminder that Mathan wasn't Kuma's father. That the blood between them was nothing.

Kuma kept his words clipped. "What do you want?"

"To know my son." Her smile was sly. "I've spent a long time searching for you."

Mathan saw the blow to Kuma's defenses. The want to believe that she'd looked for him for years. That she'd missed him. Words every abandoned child craved, no matter their age and no matter the circumstances.

Kuma glanced at the door behind him as it opened. Jake's mother stood in the doorway, wiping her hands on an apron. She wore a mask of caution. "You alright, Kuma?"

He nodded. "Yes, ma'am. We were just heading out." Kuma walked past Thyra with squared shoulders. She turned and followed him down the soft road that led to the village.

"Tell your father he's welcome to dinner tomorrow, too." Jake's mother called after them with a concerned tone.

The soft wind pressed past them, leaving a trail of teenager and woodsy Ayi that was easy for Mathan to follow. He gave them space and didn't catch their words. Kuma would hopefully tell Mathan what mattered. He considered leaving them alone, turning around and trekking through the deer paths to their cabin, but the protective part of him refused.

The sky had turned shades of deep oranges that matched the falling leaves when Thyra left Kuma standing alone in a glen close to their home. He watched her disappear with a strange expression. Mathan had left soon after, but it was over an hour before the boy returned.

Mathan was stoking the fire when Kuma entered. The boy sat at the table, fingering a single strand of wheat that he'd plucked from the ground. His gaze was far away. Mathan asked if he was hungry. Kuma grunted before glancing guiltily at him.

"You were right," Kuma said. He picked apart the grain. "She came to Jake's house."

A log shifted with a loud pop. Mathan poked it into place.

"She wants me to go with her to meet my..." Kuma bit his lower lip, words dying in the air.

"Go on," his voice was low and soft. Mathan kept all threats or wounding out of it.

He swallowed. "My father. Says she'll die if she doesn't hand me over."

Another prodding of the logs sent a flurry of sparks into the air. Mathan's chest was suddenly tight. "Do you believe her?"

He shrugged. "Why would she lie about that?"

Mathan left the fire to burn and sat across from Kuma. "Did she say who your father was?"

"Someone named Esbern. Lives in a sleuth in the north, near the river's split at the base of the mountains."

Mathan rubbed his beard thoughtfully. "You were barely two years old when she and I met. She stayed for another year before we left her and, in all that time, she never spoke of your father." He watched the boy from the corner of his eye. "It's odd that he'd make such demands after all this time. Unless she had reason to tell him of you now."

Kuma's eyes darkened. "What do you mean?"

"Esbern's a strong Ayi. He built a sleuth in the north after the hunters came," Mathan said. "But that was so long ago that I'd almost forgotten about him." The last of the southern sleuths had burned down thirty years ago, and Esbern had rounded up many of the survivors to take northward with him. He'd sent out the word to all the Ayi to join them. Most had gone, only a few, like Mathan and Thyra, had chosen not to. Esbern would have been in the north already when Thyra became pregnant. It was possible that she'd visited him and that her beauty may have charmed him for an evening or more. But the journey took months and Mathan doubted that Thyra would have made the return journey alone and with child.

"What aren't you saying?" Kuma had been studying him intently. "Tell me."

Mathan explained about the journey and how Esbern had sworn not to travel south again. "The timing doesn't add up."

A fresh wound festered behind Kuma's eyes. That he might have hoped for a better father than the one before him hurt Mathan, but he didn't dwell on it.

"So he can't be my father," Kuma said.

He hated the lies Thyra inevitably spun to her son, who clutched hope to his chest like a precious gem. "It's unlikely."

"Why would she want me to go with her then? Esbern would know she was lying."

"I don't know. I cannot presume to know her reasoning." A noise outside drew Mathan's attention. "Stay here."

"What if it's her?"

He shook his head. "It's not." The scent that greeted him was human. Familiar, like mint and fading flowers. "Vera?"

She paused beneath the sliver of moonlight. There was a cautious look on her face. "I hope I'm not intruding."

Mathan glanced around, inhaling deeply, but detected no threat. "Shouldn't you be at the tavern?"

Her hands shook on the small bundle she carried, as if it took all her bravery to stand before him. "I wanted to warn you."

"About what?" His first thought was of Thyra, that perhaps she'd bent her ear. But that would have been bold, even for her. Vera's eyes were wide. The scent of fear clung to her like a torch in the night. He stepped forward, drawn like a predator to vulnerability.

"A man came to the tavern last night after you left." Her voice quavered with each word. "Said he was a hunter. Tracked something to our village."

Mathan's breath misted in the air. "A hunter?"

She nodded. "Said he'd kill it on the new moon."

"What's he hunting?" His voice was hoarse.

"The last of the southern Ayi." The way those green eyes held him stripped Mathan bare. She offered the package to him. "Take this, spread it around your perimeter. It should give you some protection."

"What is it?"

She glanced around, aware of the music of the dying crickets. "A warding."

"You're a witch?"

"As were my mother and her mother before her. I didn't ask for the gift, and I don't use it as much as maybe I should. I'm not terribly strong with it, but a warding is better than nothing. Might send the hunter around your land," Vera said.

The package was soft and pliant. Mint, rosemary, and something richer wafted through the linen. It smelled of ominous caves and wasps' nests. Something to be avoided.

He eyed her curiously until she shrugged. Vera said, "I knew within a few months of your arrival."

"You said nothing."

"You and the boy do your best to keep to yourselves and help when you can. I've seen the new moon come sixty times and there's been no attacks, no lost cattle. If you'd meant us harm, it would have happened long ago," Vera said. "Plus, Kuma is a hell of a lot handier than half the men in this town, and he's got a better heart."

"Even if he drinks your ale and passes out?"

Her smile was genuine, fear diminishing with it. "I'll have to tell you about Frida's worst days sometime. You'll praise my patience, trust me. Did you know it was her spell that set the tavern on fire? Trust me, Kuma's got nothing on her."

A rare smile curved his lips. He studied the line of her jaw, the slight flush of her cheeks. She looked away as it spread. Mathan cursed himself for a fool. He hadn't made her uncomfortable in the way he'd thought.

"I should walk you back," he said. "Let me put this in the cabin."

She smiled, her teeth like pearls in the dark. "No need. I wear wards."

"But—"

"There's been a great decline in the large cat and wolf populations over the last few years. I'll be fine." Vera looked at the cabin door. The flickering of firelight issued through the split in the curtains. Her hand rested gently on his forearm. "Best you both stay out of sight."

With that, she turned and walked back down the moonlight spotted path. A warding would work against other humans and animals, bringing a sense of fear or anxiety that would cause them to naturally change their behavior. But wards had little effect on Ayi or wolf people. The magic wasn't strong enough. No more effective than when a few bees fought to stop a bear from raiding the hive for honeycomb. An annoyance, but not a potent deterrent.

The last time Mathan had seen a hunter was when his sleuth burned. Two dozen hunters had surrounded the village. They'd trapped the Ayi inside on the night of a full moon, when they were at their weakest, then rained poisoned-tipped arrows on them. Mathan's brother had taken one to the throat, his daughter, still new on her legs, had taken one in the back while clutched in her mother's arms.

With chaos all around, the hunters burst through the gates and cut down whoever they saw, regardless of age. Mathan had killed two of them before he'd been injured. And then, he'd taken Ana, his wife, and ran while their people died behind them.

A heavy guilt accompanied his survival. That he should have done more. Maybe he should have died with his brother. When Ana died in childbirth a few months later, it felt like fate was giving him his due. Mathan didn't deserve a happy life after his people were killed. When Esbern had taken the other Ayi's north a decade later, Mathan hadn't deserved to go with them. Instead, he chose a solitary life in the woods. When he'd met Thyra with her anger and squalling, neglected babe, it had felt like an opportunity for redemption. A chance to make it right.

He hadn't expected to love Kuma like his own. More than he'd ever loved anyone, save Ana. Kuma, despite the recent irritations of adolescence, had become Mathan's entire world.

Placing Vera's package on the table, he told Kuma to stay there, then darted after Vera. Thyra met him halfway to the village. She'd waited until Vera passed to step from the woods and block his path.

"You've settled nicely here," she said. "Even made a few friends." She inhaled deeply. "That one smells nice. Wonder what she'd think if she knew what you were."

"Thyra..." The hair on his neck rose, lips retracting into a snarl with her name.

She held her ground, her face cold. "Convince the boy to come with me."

"Esbern's not his father," Mathan said.

"So?"

"You'll only hurt Kuma with your lies. Leave him be. Let him live his life without you."

Her gaze flicked down the path. "We'll be safe in the north. You could join us."

"Why do you need him?"

"We're safer together, aren't we? These last few years alone have been hard."

"You brought the hunter." It wasn't a question, and she didn't deny it. She needed another Ayi for protection. "Why go north now?"

Thyra shifted uncomfortably from one foot to the other. "Esbern won't let me in. If I have my son with me, he might change his mind."

"Why?"

She scuffed her toe on the ground and looked away. "Kuma's his nephew." The quiet settled around them. Even the dying crickets seemed to listen. "His father died in a hunter's trap when I was pregnant."

"Why didn't you go north, then?"

"Esbern never approved of me. Thought I kept his brother from joining him."

"Did you?"

Her shrug was the only answer she gave. Mathan wasn't sure that it even mattered anymore. All that mattered was that she would use Kuma for her own gains, regardless of what would benefit him. "So you'll use Kuma to gain entrance to the sleuth?" Mathan watched Thyra's face harden. "Did you know a hunter followed you?"

Guilt flashed across her face but disappeared just as quickly. "I was hoping to lose him. He's older than the hunters I've met before."

He rubbed his beard. The determined, angular faces of the hunters that raided the sleuth in the middle of the night rose in his memory. But that felt like a hundred years ago. Most of them would be elderly. "They're a dying lot, just like we are. Why haven't you killed him before now?"

"I'm not as strong as I once was, and he's good at covering his tracks." There was a vulnerable tremble to her lips. Her voice threatened to break. "I'm tired, Mathan. Sometimes, I think maybe it would be better if he caught me. If..."

He shifted uncomfortably. There was a time when similar thoughts had overwhelmed him. Before he'd met her and Kuma. But her presence was a liability to their son. "You should move on," he said. "Lead the hunter away. It would be the kindest thing you could do for Kuma."

She bit her lip. "He's old enough to decide on his own."

Mathan looked up at the sliver of moon. "We'll be wearing the chains tomorrow. Best you find somewhere to shelter so the hunter doesn't find you." With that, he turned and left. No smoke rose from the cabin's chimney, and he knew before he opened the cabin door that Kuma was gone.

Mathan spent the night searching the village, past the tavern, and out to the western countryside, but found no trace of Kuma. The boy covered his scent and tracks well, just like he'd been taught. It was equal parts pride and disappointment that spurned Mathan back home.

Kuma would return when he wanted to, and the wriggling thought that he might not come back at all was a bitter and devouring taste in the back of Mathan's throat.

As much as he wanted Thyra gone for the boy's sake, Mathan had some empathy for her. That Kuma's father died while she'd been pregnant explained why she'd initially begged him to stay when they'd come across each other. Her look had been desperate, and it was no wonder. A single Ayi with a cub in the woods when the hunters still stalked them might have been fatal.

Having lost Ana in childbirth only a few years before, he'd been drawn to Thyra's vulnerability, but any affection had quickly faded with the familiarity of her nature. Kuma had brought something alive in him, though. A sense of purpose that he'd been lacking. When he'd offered to take the babe and she'd happily handed him over, Mathan had counted on never seeing her again.

He studied the thin seam in the wooden planks. Beneath the table was a den he'd carved with his own hands and two sets of chains that would keep him and Kuma shackled for the night. The chains weren't necessary for Mathan. He wore them as an act of solidarity for Kuma's sake. The boy was still young and hadn't had time to learn adequate control of himself on bear nights. Restraining themselves had proved the best way to keep the neighboring livestock safe and was likely why they'd been able to stay here so long. If Kuma left him, he'd have no reason to stay.

The door flew open, letting in a rich stream of golden light as Kuma lumbered inside. He paused when he saw Mathan seated at the table. Kuma's face was grey, eyes hollowed, and red-rimmed.

An initial flush of relief and anger gave way to concern as Mathan rose to meet him. "What's happened?" Kuma shook his head and moved toward his bed. "Where were you?"

Kuma dropped his coat on his bed. He kept his back to Mathan as he spoke. "There was a party at Alisom's house."

Mathan stiffened at the sadness in Kuma's voice but kept his words to himself. Kuma turned slightly.

"You were right." His voice was too low to tremble, but raw emotion broke through. He wiped his nose and hung his head. Mathan held his silence and waited for Kuma to continue. "She could invite a few friends. Jake, Frida, you know? We've all been together for a while."

Mathan stood behind him, trying to engulf him with his presence.

"I know you never liked her—" Kuma said.

"It had nothing to do with her. She's not a match for you, too much like—" Mathan was glad Kuma cut him off.

"—but I liked her, and I really thought she felt the same." He shook his head, dark curls dancing around his neck. "I misread her. I was wrong, and you were right."

Mathan deflated. "I'm sorry. I wish that I'd been wrong."

Kuma turned to him, his gaze guarded. "At the party, her father introduced a boy and his family from Gowun county." His cheeks flushed. "They're engaged. Can you believe it? She's not even twenty."

Early marriage and children were a common practice among the villagers. He'd explained this to Kuma before. "Arranged marriages aren't uncommon, especially with families of status."

A deep blush spread across the boy's cheeks. "It's not arranged. Apparently, they've been seeing each other for over a year. All this time and I...." He rubbed his eyes. "I was humiliated. I'm *such* a fool."

Mathan rested a hand on Kuma's shoulder. "You're no fool. You lead with your good heart. And having hope is nothing to be embarrassed about."

Kuma turned bleary eyes toward him. Mathan's embrace was brief and firm, hoping to convey the depth of his love in that single moment of comfort. He pulled away before Kuma stepped back and gave a weak smile.

They spent the rest of the day on the usual preparations for the new moon. Kuma cleaned the cellar, testing the chains and setting up two pitchers of water—the change always brought thirst—while Mathan went in search of food. He found the young buck at midday, shin-deep in a slow-moving creek, and broke its neck before it could do more than let out a small squeal.

Mathan hauled it back to the cabin and cut it in half before securing it in the underground den. He caught a few fish from the same stream and completed the preparations with several handfuls of berries. It wasn't as much as they usually had, but it would have to do.

Kuma was napping when Mathan spread Vera's ward around the perimeter of their cabin. It scented the ground with minty richness, creating a discomfort that rippled over his skin. By the time the preparations were complete, it was nearing sundown.

Kuma had been quiet since their discussion that morning, but as they prepared to descend into the den, he paused. His ears perked, nose lifted high, smelling the air. He looked at Mathan with a question in his eyes.

"She's out there," he said, sniffing again. "My mother." He paused, considering his words. "Do you think she needs shelter for the new moon?"

Kuma had never transitioned without great preparation. Mathan had made sure that the boy never thought it an option to not prepare for the worst and insure the safety of others. Thyra had only ever considered such things as limitations, which she'd always deemed beneath her. The ward diminished most other smells, but he caught the slightest hint of her in the breeze. And something else. An unfamiliar human scent masked beneath the fetid odor of decay. The hunter.

Mathan cursed. "Get downstairs. Chain yourself."

"But—"

"Go! Now!" He shoved Kuma gruffly. "Don't come until you hear my voice or tomorrow morning."

Thick dark hair had sprouted along Kuma's arms and neck. His ears shifted and perked, nose elongating. His clothes would tear if he didn't hurry. Still, the young bear paused on the ladder, his expression full of concern. "Father?"

Mathan shook his head. If he didn't hurry, someone's blood would spill on their lands. "Go." He closed the door atop the den and slid the table over it, making sure the table legs were clear and that, if he could not return, Kuma wouldn't be trapped.

They hadn't stoked a fire and without the moonlight, the world was pitch dark. Small croaks of frogs, eerie night bird cries, and fading crickets assaulted his ears.

The transformation always started with his ears tingling. The sensation worked its way through his scalp and down his neck. Mathan stripped his shirt and pants. Next came the full body itch, spreading down his back and limbs to his palms and feet. He winced as coarse hair erupted painfully through his skin. Joints cracked and pulled apart to reposition, forcing him to all fours. Fur-covered skin stretched taut, straining at the widening girth of corded muscles atop thickening bones. His hands grew wide and padded. Long claws burst through fingers and toes, gripping the ground with a surety that Mathan never felt in his human limbs. His grunts were low and constrained, trying to lessen his usual volume.

From the cabin, Kuma's howls and yelps were softened by the dirt and flooring. With the deer and provisions, he'd be safe for the night. Kuma had never been alone on the new moon and, leaving the boy now fought against all Mathan's instincts. He paused at the ward, then remembered Kuma was barely a boy anymore. He'd be safe in the den until sunrise.

Thyra's low growls reached him. Her muskiness beckoned to the wildness in him. Mathan raised a tentative paw and stepped into the woods, ears rotating to catch every shift of leaves or rustling brush. Thyra was a hundred yards to the south, moving slowly, but, to his ears, her steps were as loud as thunder. With the shifting wind, the other scent came from the southeast, but those steps were no louder than a beetle scrambling over a rock. The hunter had mostly disguised their natural odor with a mixture of rot and ground rodent, both of which were uncommon in Mathan's territory. But the hunter wouldn't know that. If they'd been fixated on hunting Thyra, they might have neglected to consider that other Ayi's would be in the area. At least, Mathan hoped so.

Unlike the wolf people, mature Ayis remained cognizant of each decision they made while in their bear form. Unless something triggered their animalistic instincts. Fight or flight. Kill or run. Some Ayi, like Thyra, didn't resist the bear when it took hold. But Mathan had always seen restraint as a means of survival. He slunk close to the ground and waited.

The hunter had placed himself down wind of Thyra but upwind of the cabin. He drifted, taking time with each step, cautiously shifting branches from his path, and resettling them with barely a sound. Every time the footsteps moved toward the cabin, they veered away again. Vera's warding batting him away.

Mathan followed the hunter as quietly as he could. With each of the man's smooth breaths, Mathan smelled the rot of his teeth. There was a sourness to the man, more than the odors he used for disguise. As he followed, the man's shape became clear in the dark. He was lean and worn with time, but his spine was erect and each of his movements displayed a steady resolve.

Ahead, Thyra moved through the underbrush, heading towards a neighboring farm which housed goats and sheep. If she took the animals, it would jeopardize the last five years he'd worked so hard to build here. But if the hunter took her down before she got there, Kuma would suffer her loss. There was no simple answer or response to the risks. Mathan wanted them both gone, wanted his simple, quiet life back with Kuma beside him.

The hunter's steps faltered. A stick snapped beneath his boot. All went silent and still. Mathan imagined Thyra's black head lifting, tilting, as she debated the next action. Ignoring the bow and arrows strung across his back, the hunter drew his sword. He paced forward with his blade before him.

Thyra loomed suddenly, rising onto her back legs. Most people would have flinched, but the hunter lunged toward her. She swiped at him. His blade pierced her massive paw. She yelped and stumbled backward as the sword withdrew. The iron tang of blood filled the air.

As Mathan rushed forward, the hunter spun to meet him. The blade sung before his face, barely missing his nose. The hunter slashed again, cutting a few hairs from Mathan's shoulder.

Thyra chuffed. Followed by a pulsing sound emanating from deep in her throat. Mathan lumbered sideways, placing himself protectively between the two. The man's face was hard, eyes fixed on Mathan's throat.

She chuffed again, louder. After shaking her majestic head, she collapsed to the ground. She licked her wounded hand. Her eyes were wide, black orbs filled with fear.

Poisoned.

Mathan's bellow rumbled the ground, shaking the birds from the trees. The neighbor's sheep bleated in the distance.

The hunter waved the blade again. Mathan could see him more clearly now. He was old, maybe one of the last of his kind, and his failing life was written in the lines of his face.

Kuma was safe in the den for now. For his sake, Mathan would make sure the hunter could go no further. That his sleuth would live. It was what he wished he'd done so many years ago.

Mathan rose onto his back legs, watching the man's eyes narrow with determination. The force of his bellow blew the hunter's straggly hair from his face. But the blade was poised and ready. Mathan dove for him, but the hunter vanished from his path.

Kuma tumbled over the man. They rolled as the boy growled and the man grunted. The hunter struggled, taking the gashes of angry claws across his shoulder but holding the smaller bear back. The sword dipped low, toward Kuma's ribs.

Using all his force, Mathan knocked Kuma away. The blade slid between Mathan's ribs, burning as it entered. He loomed over the hunter, whose eyes were full of desperation. Mathan pressed himself down onto the blade and opened his jaws. With a loud crunch and a curdling scream, the night went quiet.

Vera's green eyes greeted him when Mathan woke. He liked the expression that swept across her face. There was a tenderness in the way she blotted his brow with a damp cloth. He tried to speak but his breath caught in pain. She shook her head.

"Hush. It's alright," Vera said.

Mathan looked around the cabin. The slanting light told him it was late. They were alone.

"Kuma?" He whispered, wincing with the word.

"He's fine," she said as she looked away. "You've been asleep four days. Didn't think you were going to make it that first one. It wasn't until yesterday that I was sure. Kuma left only when I could assure him you'd be alright. The boy... well, he wasn't a boy then, was frantic when he appeared on my doorstep in the middle of the night."

Questions were trapped in his throat, refusing to break free. Vera patted his hand.

"Lucky he came when he did. I should have made a better warding," she said. "Given you and Kuma each one to wear. I regret I didn't do better by you." She turned back to him.

He tried to sit up. Where had Kuma gone? The sudden movement sent him spiraling back into darkness. When he woke some time later, Vera's eyes were closed, her head rested on a pillow beside him. One of her hands was splayed across his chest as if it were the most natural thing in the world.

The story unraveled over the next few days. Kuma hadn't known where else to go and had woken Vera and Frida. They'd followed him into the woods and worked to save both him and Thyra. Though she'd gotten more of the poison, he'd taken a direct hit. Vera and her daughter's spells had pulled most of the poison out that night. But Mathan's injuries required more care and tending. So, Vera stayed.

When Mathan apologized, she said she stayed because she wanted to and warned him not to do anything foolish after she'd healed him.

Kuma had gone north with Thyra. She'd insisted that it would be harder travelling once the snows came. Vera admitted with little coercing that she didn't much care for Thyra.

"Poor boy," Vera said. "His heart was strung in two directions." She pulled Mathan close as he withheld tears. "Give him time, Mathan. He's a good lad." His chest clenched, arms wrapping tight around her as he wept against her shoulder. She stroked his back and whispered, "Give it time."

The creeks and ponds froze hard that winter. If not for Vera needing Mathan to fix various things at the tavern, which seemed to always be breaking, he'd have drowned in isolation and despair. As each new moon came, Vera forced a warding around his neck and spread one around his property, whispering small incantations. Frida sometimes wandered behind her, making small inquiries about this word or that herb. They spoke little about Kuma, though his absence hung in the cabin like a shroud.

With his increased presence at the tavern brought more attention. Those men who'd been afraid of him now sought his help with other projects. It struck Mathan as both familiar and odd. He'd not been a part of a community since the sleuth burned.

When the daffodils of spring broke through the ground, Mathan considered leaving. He'd told himself he would if Kuma left. But now he worried the boy wouldn't be able to find him if he returned.

If he returned. Those three words wormed steadily in his brain. Mathan stayed.

The heat of summer brought powerful storms that flooded fields and wrenched barns from the ground. With his firm hands and skill with tools, he helped neighbors rebuild. He told himself he'd stay another winter.

In the fall, Mathan spent long days harvesting the fields with Jake. His father had perished in the gloom of winter, and Vera said the family was at risk of losing their home without help.

The sweat still clung to Mathan's back as he walked the worn path to his cabin. Red and gold leaves fluttered in the air. He paused when he caught a familiar scent. Smoke wafted from the chimney. Mathan ran, stumbling over his own feet, heart racing. He threw the door open.

Kuma sat at the table. His hair was past his shoulders, a thick stubble spread across his jaw. He stood when their eyes met, a wide grin spread across his face. Mathan crushed him in his arms, rocking from one foot to the other.

Kuma's voice was warm against his ear. "Father, I've come home."

CHAPTER ELEVEN

OH, GREAT DRAGON

Plumes of curling steam wafted from Bruce's wide nostrils. He rolled onto one side, adjusting his wings to accommodate the movement. The red silt on the cavern's floor stuck to his plated green scales as he studied the trembling armored man before him. Bruce's tail tapped once, sending a small dirty cloud into the young man's face.

The soldier wrinkled his nose. Whether from the dust or the stench of charred remains from the last eight visitors piled along the wall, Bruce couldn't be sure. Nor did he care. This one, at least, had the great sense to introduce himself rather than charge in haphazardly waving a puny sword. In fact, this idiot hadn't drawn a sword at all, though one hung from his belt. Instead of a weapon, the man held a golden statue of what might have been a poorly sculpted cow or ox. The distance made it difficult to be certain. It piqued Bruce's curiosity, lessening his annoyance at being bothered, if only slightly.

He'd probably still kill him.

"Leo, is it?" The dragon's deep voice thrummed across the walls.

The man's eyes widened beneath the confines of his too-large gleaming helmet. His arms trembled under the weight of the statue and a stench of proper fear permeated the air. The odor pleased Bruce. It harkened back to his youth when dragons were respected and avoided for their fearsomeness. When wonderfully long years passed and people avoided his kind. Now, he'd been made into a romanticized novelty that caused humans to forget what dragons could do. Especially when their inherently introverted natures were disturbed.

"L...Leopold," he squeaked. His voice was youthful, and he seemed, honestly, a bit naïve.

"Leo. Do you know what happened when there was only one unicorn left?" Bruce picked at his teeth with one great talon, loosening the burnt remains of a tunic. He tossed it atop the pile of bones in the corner. "They received some lovely accolades. Someone even wrote a book. Did you happen to read it?" Bruce's voice rumbled with age and smoke.

Leopold shifted on his feet, having the good sense to look more uncomfortable than afraid. But his incessant blinking betrayed his nerves.

"No?" Bruce asked, doubting that the boy could read. Most soldiers he'd encountered had a literacy level well below that of the average dragon. "It was charming. Absolutely charming. I didn't manage to finish it, unfortunately. But you *should* read it. I hear they even made it into a play with some lovely music. But now that there's only one dragon left, what do I get?" Bruce paused dramatically and crossed his arms. "One of two things—either threatened or patronized to."

Beads of sweat dripped from beneath Leopold's helmet. His cheeks bloomed red as the temperature in the cave swelled with each of the dragon's sulfurous words.

"Honestly, neither of those things is endearing. It's as if people aren't trying in the least to understand me. I know soldiers aren't the best at art or poetry. Unless it's poetic justice, am I right?" Bruce snorted at his own joke. Seeing it fall flat before the frightened soldier soured his mood, so he continued. "But you could *try*, couldn't you? A little poem. Maybe a sketch or painting. Some sort of metaphorical tribute that speaks of my emerald scales or amethyst eyes. Why does no one compare me to jewels or lovely metaphors?"

"I...I apologize, oh, great dragon. I thought, I mean, everyone says that your kind prefers gold to all else."

"My kind?" He snorted. "That's rather offensive. I'm assuming that you are referring to the hoarding."

Leopold swallowed and nodded. "Yes, the hoarding."

Bruce's eyes narrowed into purple slits with thin, elongated pupils. Swirls of steam rose from between his long teeth and partially opened mouth. "Have you ever *seen* my hoard?"

"N...no..."

"No, of course not. No one has. It's very rude to assume, isn't it?" Beneath the lighter verdant scales of his throat, a glow grew. Bruce could roast him in his suit, have the poor man for a tasty snack later. But the dragon feared it would leave a bitter taste in his mouth, like the last one had. He wondered if Leo was a vegan, there'd been too many of them lately and they tasted exactly as one might expect, like soggy brussels sprouts. "You know, plenty of dragons don't even like gold. I don't. It's garish and rather impractical."

"What?" Leo looked stunned. The genuineness of emotions that played across his face was endearing. Perhaps Bruce wouldn't kill him. He was a different sort of soldier, entertaining in his own way. Softer. And that was worth something.

"I did when I was younger. All young dragons do. But we grow. Our interests change. Do you still play with the same toys you did as a child?"

Leo shook his head. Between the weight of the statue and the heat, his face was looking more and more like a ripe tomato beneath a summer rain. "What do you hoard then? I'm sorry, I'm assuming again. Do you hoard... anything?"

Bruce's chest brightened. Heat seared the room. "What do you see when you look at me, Leo?"

He cleared his throat, shifting nervously on his feet again. "Beautiful emerald scales. Amethyst eyes. Talons like sharpened obsidian."

Bruce chuckled. "Such flattery. You're a quick learner, aren't you? Appreciate the effort, I really do. But what am I?"

"A... dragon?"

"Yes, a dragon. Very good. And what are dragons known for?"

Leo readjusted his grip on the statue and licked his lips. "Flying?"

Bruce pressed himself onto his haunches with a sigh. Great leathery wings widened, engulfing the enormous cavern and buffeting the sweaty hair stuck to Leo's cheeks. "Flying, of course. But, what else?" He tapped his long talons on the floor, the sound echoing like ticks of a clock. "Come on, you can do it."

"H...hoarding?"

"There you go again. Why don't you be a good lad and set the statue down? You're looking tired," Bruce coaxed. "What else?"

Leo placed the gold figure on the floor and shook out his arms, mumbling.

"Speak louder, Leo."

"Fire?"

"Yes, Leo. We breathe fire. Creatures of destruction, right?" Bruce's tone was condescending. All humans eventually revealed themselves to be the same. But he supposed he should be glad this one came bearing gifts and not trying to kill him. Or worse, trying to find and steal his mythical, shining hoard. A deep inhale fed the flames in his belly, escalating the temperature another twenty degrees. "If only people could change the way they see creatures unlike themselves. You ever think that maybe we'd like to create something?"

"Sir?"

Bruce sighed. The boy still didn't get it. "'Oh, great dragon' worked just fine, Leo." The talons ceased their tapping. The prickling anticipation that blooms before violence filled the air. "You have exactly five seconds to ask one more question before I roast you in that shiny suit of yours."

Leo paled. Armored joints clattered against each other as his legs trembled. He didn't move.

"Or you could run."

"Thank you, oh, great dragon!" Leo turned, legs moving clumsily as he hastened back up the long passage that led to the surface.

For good measure, Bruce blew a stream of fire after him. He cocked his head, listening to the departing steps, and smiled. "I'm too merciful."

He had no sooner lay his head back on the ground when a fresh clattering of armor rushed into the cavern. A sword gleamed in her hand as she yelled, "Die, foul beast! I claim your treasure as my own. Let it be known that Belinda the Brave was the last face you ever—"

A gust of flames stole her words, hot enough to end her life without an abundance of screaming. Bruce thought that was merciful, too.

One massive paw nudged the corpse to the corner, adding to his collection of blackened armor and broad swords with bejeweled hilts. Twenty-three in total over the last month. If this kept up, he'd have to move soon. That thought filled him with dread and worry. Moving would be no easy feat. His belongings required delicate handling. And what would happen if he left his cavern unprotected?

He shook his head. They'd come in and, when disappointment struck, they'd destroy everything. Then, being the dragon that he was, he'd have no choice but to burn their villages and castles. Killing as many as he could. It all sounded so tedious, but those were the expected codes of conduct taught to every scaled youth in Dragon Primary, Volume I.

One couldn't break with tradition just because they were the last one left. Even the unicorn knew that.

The humans would blame him, the way they had with Cousin Lucinda, before their gigantic arrows struck her throat. Then there would be no more dragons. He didn't think anyone would even write a book about him.

No, he would have to think of another way. Bruce nestled his head beneath his wing and drifted to sleep, hoping for the quiet to last.

A week and four more suits of armor later, Leo's voice whispered from the cavern entrance. His words had a respectful tone as they echoed down the tunnel.

"Oh, great dragon?"

Bruce finished picking the meat from his teeth with a femur bone and tossed it into the pile. Maybe he shouldn't have let the boy live. Was this a lesson on the bad dealings of mercy that Bruce had yet to learn? Mother always said he was too soft-hearted for a dragon, that he would do better if he'd tried to emulate his cousin's ferocity. But he was the only one left, so, in that regard, his mother might have been less than right. Not that he ever would have said that to her.

Leo called again. No point in being rude, he supposed. "Did you think of a final question, Leo?"

"No, I have something for you."

Bruce grumbled. He supposed he'd have to let the boy live a bit longer. No one ever gave him gifts other than their dying screams, which only sometimes had a nice ring to it. Occasionally, someone would try being overly complimentary, but that never ended well for them. The last thing a dragon ever wanted was insincerity. Authentic hate was preferable to a lousy, contemptuous attempt at manipulation. But the soldier had returned, and that was a first.

"Enter, Leopold, the last of his line." Bruce snorted.

Leo's steps were soft and light. He rounded the corner in plain linen pants and a tan shirt that nearly matched his complexion. He wore no weapon. In his arms was a medium-sized square object wrapped in a tarp.

Bruce sat up, cocking his head curiously. His breath moistened the room. "What's all this? No armor?" Poor confused human. Didn't value his life. Perhaps their last visit had left him in an existential crisis. "Leo, have you considered seeking help from a qualified professional?"

He frowned. "Qualified professional?"

"You could still have a long life ahead of you, but only if you stop bothering me. And, frankly, I don't appreciate being used as a means to your doom."

A small smile loosened his face. "Oh. No, it's nothing like that. Apologies for the misunderstanding." He hefted his arms an inch. "I brought you something that isn't gold."

Bruce sat a little taller, suspicious. "Why?"

Leo set the bundle on the floor and began unwrapping it. "Our last conversation got me thinking. I mean, what do I really know about dragons? Only hearsay and outdated tales. It made me question myself and everything I'd ever heard."

"Ah, well. Glad our little talk affected you, I suppose. But why bring another gift?"

He pulled the tarp away, revealing a canvas. "As a thank you for letting me live." He turned the painting around proudly.

Bruce squinted at the image on the canvas, barely making out the greenish shape and outline of dark wings. Two purple dots for eyes in the center of the face. Surely, he didn't... "Is that supposed to be me?"

Leo's smile faltered. "Yes. You, being the only dragon I've ever met, were the inspiration."

Dragons weren't known to be grateful creatures, and feigning appreciation was beyond his capabilities. But Leo looked so proud of his gift, and Bruce had to give credit where it was due. The soldier had listened to Bruce's musings and tried to redeem himself. Bruce wasn't sure how to respond. Instinctively, he wanted to roast the man. But Leo stood there, vulnerable, with a look of hopeful anticipation. Like a puppy begging for a pat on the head. It was endearing.

"It must have taken you quite a long time to create something so...interesting." He coughed smoke on the last word.

Leo's face lit with excitement. If he'd had a tail, Bruce was sure it would have wagged. "Almost five days. This is the third version. The first two didn't capture your glory. I'm so glad that you like it."

Bruce had to quell the fire that rose in his throat. He choked again. "Yes, yes. My glory." He squinted, elongating his neck to get a better view.

"Do you want me to bring it closer?"

"What? No, it's fine from over..."

Leo picked up the canvas, and holding it before him, scuffled across the room. "I want to make sure you have a clear view."

Bruce frowned, was about to protest, but as the painting moved closer, he thought better of it. The painted outlines of his body were crisp. His back was a darker forest green while the scales on his chest were a bright emerald. The eyes were amethyst purple with vertical ebony pupils. It was actually a wonderful likeness. The young man had talent.

"It's quite well-done," he finally admitted. He studied Leo, cocking his head with increased curiosity. "This is no work of a novice. How long have you been an artist?"

A bright blush crept from his collar and burned his cheeks. He looked bashfully at the floor. "I don't remember when I wasn't one, to be honest."

Bruce huffed. Dual puffs of smoke issued from his nostrils. "And yet you chose to be a soldier?"

"Wasn't really a choice. My father insisted I needed a career to fall back on."

"Hm. Parents think they know what's best for us, don't they? Don't realize that their smothering stifles the soul. They always encouraged me to do more dragonly-type things. You know, wreaking havoc and burning down villages. That sort of stuff never suited me. I imagine soldiering cuts into your creative endeavors?"

Leo nodded glumly.

"Why don't you quit? If this piece is any indication, you're quite talented."

"I'm not sure I could make a living, to be honest."

"Don't know until you try."

Leo's sigh was thick. He glanced at the walls, scarred with thick scorch marks and deep cracks. "Would you like me to hang it somewhere?"

Bruce assessed the space. There was no wall unburnt and with the increase in unwanted visitors, it was likely to get worse. "There's a smaller cave behind me." He arched his back, stretching his neck and legs, filling up the space in front of Leo. "It's where I keep things most precious to me. Just let me move out of the way."

He lumbered sideways, his long tail knocking over the largest pile of corpses and bones, spreading them across the floor with a sickening crash. They crunched and broke beneath the dragon's enormous feet and long claws. "Pardon the mess. It's just through there."

Leo eyed the arched doorway, barely large enough for the dragon to get his head and shoulders through. Long scrapes along the ceiling were proof that someone had painstakingly carved the room out. It was dark and quiet, relatively cool compared to the rest of the cavern. He entered and returned a moment later, wearing a look of confusion. He held a thick, leather-bound book aloft.

"What is this?"

Bruce's eyes glowed with warning. His voice rumbled. "First edition in French. Signed. You'd best put that back, Leo. I thought we were making progress in our relationship. Don't make me kill you now."

Leo darted back into the room, returning the book carefully to where he'd found it. He muttered apologies. "There must be thousands of books in there, oh, great dragon."

Bruce sat on his haunches, face beaming with pride. "Seven thousand eight hundred and sixty-two, to be exact. And now one painting." He didn't care for the surprised look Leo gave him. "Speak your mind, Leopold. I can see a thought tickling your small brain."

"It's just—no offense—I didn't know dragons could read. Or even enjoyed reading."

"No offense taken, boy. To be fair, most dragons don't..." He paused, frowning slightly as he caught his words. "*Didn't* like to read. Too busy with other pursuits that I've already alluded to. Myself, though, I've always loved a good story. Those who can string a series of phrases together to make me forget the world and predicament I find myself in." He snapped a bone that had rolled beneath his talons in excitement. His eyes cast a warm glow. "Now *that* is true magic."

Leo smiled. "So, you do have a hoard."

Bruce gave a one-shouldered shrug. "I like to think of myself as a collector. It sounds less judgmental, don't you think?"

"I doubt there's a tremendous difference between hoarding and collecting, to be honest. But I'm not here to argue semantics."

"Semantics? Did you just use the word 'semantics'?" Bruce edged slightly closer, blocking the exit. Most of the soldiers that he'd had experience with barely uttered more than one or two syllables strung together. He used to recite poetry to them, but anything other than limericks made their eyes glaze over. In the end, it had been less frustrating to just burn them. He considered it a mercy done for the greater good. And a might more satisfying too. With an eager voice, he asked, "Leo, you can read?"

Leo nodded, eyes darting to the narrow space between the dragon's body and the wall. Bruce ignored his obvious nervousness.

"It seems we share a kinship of ignorance, Leo. I didn't think soldiers could read, either." Bruce's voice boomed. "I am absolutely *delighted* to hear it."

"You are?"

"Yes, dear boy. Do you know how difficult it is for a dragon to..." His voice trembled with emotion. Vision blurring as he gazed at the young man. "Leopold, I would like to offer you employment."

Leo hugged the wall, stepping sideways in an attempt to squeeze past the dragon. His face had gone red again. Bruce could smell the boy's mounting fear. "Wh...what sort of employment? I don't want to kill anyone."

Bruce shifted, allowing more space for him to move, trying not to scare him off. "No, no. I can handle all that, though it is tiresome. I need someone to read to me."

Leo froze. "Read to you?"

"Yes. You see, the trouble with my chosen passion is that—as you well know—I breathe fire. Sometimes accidentally. And books, the things I love most in this world, are highly flammable. If you only knew how many stories I hadn't finished reading because of a sudden sneeze or cough." Bruce shook his head. "Caves are dusty things, you know, and I am allergic to dust and mold."

"What about those books?" Leo gestured toward the smaller room.

"I've been too afraid to read them. And with the recent disruption to my quietude, I've been trying to determine how to move them to a new cave where I can read in peace. But that comes with its own set of problems."

Leo squirmed past the dragon and hopped over a few sets of remains. One skull still wore its battered helmet. He chewed his lip, studying the corpses with a look of repulsion.

Bruce saw him wavering and hoped to sway him. "I can pay you enough to stop soldiering. And dragons are sort of like cats. We sleep for around eighteen to twenty hours a day. Plenty of time for you to paint or do whatever humans do when they aren't trying to kill other creatures. What do you say?"

"Will you stop killing people?" Leo's whisper dripped with fear.

"Believe me, I would be more than happy to. But they should stop trying to kill me first."

A frown tensed his jaw. "That might be difficult. The king has promised a substantial reward to anyone who delivers the last dragon to the castle."

Bruce slumped. No choice now. He'd have to move. But all the other caves probably still held the scents of his dead kin. With a piteous voice, he said as much.

After a lengthy silence, Leo spoke. "Oh, great dragon, could I ask you a personal question?"

"Really, Leopold? Now is not the time to discuss my sexuality. I'm saddened that is where your mind—"

"What? No! I don't care about that. I'm curious, naturally, but what difference does it make?"

"You'd be surprised how often the question gets asked. What then?"

"Are your scales impenetrable?"

"Excuse me? How does that have anything to do with my offer of employment?" Bruce inhaled deeply. This was taking a turn for the worse. Now the boy wanted to know how to kill him. It was his own fault for getting his hopes up. Best eat him now and figure everything else out later.

"The king wants the last dragon brought to him." The words hurried from Leo's mouth. Sweat trickled down his face with the sudden increase in temperature. "He never said the dragon had to be dead."

The fire in Bruce's gullet quelled. "Leopold, is that why you brought me the gold statue? Trying to bribe me. You little trickster. I appreciate this opportunistic usage of a loophole, but what do you expect will happen when I show up at the castle fully alive?"

Leo smiled slyly. "I expect you to do what dragons do."

Bruce tapped his talons, studying the man with renewed appreciation. "I thought you wanted me to stop killing people."

"Oh, I do. Truly. But if it weren't for the king and his stupid proclamations, none of these people would have come here and bothered you. He's a coward that has never once sullied his hands."

"You blame him for the violence. I can appreciate that," Bruce said. Leo's words provided a sense of vindication he hadn't realized he craved. But to leave his cavern and purposefully expose himself was unsettling. It was very dragon-like. The type of action that would have made his mother proud. Still, he doubted. How would he protect the loose scales at his throat? "I can stay here and keep killing the fools who come. Or I could move somewhere else."

"You could do either of those things, but it won't bring you peace. They'll keep attacking you or they'll find where you move to. It's likely one of them will kill you eventually. And what about the risk to your books? If you take over the castle, you could defend it for centuries with little effort."

Bruce scowled. It sounded like too much work. "Taking over the castle... I don't know, Leo. With great stone buildings comes great...well, you know."

"Have you ever seen the castle? It's gigantic. In the middle of a hundred thousand acres, at least. Lots of buildings or turrets to choose from. And the largest library in five kingdoms."

"Library?" Bruce's eyes glazed over. His tongue slicked across his teeth. He shook his head to clear it, sending a bit of drool onto the wall. "What do you hope to get out of all of this?"

"The south tower has a beautiful view of the valley and mountains. Glorious light for painting. That's all I want and I think I know a way we can avoid killing most of the people."

"Enlighten me."

"I'll send word that I've captured you, but that you are too magnificent to fit through the gate. Truthfully, there'd be no way to squeeze you over the bridge and into the outer bailey, anyway. I'll request that the king and court set up something outside the castle to admire you. That should get most of the people outside, except for some soldiers and servants. I suspect not all of them will be sorry to see the king removed."

"What about the archers?"

"Pretty arrogant lot, to be honest. They'll be in the towers. Sitting ducks for roasting, so to speak."

"You think the king is foolish enough to fall for this?" Bruce asked.

"He'll never see it coming."

"What will your family say? You'll be betraying your own kind."

Leo shrugged. "I've never given my paintings to anyone before. And certainly no one has ever encouraged me in my whole life as much as you have in one day. My family lives close to the border. Even if they must flee, they'll be satisfied if I send them a monthly stipend."

Bruce's talons ticked on the ground as he pondered the situation. He would have to trust the young man, something that went inherently against his nature and was warned against repeatedly in Dragon Primary Volumes 2 through 7.

The memory of Lucinda's demise made him blink away tears and shudder. "We'll have to protect against the archers."

"How?"

Bruce eyed the scrapped armor along the wall. "Ever done any welding?"

Leo followed his gaze. "No."

"Can I trust you, Leopold?"

A hopeful smile pulled at his lips. "Yes, oh, great dragon. You can trust me."

The dragon smiled back. "Call me Bruce."

Bruce perched atop the blackened turret, watching horses drag three covered wagons across the drawbridge. The edges of his leathery wings rippled in the light breeze, scales glistening in the amber hues of the setting sun. A thick plate of armor was strapped to his chest and throat, like a stiff, uncomfortable turtleneck. It chafed but the thick dents marring the metal surface around his neck were evidence of the archer's good aim and nefarious intent.

"Is that the last of it?" The dragon asked while maintaining his watch over the stragglers that had camped outside the grounds for nearly three weeks. He kept hoping they'd leave but they were terribly stubborn and still insulted at the trick they'd been dealt. It had only taken a couple bursts of flame to keep them in line and allow Leo to pass with the wagons. A few tents still smoldered, sending black smoke into the sky. He worried he might have to feed them when winter set in.

Leo jumped down from the horse-drawn wagon to greet another man, an older soldier who'd been happy to lay down his sword. Together they pulled the ropes that dragged the drawbridge up. A young woman scurried from the wagon's seat. Bruce scowled. Another stray Leo had found.

The young man tossed back the tarp that covered the last of the dragon's hoard. Rows of books were stacked carefully, bound together by cloth cords. The last wagon was weighted with piles of gold statues and coins, some of which slid over the side to roll across the ground.

"I thought you didn't like gold?" Leo asked Bruce and tossed a coin to the other man.

"It would have been impractical to completely discard such wealth. You never know when it might be useful. Who is that?"

Leo blushed, glancing casually at the mousy girl who clutched a bag to her chest. She gaped at the dragon with wide eyes. "This is Penelope."

"Another mouth to feed, I see."

"We've plenty of food to eat. Besides, you and she might have a lot in common."

"How so?"

"She was forced to relocate here after her family died. An avid reader, she managed to keep hold of a first edition that I knew you didn't have. When she peeked at your collection, she nearly fainted."

Bruce studied Penelope warily as she drifted back toward the wagon. He briefly considered roasting her, but she stood too near the books, and he was curious about that first edition. "So, you brought her here?"

"Speaks three languages and likes to read aloud. She has a nice voice too." Leo smiled sheepishly. "She's a bit of a writer, too. Thought she might be able to help you put your stories down, given your propensity to burn things."

She tenderly traced the gold embossed lettering of a second edition. Leo said something to her. Penelope smiled shyly before tugging a thick book from her bag and raising it toward the dragon. The cover was slightly worn but the image was unmistakable. A lone unicorn stamped one hoof.

A strange sound echoed through the castle and grounds, a reverent euphoric mix of squeal and coo as it left Bruce's throat. His vision blurred.

"Leopold, I...I don't know what to say."

The young man smiled. "Just tell your story, oh, great dragon, so that we can give you the accolades you deserve."

Bruce's lip trembled. "Leopold, I told you. Call me Bruce."

CHAPTER TWELVE

THE MYSTICAL FARRAGO

Winning story published in Writers of the Future Volume 38, 2022.
Edited by David Farland.

I stood outside the fading blue and gold striped tent, studying the thinning canvas and fraying edges, a result of time and too much wear. The creatures I passed after entering the exhibition appeared well tended and healthy, even the charbulls, which were notoriously spiteful during feeding times. The staff was agreeable, as always, charming the locals with false smiles and flattery. They leaned in to share secrets with some of the more respectable men, while others flirted with doe-eyed ladies. The sharp-edged pink lizards watched me pass, catching my scent with open mouths and flicking tongues, while the triple headed mandrils lazed in the hot sun, ignoring the prodding of overly curious children.

I did not want to believe the rumors, had wanted to hold on to the echoes of childhood feelings and believe the best of old man Goddard. But, as I entered the tent, there was no disputing the evidence and horrible truth laid before me.

The crysallix was over six feet tall- small for the species- and anchored to a large perch by a golden chain shining around one slender ankle. Her wings shimmered in the dull light of the tent's interior, like an oil slick that morphed from green to purple to blue depending on the angle of light. The pinnacle of those wings arched toward the ceiling canopy, while the tips brushed the beige, silty floor. The right wing was missing several large pinions, making it impossible for her to escape easily.

The scent of mountain ginseng and hard nut bread filled my nose- not easily procured with local ovens, the kind only found in the tribal ovens of the western mountains. It reminded me of my grandmother's fondness for the tasteless fare.

The large creature, equal parts bird and human, watched me with glittering, golden eyes. Fine feathers coated her face, hiding any expression. Someone had hastily draped a long swath of linen around her, hiding her breasts and genitals in folds of cloth. I circled her, maintaining professionalism while my stomach knotted. I noted the bloodstains on the linen as Goddard coughed behind me.

"You can't have this here." I took an authoritative tone, levelling a hard gaze at the ringmaster, who clutched his black hat.

The crysallix eyes flicked between Goddard and me, her feathers ruffling down her spine. There was something wrong, more than the wounds, and though my personal knowledge of the creatures was superior to the average citizen, anyone who paid admission could see there was something amiss here. How many had paid admission at Goddard's Mystical Farrago to bear witness to her imprisonment and done nothing? How many had she suffered under? If they had seen the creature as equal to human, those who had abused her would have felt the slice of the guillotine. But because her kind did not speak a language easily understood, they were treated as less than. And the only voice she had in this world was when decent people saw wrong and strived to right it, but that did not happen often enough.

Goddard stammered, filling the air with excuses that wreaked of falsehoods. They rescued her from a smaller carnival that had been sacked in the night. She was the last creature left, he said, and would have died tethered to the wagon that held her, if they had not come along.

"How long have you had her?" I opened my notebook, making notations of her condition, documenting all that he said.

"Only a month or two, lieutenant." Goddard moved closer to me, calloused hands warping his felt hat. He blathered on and, while my pen continued to dictate his words, I was no longer listening.

She could have shredded him and the rest of the staff with her talons or torn them with her hidden beak. Their ferocity was legendary. Her feet were scaled and thin, but with five three-inch talons growing from her toes that splintered the wood she perched upon. Her arms hugged her torso, hiding the talons that should have been there. But Goddard had probably filed them down. I wondered how he had kept from being killed.

I interrupted the man's monologue, abruptly cutting him off mid-sentence. "She might have made her way back to her tribe if you released her when you found her. As it is, you have dragged her leagues away from her native lands."

"She could not have survived on her own, sir. I couldn't abandon her." He brushed the uneven wing with stubby fingers, and she flinched, tucking it closer to her body. "She might have died without me."

The possessive tone of Goddard's voice stabbed a deep discomfort in my chest.

"Mr. Goddard, it is illegal to keep a crysallix. You, being a man of the world, know this simple law. Are you telling me that you did not pass any other tribes that might have taken her? Or any rehabilitation farms?"

His hands continued to worry at the hat while she examined me with discerning eyes. She shifted on her perch, talons and toes crunching the beam that stood three feet from the ground. Large breasts moved beneath the draping fabric as she strained to sit a little taller. I wonder what my scent was to her.

"What have you been doing with her?" I asked. Perhaps it is the quiet language of distant cousins, or the way she stared at me in recognition of another female, or the blood on the fabric. But I knew her story. Every woman knew this story. It did not matter that we did not speak the same tongue.

"Just trying to make a bit of extra coin to pay for her care. She's expensive to feed, and healers don't come cheap." His voice trailed off as I turned on him.

"What were the names of the healers you employed? There are few who understand the species."

He shifted on his feet, continuing the abuse of his sad hat. "They were in the last town…"

The crysallix issued a soft coo and I met her eyes. A promise settled between us.

"Close the exhibit."

"But…"

"No more shows, no more displays." I gestured to the blood. "No more of whatever happened here."

"Sir..." he stammered, and I was too incensed to correct him.

"I will arrange care for her at the regional exotic creatures' clinic." She flexed her wings slightly as I spoke, strained a little taller, understanding the essence of what was being said. "What tribe does she hail from?"

"I don't know." Goddard's face had gone sallow, but his eyes flashed.

"Where are her leathers? Surely she wasn't naked when you found her." Without the distinct colors of her leathers, it would be difficult to discern which troupe she came from. Though, if we could replace the pinions she might find her way home.

"Perhaps, sir, if we could come to some sort of arrangement."

There it was again. He did not stop to wonder why I was unaffected by the crysallix, unlike most men. Or why I could breathe her scent and not desire her. For those not exclusively drawn to mate, the pull to her was different.

"Arrangement?" I asked. This was why she had yet to be returned to her tribe- because of bribes and temptation. How many fellow officers had succumbed to it? It was an odd thing to scold someone I once revered, but I was not a child, and he was proving my childhood idolizations to be grossly misplaced.

"Mr. Goddard, if you would like to add bribery to your charges, please continue." I wrote in quick, clipped script describing the offences and tearing off a piece of the triple layered parchment. "I will return in three hours, and you will hand her over, unscathed, with all of her belongings."

"But I haven't...."

"Three hours. And I will have reinforcements with me. Do I make myself clear?"

Goddard's face puckered, and he spit on the ground. "You little shit. How dare you come into my business and tell me what to do? I remember you. Remember the free tickets and rides I gave you and your friend? And every year I would come back, you would be waiting." He spit again, hitting my boot. "And this is how you repay my generosity? I remember your little friend, too. I remember what happened to her."

He attempted to rattle me by mentioning Judeth, but I had years to deal with her loss and would not be swayed. She would be just as disgusted as I was with the scene.

I shoved the paper into his hands, my eyes never leaving the crysallix.

"When someone demands a kindness be repaid, it is proof that it was never a kindness at all." I said, "Instead, it is a revelation of one's true character." I towered over him, staring into his black eyes until they looked away in shame. "And cover her properly or I'll strip the coat from your back."

Stepping outside the tent, the crowd continued to mill about. Children ran to the next exhibit, laughing and dripping creamsicles down their dirty hands as well-dressed couples strode by, leaning towards each other donned in long skirts and tall hats. The air was filled with childhood memories, now forever tainted.

My mouth was dry with the knowledge there was something here that I was missing, but he would give me only what I could discover on my own. Perhaps the crysallix would speak to me when she was in a safer place. I thought it as likely as being struck by ball lightning on a cold summer day.

They were notoriously private creatures, untrusting of outsiders and, after incidences like this, it was understandable.

They lived in tight-knit tribes in the mountains and valleys to the far west, but there were rumors of other groups nestled in the east and south as well. It was a matriarchal society, with their own written language, their own ways, their own strange foods. They took one love mate in their lifetimes, but could breed outside of that relationship and outside of their species. And, according to my mother, those that did not find a love mate continued to attract unwanted attention. There was something about the creatures that drew the gaze of the human male. Perhaps it was the wild feminine, the fierce winged warrior that defied the male order and gave no unearned respect. Perhaps it was the scent of their pheromones that were used to find a mate. It was said that once love mated, the crysallix ceased the production of their pheromones, but I offer no opinion on that.

I had listened in school as one teacher romanticized them, his tone lilting as he described a lucky meeting with one as several boys leaned forward, entranced. Judeth and I had wondered at their reaction, and it disturbed me in a way I was too young to define. Mother once said there was a reason we lived so far from town, especially after father died. She said we were always in danger amongst men.

I often thought of Judeth and considered that if she had been granted even a fraction of the crysallix strength, perhaps she might still be alive. As it was, I had consigned myself to a quiet life without her. There was nothing more to be done about it. I moved away from the Farrago, recalling the way the creamsicles dripped down her knuckles as she tossed her head back in laughter, green eyes shining with affection.

Three hours later, ten officers returned with me, a mix of male and female, per my request. Aggie, the healer who ran the exotic clinic, already stood before the tent when we arrived. She was a short, thick woman with disheveled hair and dirt under her fingers. Her dress was torn in three places and spattered with, what I hoped was, dirt. The messenger reported she had nearly knocked him over when she received my request and beat us to the tent in her haste. When I arrived, she was guarding the entryway like a goose and its nest, preventing any man from entering until they had inhaled a pungent herb that she forced upon them by threat. It negated the effects of the pheromones in the air and would last for several hours.

Aggie's familiar smile warmed me. It was the type of warmth that could settle crying children with a single look. She gripped my hand, daring to pull me in close for a quick hug.

"I was happy to hear from you, *lieutenant*." She winked. "My Jude would have been so proud."

My cheeks grew hot. "I should have stayed in touch." I said flatly.

She patted my hand. "Life is hard enough without being reminded of our losses." The same softness that Judeth had inherited swam in her eyes. She nodded towards the tent. "Tell me about her."

I conveyed all that Goddard had said, indicating I believed it all to be fabrication. She listened intently, murmuring that he probably pulled out the pinions to keep her grounded.

She rubbed her chin. "Why didn't she kill him? Rip his spine through his throat, or sever an artery?" She frowned, "It's out of character for the crysallix."

"I thought so as well. That is why I sent for you." Creatures trusted Aggie, they knew her good intent by her smell. Well, except for the charbull that took two of her fingers. But she reckoned he was hungry at the time.

Officer Vinja, on loan from a different department, stuck his head through the flap of the tent. His greased hair jutted in unintentional directions, and one side of his moustache drooped down while the other side curled upward in unnatural cheerfulness. "We have unchained it, sir, but it's fighting our attempts to move it. We can't coax it off the perch."

"Sir?" Aggie demanded, puffing up her chest and scowling. Her tone caused Vijna to step back in concern. "What do you mean by 'sir'? Have you no eyes to see, nor wits to think?"

"Aggie, it's okay."

But that would not soothe her. "Sir? Well then, I suppose you might be a young lass? Or I, a plucked eagle? Perhaps that's not an exotic creature at all but a…"

"Aggie, the crysallix." I breathed. She huffed, tossing a few more curt words at him as he opened the tent for us. He mouthed apologies, his cheeks flushed, but I waved him away. He had intended no harm, and it happened too frequently for me to react to anymore.

They had clothed the crysallix in a clean dress, tearing the back out to accommodate the wings, but the rest of her was covered. Her wings spread wide, flapping at anyone who came too near as her talons gripped the perch. Goddard stood in the corner, sneering at the officers, who ducked away from each swipe of her hand. Though the claws were too dulled to slice, they could still rend flesh with enough force behind them.

The scent of ginseng and nut bread was thick in my head, reminding me of quiet nights and warm hugs. I knew their scent registered differently for each person.

"You, moustache!" Aggie waved over an anxious Vinja, whispering into his ear and pointing at the door, which he disappeared through with some urgency.

I should have been the first one in, but had stayed back to make sure Goddard didn't run for it. She narrowed her eyes at me, then switched to watching Aggie, who was pointing a finger in Goddard's face. She had backed him into a corner but kept advancing. I thought she might bite him.

"What have you been feeding her?" She shoved herself into him. Goddard glanced to me, but I offered no rescue.

"Bread and cheese. Sometimes fruit." He stammered.

"Bread!" Aggie rolled up her sleeves, her eyes wide with fury. "She's starving, that much is clear. Bread and cheese aren't part of their diets, you numb-knuckle. They are predators. They need meat- liver and organs- to live. If not, then nuts and specific fruits, but bread? They can only digest nut bread from their recipes, not ours. Are you daft or heartless? Are you trying to kill her?"

"No, no ma'am. I was trying to save her." His hat lay trampled under their shifting feet. "We found her trapped and injured. Surely you don't think..."

"Even I can see that you are a terrible liar, and I don't have the sight." The force of her voice sprayed spittle into his face. "And what did you do with her pinions? Where did you hide them?"

"I don't have them." He stammered, grateful when she stepped back at Vinja's return. He held a large bag under one arm.

Tugging the bag from the young officer, Aggie held a yellow persimmon aloft, making a tut sound as she advanced cautiously towards the creature. She was whispering as she moved, stopping arms-length away and offering the fruit to the crysallix, as she bowed her head.

Gold eyes flicked from the woman to the fruit, then to me. I nodded, imperceptible to the others in the room and she swiped it from Aggie's palm. If you have never seen a crysallix eat, it is unlike anything you might have experienced. I would recommend something like a fruit or nut your first time, because watching them rend a dove or rodent with their beaks will turn you sour for days.

Her seemingly human jaw opened wide, a black beak extending from the maw, its long point sharp as steel. She devoured the fruit in two bites, her beak, gleaming slick with juice, disappeared again. Aggie held up another, the scene repeating as a few of the officers shifted uncomfortably. Stepping backwards, she continued to coax the creature. She offered two hard-shelled nuts, freshly roasted by the smell of them. The crysallix stepped down from the perch, warily watching the surrounding officers, but unable to resist. Aggie produced a piece of jerky, leading the creature through the door, into the bustling crowd of the afternoon.

"We are not done here, Goddard." I said in a steady voice. "I'll be back for those pinions, or I'll be removing something of yours."

I stationed two guards around the Farrago to dissuade any attempt at running. It was a long walk to the clinic. The officers kept the crowd at bay as we moved. Hungering eyes of men that drew too near were met with harsh words and the barrel of a rifle. The frustration of desire as the local men caught her scent and were rebuffed grew angry curses, but no violence.

We saw her settled in a large enclosure as Aggie gave her the rest of the food and the officers returned to their prospective stations. I lingered behind, watching her and wondering at her odd behavior.

"What do you smell?" Aggie smiled as the crysallix beak extended again, tearing through the bag and devouring its contents. "For me, it is the scent of a fresh born babe, my babe. And fresh dirt, with a hint of mint."

"Mountain dug ginseng, and the hard nut bread that my mother baked for my grandmother." A tug of nostalgia crept into my voice. "She smells like home."

She nodded, glancing around to make sure we were alone, and whispered anyway. "How are the feet holding up?"

"No issues, thanks to you."

"And the shoes?"

"Still go through them quickly, but not like I used to. Ever since you trimmed them down, it's been fine. I'll probably need your services in another year when the nails break through again."

"My home is always open to you." She looked satisfied, but her gaze shifted back to the enclosure. "Can you hear her?"

She flexed and extended her wings, watching us curiously.

"No. I don't know that she will speak to me."

She shrugged. "Don't know that she won't until you ask. Did you see the way she looked at you in the tent? She recognizes kin."

There was a squawk from another enclosure, followed by a louder grunt, and Aggie bustled away, shouting reprisals as she went. I was turning to follow when I heard a breath of wind behind me, the whisper of wings. I hadn't considered my proximity to the bars of the enclosure when I turned and stared into intelligent, golden eyes. Greenish blue bristles and filoplumes surrounded her eyes and nose, leading outward to brighter contour feathers. Too much like my grandmothers, but brighter and fuller than mother's had been.

She extended dulled talons in greeting. I hesitated, unsure, before reaching back, allowing my fingers to entangle with hers. She raised her head, sniffing the air before jerking me in close. The sharp beak extended too fast for me to react as she nipped my cheek, drawing a bit of blood before releasing me. It was a bonding ritual. Though I had never experienced one before, my grandmother had spoken of it in her more wistful moments.

I stumbled back as she ambled away and nestled in the soft bedding in the corner. Finding Aggie, I made my excuses and stopped at the station to file my report before heading to my simple apartment.

She found me in my slumber, lulling me into her dream with a voice as soft as wind. We perched naked in a high tree, the blue tipped mountains spread around us in a twilight sky. Her name was Nyla and, like many of her kind, she was a curious creature.

'What are you?' she asked.

'Distant relation.' I answered.

She laid a hand on my chest. 'I can smell our ancestors in you.'

I shook my head. 'My ancestors are gone. I have no connection to a tribe. I was raised alone and schooled with the humans.'

Her wings stretched wide, matching the iridescence of the mountains before resettling. 'But you do not belong with these people. It must be difficult. How do they not see you?'

I swung my legs in the air, explaining that it was not as difficult as it had been for my mother or grandmother, who could not walk down the street without unwanted attention and lived in isolation, devoid of any tribal connections. Mother began shaving my face at a young age so that I could make trades and sell goods for the family.

'What of your wings?' She cocked her head in a stilted way, leaning around me to eye the fragile, undergrown things.

'Useless, too small to serve any purpose. I keep them strapped down most of the time.'

Gently, she ran a tough hand across my cheek. 'I can feel the rachis and calamus of the feathers, the barbs trying to sprout. Why do you dispose of them?'

'It is easier for them to accept me if I look like them.'

Her eyes narrowed, but I sensed no judgement. Wild creatures understood the motivation for survival in strange environments.

'How do you eat?' she asked.

'Same as you, though my beak is small and weak. I cannot manage the unroasted nuts or hard seeds, but I can eat fish and meat, fruits and vegetables.' I shrugged, looking around at the landscape she had brought me to. 'Is this your home?'

'It was.' Nyla sighed, drawing a single knee to her chest as she gazed about at the mountains. I could almost hear the songs of her sisters crying out to her. She leaned toward me in a gesture of intimacy. 'What happened to your mate?'

Not ready to speak of something so painful, I countered, 'Why didn't you kill Goddard when you had a chance?'

Her eyes held sadness. 'He has something precious of mine. I should have stayed and fought, but no one would have understood. They do not hear me like you do now. So, I left to build strength and re-strategize.' She lay a firm hand on my shoulder, staring into my eyes. 'Will you help me get it back?'

A pounding on my door pulled me from my answer, tugging me from our dream into unwanted consciousness. Vijna stood on the threshold, hair greased into place and moustache symmetrical in its upward curls. Behind him the sky was brightening into dawn.

"They're gone." He panted.

"Who?" My muddled brain was still half trapped in Nyla's dream.

"The Mystical Farrago. Durgin and Eads were stationed outside to keep them from leaving, but when their replacements showed this morning, they were gone."

"Durgin and Eads?"

He shook his head. "Dead, skulls bashed in. Goddard took an assortment of creatures and the wagons but left most of the tents."

I rubbed my eyes. "A moment." I said, closing the door and donning my uniform before stepping outside. There was no time to shave off the stubble that poked through my skin. I would have to hope that no one looked too closely.

They draped the bodies in white linen spattered brown with drying blood. I did not look beneath, instead focusing on the wheel tracks that lead away from town, following the smaller road through the forest. They could be heading north around the western mountains by now, or worse, gone into the deserts to the south. But I doubted Goddard was that foolish.

The hasty departure and abandonment of several exotic creatures made me ponder what he was running from, or running with.While I studied the tracks and dealt with the assignment and care of the abandoned creatures, a message arrived from Aggie.

'I have completed my examination of our guest and need to speak with you. Come as soon as you can.'

My mouth was dust as I stared down the road for a moment, deciding my course of action. Issuing orders to the remaining officers and organizing a search party, I specified their route and what to look for. I knew what Aggie would tell me. I knew from the experiences of my grandmother and mother there was only one thing that caused a crysallix to stay with someone they loathed.

It took an hour for me to reach my old home in the woods. Carved between two boulders and shaded by towering conifers, the cave sat undisturbed for the last five years. Ever since mother had wandered away into the woods, it had sat empty of life and I had lacked the heart to tend to it. Home was a painful reminder of things lost, and I told myself that I now lead a different life, and had become a different person. But we are skilled at convincing ourselves of our evolution until the past pulls you back and forces you to deal with those things you never speak of.

It was much like I remembered, perhaps a little mustier and lacking the warm scents of the people I loved. It took thirty minutes of searching to locate grandmother's old trunk, then took me an hour and a half to get to Aggie. Nyla waited for my answer.

"She's had a bantling recently- less than a year, I'd wager. It wouldn't be strong enough to fly yet, and still vulnerable to the elements,"Aggie said. The concern on her face was evident, her hair more wild than usual. I imagined the handwringing when she realized the situation.

"How is Nyla?"

"Nyla? Aw, that's a lovely name." She crooned before her expression slagged into sadness. "They don't do well when separated from their off-spring, typically they stay together until the bantling begins its first cycle." It must have been the look on my face that showed my confusion. "Wasn't that true of your mother?"

I didn't answer. I honestly couldn't recall how old I was when she first left, but she came and went so often after I met Judeth. "Are you saying that all crysallix have a cycle? Even the males?"

It was Aggie's turn to look confused. "There are no male crysallix born, dear. When the cycle comes, they can choose to carry more masculine or feminine traits. Didn't your mother teach you?"

Nyla was sitting up, hugging her knees close, observing us from inside the enclosure. The dress she wore was torn in places, probably ripped by her talons while she slept.

"I have something for you," I said.

Nyla sniffed the air before moving toward us. I pulled the leathers from my satchel, running a hand over their faded blues and greens. There was a heart worn tug in my chest before I handed them to her. She cocked her head from side to side, wings shuffling down her back as she alternately studied my face and the garments. Crysallix did not give up their leathers, and it was abnormal to wear another's. I nudged the clothing through the bars. She hesitated for a fraction of a second before clutching them to her chest.

She tore the dress from her back, rending it in long strips, before tugging the leather breeches on and pulling the breastplate over her chest. The straps crisscrossed between her wings, latching the buckles at either shoulder. The colors were a near match to her feathers. If she wasn't of my grandmother's tribe, she was from a neighboring one, and my sadness lessened at letting them go.

Aggie patted my shoulder. "They fit her well. It must have been difficult to part with them. I thought Ardan would have taken them when she left."

"Mother had her own leathers, and these have been hidden away for too long. It seemed appropriate they find a new owner." Nyla smoothed down the pants and tucked the straps underneath the breast plate edges. When she finished, she stood taller. The wings seemed stronger, despite the missing pinions. "This would have made her happy."

"What about the bantling?" Aggie asked.

Nyla listened, though she did not show it. "I've sent a search party into the desert trails, it won't take long to realize the caravan did not go that way. They are only searching for Goddard and know nothing of the offspring. Hopefully, by the time they return, the bantling will be safely reunited with its mother."

"And Goddard?"

I shrugged, remembering his face when he mentioned Judeth. "His well-being is not my concern."

Nyla stared through the bars, reaching out with her dulled talons. I nodded. She could smell her offspring and track it faster than anyone else could. It was dangerous to smuggle her out of town, a risk to both of us, but it was the only sure way to locate Goddard and the child.

I rented a dapple-gray draft horse, powerful and able to bear the weight of both of us on his back. We skirted the town through old pathways, avoiding the locals. Nyla allowed me to cover her with a cape, but the tips of her wings brushed the haunches of the horse. She was used to being around horses from being in the wagons,but I don't think she had ridden one before. Her arms latched around me as we rode.

Nyla kept her nose angled upward, occasionally opening her mouth to get a better scent, and pointed which direction to turn. It took several hours, but eventually we found the wagon tracks heading toward the western mountains. The wagon train then split, three wagons heading to the long path to the desert, two wagons continuing on.

Nudging the draft horse to move faster, we followed the trail into the woods. It would be dark in a couple of hours, but the air still held warmth and Nyla would have an advantage come nightfall.

Two of Goddard's men sat around a small campfire, while the old man paced from one wagon to the other, worrying his hands. Stopping at the far wagon, he pulled back the bonnet before re-securing it and continuing his pacing.

"Relax, boss. No way they find us, not with the side roads we took." The younger man said. He was the type of leanness that could be misperceived as weak. He had grown an unruly beard that snuck up on either side of a crooked nose to appear older.

Goddard shook his head. "We rest for a few hours and leave with the first light. "

There was a sound from inside the wagon, like a whimper or a weakened chirp. Nyla bristled beside me, the sharp nails of her toes and fingers dug into the ground as we watched and waited. The horse was a half mile behind, tethered lightly to a tree and happy for the rest, while they settled their horses on the far side of the wagons. They had not caught our scent yet.

The other man was older, clean shaven, but with a face full of scars. He poked the fire, asking, "Is it worth bringing with us?"

Goddard paused, moving closer to the speaker and distancing himself and the wagons. "What are you saying?"

Nyla darted away, skirting the clearing, and heading toward the wagon, quiet and quick. I could not have stopped her had I tried.

"All this trouble." The man spat on the ground. "We should cut our losses and be rid of it."

Goddard stormed forward, brandishing a small knife. "Do you know how much money that little thing will fetch us?" The man did not react to the blade being wagged at him. "The foreign markets will pay a fortune for it. I was planning on selling the set by winter, but perhaps this way is better."

The younger man squirmed. "Will it live without its mother?" He avoided looking at his companions. "It seems to be getting weaker."

The blue of Nyla's feathers caught the light as she paused behind the brush beside the wagons, but the men did not notice. To reach the opening of the wagons, she would have to be in the open, exposed. If they trapped her in the wagon, she would lose the advantage we had counted on.

Goddard turned on the younger man. "They didn't leave us much choice, did they? Stole her away with food. How was I to know what she ate? It's not like the damn things talk." His face shifted into a half smile. "Nice of that hag to educate me. The little thing ate up half my jerky before it fell asleep."

Unlatching the clip on my holster, I withdrew the flintlock pistol. It was not as powerful as a rifle, and I would only have one shot before they were on me. So far, I could not see a pistol on either of them, but I suspected at least one of them to have something concealed. Nyla slid from the shadows toward the wagon. The rustling of the bush caused the young man to turn when I leapt from the bushes.

"Goddard." I leveled the pistol at him, releasing the safety. He paled while the other men startled to their feet. "Thought you would escape?"

Goddard sneered as his older companion brought his hand to his hip. "Lieutenant. Didn't expect you to come all this way just for me. You'd think they would better spend our tax money on actual crimes, rather than trying to bring in a small crook like me."

Nyla slipped into the tent. A coo echoing from inside. The young man turned again, but was drawn back by my words.

"I don't plan on taking you back." I said, eyeing each of them in turn. It was a lie, of course. My intention was only to grant Nyla the opportunity to get the bantling and then be on our separate ways. I did not come with murder on my mind.

"You mean to kill me?" He glanced at his companions. "And what of them? You can't kill us all."

"I don't plan on killing them." I cocked the gun, trying to keep my nerves and aim steady. Nyla was taking too long. She should have been out by now.

"Is this about that waif that used to come around with you?" Goddard asked, his face done up in a cruel smile.

My stomach knotted.

"She was a sweet thing, wasn't she?" The smile turned wicked as he spoke. "What was her name?"

The gun trembled with my voice. "Don't."

He snorted. "Jude…"

The explosion from my hands drowned out his voice. He stumbled backwards as the bullet struck his shoulder.

The smoke wafted from the gun as Nyla paused outside the tent, a bundle in her arms. Pinions evened out the drape of her wings. Her eyes narrowed at the scene before she launched upward, and I knew I would not see her again.

The scarred man leapt over the fire, wrapping his arms around my gut. We landed in a heap of curses and fists, wrestling one way, then the other, as the pistol disappeared into the brush. I flipped him beneath me, pummeling his face. Blood spattered from his nose as bone crunched and gave. But he did not relent. His fist met my cheek as I landed a hit to his ear and, for a moment, I had the better of him.

A hit to the back of my head knocked me sideways. I had forgotten about the younger man. He kicked my ribs, knocking me to the ground as he continued his assault. I gripped his foot, twisting his leg and knocking him off balance before the other man was up and joining in. One boot met my ribs, another my stomach, knocking the air from my lungs. They hailed fists and boots upon me as I covered my head. Blood dripped into my eyes as the world threatened darkness.

"Enough." Goddard said. One arm hung limp, blood dotted the ground beneath his feet. He leveled a small pistol at me as the men stood beside him, their breath labored. "You won't be leaving these woods. Maybe I'll feed you to the little crysallix we've got."

He cocked the pistol, and I closed my eyes.

A scream between a hawk and a mountain cat split the air. A flurry of oil slick wings shot above me as Nyla slapped the pistol from Goddard's hand. Her wings unfolded, knocking one man to the ground while shredding the face of the other with her talons as she spun.

Goddard stumbled back, searching for the lost pistol as she advanced.

"Please." He begged, holding one hand up. "I was trying to help you."

She stopped, tilting her head as her wings shivered again.

The younger man rose to his feet behind her, a knife in his hand. I struggled to reach him, dragging myself on the ground and gripping his leg. The knife glinted in the firelight as he raised it. I screamed her name.

Warm blood pooled onto his boots, coating my hands and splattering my face. The man fell before me, lifeless eyes staring at the sky. White ovals of bone were pulled through the torn gap in his throat. There was a soft gurgling as his last breath struggled to exit and found itself trapped.

Goddard screamed as she leapt upon him. I closed my eyes until his cries ceased, replaced by a sound I knew too well. It was the sound that my mother and my grandmother made when they feasted on ferrets or lambs.

I pressed myself up. Nyla was perched upon his chest, the rest of the scene blocked out by the drape of her wings. Goddard's head lay twenty feet away, expression frozen in terror.

The remaining man watched in horror as his face bled down his shirt. Slowly, he pulled himself to his feet and stumbled into the woods. He would have to seek a healer in the closest village, then tell his tale of the crysallix. A vastly different tale than other men told. I hoped it was a warning to others.

Nyla nudged me awake sometime later, helping me to sit and fussing over my cuts and bruises. Preening me like my mother used to. Once satisfied, she darted into the wagon that our draft horse was now hooked to. She had cleared the bodies away. Long smears of blood led into the trees and the wheel tracks that led us here were swept away.

Emerging from the bonnet, she squatted down before me, holding out the small babe to me. Its hands already sported soft talons, slender limbs covered in a dull gray down with shades of blue surrounding golden eyes. Bringing the creature to my chest, one hand reached my face as I smiled. Nyla leaned close, resting her head on my shoulder with a gesture of pride.

They smelled of mountain ginseng and hard nut bread, of fresh meat and soft down. They smelled of home.

AUTHOR BIOGRAPHY

N.V. Haskell is an award-winning author of speculative fiction. When she manages to step away from her computer, she can be found at Comic Cons or Renaissance Fairs donned in her favorite costumes, reading multiple books at a time, running badly, travelling, or teaching yoga.

She lives somewhere between civilization and haunted creeks with her long-suffering spouse, rescue dog, and too many squirrels that she can't help but feed. She is open about her struggles with mental health and is a staunch advocate for mental health awareness and LGBTQ rights.

After many years working in healthcare, she remains stubbornly (or foolishly) optimistic. To find out more please visit her website https://nv haskell.com/and sign up for her newsletter.

Book 1 of *The Broken Bonds of Magic* Series will be available in February 2025 with Cursed Dragon Ship Publishing.https://curseddragonship.com/